KT-579-524

A Bespoke Murder

By Edward Marston

THE HOME FRONT DETECTIVE SERIES

A Bespoke Murder

THE RAILWAY DETECTIVE SERIES

The Railway Detective

The Excursion Train

The Railway Viaduct

The Iron Horse

Murder on the Brighton Express

The Silver Locomotive Mystery

Railway to the Grave

Blood on the Line

The Railway Detective Omnibus:
The Railway Detective, The Excursion Train, The Railway Viaduct

THE RESTORATION SERIES

The King's Evil

The Amorous Nightingale

The Repentant Rake

The Frost Fair

The Parliament House

The Painted Lady

THE CAPTAIN RAWSON SERIES

Soldier of Fortune

Drums of War

Fire and Sword

Under Siege

A Very Murdering Battle

a&b

A Bespoke Murder

EDWARD MARSTON

First published in Great Britain in 2011 by
Allison & Busby Limited
13 Charlotte Mews
London W1T 4EJ
www.allisonandbusby.com

A CIP catalogue record for this book is available from
the British Library.

10 9 8 7 6 5 4 3 2 1

13-ISBN 978-0-7490-0990-8

Typeset in 12/18 pt Adobe Garamond Pro by
Allison & Busby Ltd.

Paper used in this publication is from sustainably managed sources.
All of the wood used is procured from legal sources and is fully traceable.
The producing mill uses schemes such as ISO 14001
to monitor environmental impact.

Printed and bound by
CPI Group (UK) Ltd, Croydon, CR0 4Y

To Doug Emmott
friend, philosopher and tennis star
who bears no relation whatsoever to his namesake in this book

CHAPTER ONE

They all knew the danger. When the *Lusitania* sailed from New York on 1st May 1915, passengers and crew alike understood the risk that they were taking. Spelt out with cold clarity by the German Embassy, the grim warning had been widely circulated.

> *Travellers intending to embark for the Atlantic voyage are reminded that a state of war exists between Germany and her allies and Great Britain and her allies; that the zone of war includes the waters adjacent to the British Isles; that, in accordance with formal notice given by the Imperial German Government, vessels flying the flag of Great Britain, or of any of her allies, are liable to destruction in those waters . . .*

The threat did not deter 1,257 passengers from making the trip, though there was a measure of disquiet. The general feeling was that a ship capable of twenty-six knots was far too fast to be caught by any of the German U-boats lurking in British waters. Besides, it was argued, the *Lusitania* was essentially a passenger liner and therefore not a legitimate target for the enemy. The further they sailed across the Atlantic, the stronger that argument seemed. They were safe.

Also aboard the *Lusitania* on her fateful crossing was Irene Bayard, one of the hundreds of crew members. Irene had an unshakable faith in the Cunard vessel, having worked on her as a stewardess since her maiden voyage from Liverpool in September 1907. She was fiercely proud of being associated with a ship that had established so many startling precedents. RMS *Lusitania* was the first British four-stacker, the first to exceed 30,000 gross tons and the first to cross the Atlantic in under five days, securing the prized Blue Riband, the unofficial award for the fastest crossing. As such, she was the first quadruple-screw speed record-breaker and her achievements had made her the first choice for many passengers. That was a source of great satisfaction to Irene.

She was undisturbed by warnings from the Imperial German Government. Employed to look after passengers in first class, Irene was far too busy to worry about any notional dangers. It was hard work but so full of interest that – even though she was now in her late thirties – she never felt the slightest fatigue. Among those whose every request she met with smiling efficiency were a famous dancer, a celebrated American fashion designer and an ancient lady with two spaniels and an unspecified connection to the higher reaches of the British aristocracy. Each day brought new surprises. It was why Irene found working on the *Lusitania* such a pleasure.

Ernie Gill was less happy in his work. Taking a last pull on his cigarette, he flicked it overboard before turning to Irene.

'Who says that Americans are generous?' he moaned.

'I've always found them so,' said Irene.

'That's because you've never had to cut their hair. I spend at least ten hours a day on my feet and what do I get for it? Most of them won't even give me a proper thank you, let alone a decent tip.'

'What about that Belgian you told me about?'

'Ah, yes,' conceded Gill, brightening, 'that was different. Now he was a real gentleman. Back home, he's some kind of diplomat. I mean, he must be worried sick about what happened to his country when the Germans trampled all over it, yet he still remembers that a barber deserves a reward. He slipped me a sovereign.'

'He was obviously pleased with his haircut.'

'So he should be, Irene. I know my trade.'

Gill was a tall, skinny man in his forties with a sallow complexion. Though he and Irene had become friends, she was wary of his sudden bursts of intensity. He had offered her two proposals of marriage and, when inebriated, propositions of a different nature but she had turned him down politely each time. Since the death of her first husband, Irene had resolved never to marry again, least of all to a lustful barber with a fondness for strong drink. She was quite happy to limit the relationship to the occasional pleasant chat.

It was afternoon on 7th May and the ship was steaming along with unassailable confidence. After a steady and uneventful voyage, anxiety aboard had more or less evaporated. They were only ten miles from Queenstown, their first port of call. Like many of the passengers, Irene had come out on deck when land was first sighted. The barber had joined her.

'Not long to go now,' she observed. 'Since that fog lifted, the Irish coast is clearly visible.'

'Don't talk to me about the Irish,' said Gill, sharply. 'They're even worse than the Yanks. I've had three Micks in my chair and not a penny in tips from any of them. That Irish composer whistled his latest song at me as if he was doing me a favour. The only favour I want,' he added with a sniff, 'is silver coins in the palm of my hand.'

'Can't you think about anything but money?'

He grinned slyly. 'I think about *you* sometimes, Irene.'

'That's enough of that,' she said, firmly.

'A man can still hope.'

He ran a covetous eye over her shapely figure.

'You know my decision, Ernie, and it's final.'

She was about to explain why when she was interrupted by a shout from the young lookout on the bow. Having seen the telltale shape hurtling towards them through the water, he bellowed into his megaphone.

'Torpedoes coming on the starboard side!'

Before anyone could react to the news, the ship was struck with such violence that it was rocked from stem to stern. The explosion was deafening. Panic set in immediately. Passengers screamed, shouted and ran in all directions. Electricity had been knocked out, leaving cabins and public rooms in comparative darkness. Worst of all was the fact that the ship began to list dramatically, making several people lose their balance and fall over. On a command from Captain Turner, an SOS message was sent by the wireless operator but there was no chance of a rescue ship reaching them in time. The *Lusitania* was holed below the water. She was sinking fast. A second explosion caused her to keel over even more. In some parts of the ship, panic gave way to hysteria. This, they all feared, was it.

'Blimey!' cried Gill. 'The Huns have got us.'

'Think of the passengers,' urged Irene. 'Get them to put on their life jackets and move to the boat deck.'

'We're going down, Irene. It's every man for himself.'

'We have to do our duty.'

But he was no longer listening. Gill had charged off to collect what he could from his quarters. Irene snapped into action. Rushing to the nearest supply of life jackets, she put one on and grabbed several others so that she could hand them out to people she met on the way. When she got to the boat deck, she found it in complete disarray. There were twenty-two standard lifeboats but the ship was now at such a crazy angle that it was impossible to launch several of them. The other problem was that the ship was still maintaining an appreciable speed, making it difficult to control any lowering. Of the lifeboats that were actually launched, some met with instant disaster, tipping over and spilling their passengers into the sea or hitting the water with such a shuddering impact that people were hurled uncaringly over the side.

Irene did what she could, helping to fasten life jackets, spread reassurance and assist people into any boats that looked as if they might be lowered without mishap. She was pleased to see that Ernie Gill had also decided to do his duty now that he'd retrieved his few valuables. The noise was ear-splitting and the confusion almost overwhelming. The constant boom of the engines was amplified by the rhythmical gushing of the waves and the stentorian yells of the sailors handling the falls, the ropes that lowered the boats from the davits. Yet a strange calm was slowly starting to spread, born of bravery and an acceptance of the inevitable. People were making allowances for the most vulnerable, yielding up their places in a boat to the old and infirm. Frightened children were herded together and strapped into life jackets. Pet animals were gathered up and cuddled by their owners. Irene saw countless examples of courage and kindness from crew members as they went through survival drills they'd practised for such an emergency.

In addition to the lifeboats, there were twenty-six collapsible boats and they would play an important part in saving lives, but it was clear from the start that casualties would be extremely high. Several people had already perished, dashed against the side of the ship or killed by a falling lifeboat. Others had drowned in the cold unforgiving water. Seated in one of the last lifeboats, the titled old lady with the two spaniels was knocked overboard when a man who leapt from an upper deck landed directly on top of her. Yapping piteously, the dogs swam madly in small circles but their owner was already dead and they were doomed to join her in a watery grave.

Having gradually slowed, the *Lusitania* rolled over even more and was patently close to her end. In less than twenty minutes since she was hit, one of the largest and finest vessels ever to be built in a British shipyard began to founder. It was time to go.

'Jump, Irene!' shouted Gill, taking her by the arm.

'I'm needed here, Ernie,' she said.

'There's nothing else we can do. She's going down.'

Irene felt the deck lurch. 'You may be right.'

'Jump while you can or you'll be sucked down.' He pulled her to the rail. 'Try not to hit anyone.'

It was a tall order. Hundreds of heads were bobbing about in the sea and some of the collapsible boats were directly below Irene. She could see no inviting space. After snatching a farewell kiss from her,

Gill jumped over the side while pinching his nose between a thumb and forefinger. Dozens of other people were abandoning the ship as well. Irene offered up a silent prayer for her salvation then joined the general exodus. As she fell through the air, she was overcome by a sense of righteous indignation at the enemy for daring to attack her beloved *Lusitania*. It was sacrilege.

She hit the sea hard and sank beneath the green waves before coming to the surface again and expelling a mouthful of salt water. All around her were people desperately trying to make their way past those who had already given up the fight. When a corpse floated helplessly against her, Irene saw that it was one of the mess stewards, his eyes gazing sightlessly up at the sky. She remembered what Gill had said. As she finally went down, he warned, the *Lusitania* would take anyone nearby deep into the vortex she had created. It would be a hideous way to die. That thought spurred Irene on to swim away as hard as she could, heading towards a collapsible boat she could see. Because it was being rowed away from her, however, Irene never reached the boat and its vague promise of safety. Instead, she kept flailing away with both arms until she barely had the strength to lift them. Her head was pounding, her lungs were on fire and her legs were no longer obeying her. All that she could do was to tread water.

A collective shout of horror went up and Irene turned to take a last glimpse of the ship on which she'd spent so many happy years. One end suddenly dipped in defeat, the other rose high, then the *Lusitania* dived below like a gigantic iron whale, sucking everyone within reach in her wake. Irene was still staring at the massive circle of foam when she collided with a wooden object and automatically grasped it. She was holding on to a large chair that gave her extra buoyancy. It had not arrived by accident. Using his other arm to swim, Ernie Gill had guided it over to her so that both of them had something to cling to. Shivering with cold, Irene was unable to express her thanks in words. Gill, however, was shaking with fury and the expletives came out of him like steam escaping from a kettle.

'Bleeding Huns!' he exclaimed. 'I'll fucking *kill* the bastards!'

CHAPTER TWO

Reaction was immediate and savage. As soon as news of the disaster reached Liverpool, mobs went on the rampage. Because the *Lusitania* was held in great affection in her home port, her sinking produced outrage, disbelief and an overpowering urge for revenge. Anyone with a German name became a target. Shops were looted, houses raided and people beaten up at random. The fact that they were naturalised British citizens was no protection. They were hunted indiscriminately. When one man protested that his family had lived in the country for generations, he was grabbed by the mob, stripped naked then tarred and feathered. Many policemen shared the feelings of the vigilantes and chose to turn a blind eye to their campaign of destruction. As the homes of German families were plundered then set alight, a pall of smoke hung over the city.

Liverpool was not alone in its fury. All over Britain, a German birth certificate was the mark of a victim. When it was learnt that over a thousand people on the *Lusitania* had lost their lives, the search for scapegoats was intensified. London offered an unlimited supply of them. In the East End, where many German immigrants had settled, vengeful gangs stormed along a trail of terror, meting out punishment with remorseless efficiency.

Nor was the West End immune to attack.

'Why do they hate us so much?' asked Ruth Stein.

'They don't hate *us*,' replied her father. 'They hate Germany for killing so many innocent people in the *Lusitania*. It's a question of guilt by association, Ruth. We should have changed our name.'

'Would that have made a difference, Father?'

He heaved a sigh. 'Who knows? Your Uncle Herman changed his name yet they still wrecked his warehouse.'

'It's the way people *look* at me,' she said. 'It's frightening.'

'Try to ignore it.'

They were in the upstairs room at the front of the shop. Thanks to his skill as a bespoke tailor, he had one of the most flourishing businesses in Jermyn Street. He was a short, stout man in his late fifties with rounded shoulders. There was usually a benign smile on his face but it was now corrugated by concern. It was mid-evening and his daughter had joined him when the shop closed. Ruth was a slim, angular, pallid and undeniably plain girl of eighteen. Her father had been teaching her the rudiments of bookkeeping so that she could in time relieve her mother of that aspect of the business.

Ruth started. 'What's that noise?'

'I heard nothing,' he said.

'It sounded like the roar of a crowd.'

'Some lads have probably had too much to drink.'

'It was a loud cheer.'

'Was it?'

Stein had heard it clearly but tried to show no alarm. If a gang was on the loose, he could only hope that his shop would be spared. He had put up two large posters in the window. One declared that he and his family were naturalised and in full support of Britain in its fight against Germany. On the other poster was an enlarged photo of his son, Daniel, wearing the uniform of the British regiment he'd volunteered to join only days after war was declared. Stein felt that his credentials were impeccable but he knew that a lawless mob would take no account of them. The thirst for revenge imposed blindness.

Ruth crossed to the window and peered nervously at the street.

'I don't see those policemen outside,' she said.

'They'll still be nearby.'

'What can two of them do against a big crowd?'

'I trust that we'll never have to find out.'

'Are you afraid?'

'We're British citizens. We've nothing to be afraid about.'

'Mother said it was too dangerous for me to come here.'

He smiled tolerantly. 'Your mother worries too much.'

'She wanted you to close the shop today.'

'We had customers to serve, Ruth. We can't turn people away.'

She recoiled from another burst of cheering.

'The noise is getting louder – they're coming this way.'

'Stand away from the window,' he said, trying to keep the anxiety out of his voice. 'Let's do some work.'

'Look,' she cried, pointing a finger. 'You can see them now – dozens and dozens of them. They're heading up the street.'

Stein looked over her shoulder. The crowd was large and volatile. Its jostling members were either inflamed or drunk or both simultaneously.

They were chanting obscenities about Germans that made his daughter blush. He pulled her away. The baying got louder and louder until it was directly outside. Stein quivered in fear. The mob had not stopped in order to read the two posters in the window. The only thing that interested them was the name painted in large capitals above the shop – Jacob Stein.

'German killer!' yelled a voice. 'Drive him out!'

Someone threw a brick at the window, smashing it into myriad shards. The first people to clamber into the shop grabbed the suits on display on the models, expensive garments that were well beyond the reach of low-paid working-class men. There were shouts of triumph as more looters climbed into the premises.

'They've got in!' cried Ruth in alarm.

'Leave at once,' ordered her father.

'But they're stealing your property.'

'Go out by the back door. Run to the police station.'

'Why not ring them?'

'The telephone is downstairs. I'd never reach it. Off you go. I won't be far behind.' He scurried across to the safe and pulled out a bunch of keys. Aware that she was still there, he adopted a sterner tone. 'Don't just stand there – get out now! There's no telling what they'll do if they catch us still here. Run, girl – run! This is an emergency.'

Snatching up her handbag, Ruth did as she was told and ran down the stairs. From inside the shop, she heard the bell tinkle as the till was opened, followed by a groan of disappointment because it was empty. A far more ominous sound ensued. When Ruth heard the first crackle of fire, her blood froze. They were going to burn down the shop. She opened the back door and fled, intent on racing to the police station to raise the alarm. But she got no further than the end of the alley. Two scruffy young men were lounging against the wall, taking it in turns to swig from a flagon of beer. When they saw Ruth, they stood up to block her path.

'Let me pass,' she said, bravely.

'What's the hurry, darling?' asked one of them.

'They've broken into our shop.'

'Who cares?' He leered at her. 'Give us a kiss.'

'I have to get to the police station,' she wailed.

'All in good time,' he said. 'Come on – what about a farewell kiss for Gatty and me? We're sailing off to France with our regiment tomorrow. This is our last chance for a bit of fun.'

'Yes,' added his friend. 'One kiss is all we want.'

'I'm first,' said the other, putting the flagon down.

He lunged forward. When he touched her shoulder, Ruth lashed out on impulse, slapping him hard across the face. It stung him into a rage. He grabbed her with both hands.

'We'll have a lot more than a kiss for that,' he warned, pulling her to the ground and knocking her hat off in the process. 'Come on, Gatty – hold her down.'

His friend hesitated. 'Don't hurt her, Ol,' he said, worriedly. 'Let her go.'

'Not until I've had my money's worth. Now hold her down.'

The friend reluctantly held Ruth's arms but she did not struggle. In a state of shock, she was unable to move. She could not believe what was happening to her. Her skirt was pulled up and her legs were forced apart. As the first man loomed over her, she could smell the beer on his breath. He was giggling wildly and undoing the buttons on his trousers. When he pulled them down, he was already aroused. Ruth was aghast. She didn't hear the explosion in the shop or wonder if her father would escape in time. She forgot all about the fire. Held down by the sheer weight of her attacker, she was revolted by the taste of his lips when he took a first guzzled kiss. Fondling her breasts, he plunged his tongue into her mouth and rolled excitedly about on top of her.

'That's enough, Ol,' said the friend. 'Somebody will come.'

'I haven't even started yet.'

'Be quick – we've got to go.'

'She asked for this.'

Using a hand to widen her thighs still further, he manoeuvred into position then suddenly forced his erect penis into her. The stab of pain made Ruth cry out. He silenced her with another kiss and pumped away madly inside her. It was excruciating. She was pinned down and groped all over. She was being defiled, yet nobody came to her aid. Torn between agony and humiliation, all that she could do was to lie there and endure the ordeal. The only consolation was that it was short-lived. Panting heavily from his exertions, the man soon reached his climax, arching his back and letting out a long howl of pleasure. After a final thrust, he needed a minute to recover before pulling out of her with a grunt of satisfaction.

'Your turn, Gatty,' he said, rising to his feet and yanking up his trousers. 'You'll enjoy it – she's nice and tight.'

'We've got to go, Ol,' urged his friend. 'Leave her be.'

'Don't tell me you're scared to do it.'

'We don't have time. That place is on fire.'

As if to emphasise the point, the wail of a fire engine could be heard approaching from the distance. The first man nodded his head then looked down at Ruth.

'Goodbye, darling – remember me, won't you?'

His friend tugged him away. 'We've got to go.'

The two of them skulked off, leaving Ruth still on the ground. She was too stunned even to move. She'd been raped less than twenty yards from the family shop. Pain, confusion, fear and shame assailed her. She was in despair. At that moment in time, Ruth felt as if she'd lost absolutely everything. She'd lost her virginity, her innocence, her respectability, her confidence, her hopes for the future and her peace of mind. Unbeknown to her, she'd suffered a further loss as well. Stretched out on the carpet in the room above his burning shop was her father. Jacob Stein had never lived to hear about the brutal assault on his only daughter.

CHAPTER THREE

'I want you to take charge of this case, Inspector.'

'Yes, Sir Edward,' replied Harvey Marmion.

'Initial reports say that the shop was broken into then set alight. Anything that was not stolen was destroyed in the fire. More worrying is the fact that a body has been seen in an upstairs room. The fire brigade has been unable to reach the corpse in order to identify it but the likelihood is that it belongs to the proprietor, Jacob Stein.'

'I've walked past his shop many a time.'

'You won't be able to do that anymore,' said the commissioner, sadly. 'From what I can gather, the place will be burnt to a cinder.'

'Was it another mob out of control?'

'Yes, Inspector, and I won't stand for it. I'm not having the capital city at the mercy of roving gangs with a grudge. Somebody must be caught and punished for this.'

'That may be difficult, Sir Edward,' warned Marmion.

The older man smiled. 'Why do you think I chose you?'

They were in the commissioner's office at New Scotland Yard, the red and white brick building in the Gothic style that was the headquarters of the Metropolitan Police Force. Now in his mid sixties, Sir Edward Henry, the commissioner, should have retired but his patriotism had been stirred by the outbreak of war and he'd agreed to stay in a post he'd held for twelve productive years. Marmion had the greatest admiration for him, not least because the commissioner had survived an attempted assassination three years earlier and, though wounded by a bullet, had soon returned to work.

Harvey Marmion's father had been less fortunate. A policeman renowned for his devotion to duty, Alfred Marmion had been shot dead while trying to arrest a burglar. The incident had persuaded his son to give up his job as a clerk in the civil service and join the police force. Marmion was a chunky man in his forties with a physique that belied his bookishness. Astute and tenacious, he had worked his way up to the rank of detective inspector and was tipped for even higher office. Though he was well groomed, he was not the smartest dresser. Indeed, he looked almost shabby beside the immaculately attired Sir Edward Henry. Marmion's suit was crumpled and his tie was askew. His shirt collar had a smudge on it. Fortunately, the commissioner did not judge him on his appearance. He knew the man's worth and rated him highly.

'There's really nothing else that I can tell you, Inspector.'

'How many other shops have been attacked?' asked Marmion.

'Far too many,' said Sir Edward.

'Presumably, they were mostly in the East End.'

'The West End had its casualties as well. Windows were smashed in

Bond Street and in Savile Row. Luckily, the crowds were dispersed after a scuffle with our officers.'

'But that was not the case in Jermyn Street.'

'Alas, no – witnesses talk of a sudden burst of flame.'

'That means an accelerant like petrol was used.'

'If it was,' said Sir Edward, seriously, 'then I want the man who took it there. Arson is a heinous crime. I don't care how upset people are by what happened to the *Lusitania*. It's no excuse for the wanton destruction of private property.'

'I agree.'

'Get over there at once.'

'I will,' Marmion said. 'I'll take Sergeant Keedy with me.'

'Good – I know I can rely on the pair of you.'

'Thank you, Sir Edward.'

The commissioner walked to the door and opened it for his visitor. He put a hand on Marmion's arm as he was about to leave.

'This case has a special significance for me, Inspector.'

'Oh? Why is that?'

'Jacob Stein was my tailor.'

Ruth had no idea how she managed to drag herself to the police station in Vine Street. Nor could she remember what she actually said. She was still too stunned by the horror of her experience to speak with any articulation. When she mumbled something about her father's shop, she was told that the fire brigade was already attending the incident. The station sergeant eyed her shrewdly.

'Is there anything else to report, miss?' he enquired.

'No, no,' she said, flushing at the memory of the assault and feeling her heart pound. 'There's nothing at all.'

'You seem distracted.'

'I must get home.'

'And where would that be?'

'We live in Golders Green.'

'Can you tell me the address?'

'Well . . .'

Ruth's mind was blank. She had to rack her brains for minutes before she could remember where she lived. Ordinarily, she would have been driven home by her father but he had been trapped in the burning building. Seeing her bewilderment, the sergeant took pity on her. He signalled to a uniformed constable.

'PC Walters will see you safely home,' he said.

'I can manage,' murmured Ruth.

'I don't think that you can, miss. You're obviously distressed. You need help. Golders Green is on the Northern Line.' His head jerked to the constable. 'Take the young lady to her front door.'

'Yes, Sergeant,' said Walters.

'See that no harm comes to her.' He smiled sympathetically at Ruth. 'There are strange characters about at this time of day. We don't want you falling into the wrong hands, do we?'

It's too late, said Ruth to herself.

'Off you go, then, and thank you for coming.'

Walters extended an arm. 'This way, miss.'

Ruth accepted his help with profound misgivings. Though he tried to strike up a conversation with her, she maintained a hurt silence. Having a policeman beside her on the tube train was a mixed blessing. It prevented anyone from bothering her but, at the same time, it raised the suspicion that she was under arrest. Ruth was embarrassed by some of the glances that were shot at her. When they alighted at Golders

Green station, she was afraid that she might be spotted with PC Walters by someone she knew. Rumours would immediately start. All she yearned for now was the safety and the anonymity of her own home.

'I can manage from here,' she said.

'But the sergeant told me to take you all the way.'

'It's only a minute away.'

'Are you sure?'

'Yes – thank you very much.'

And before he had the chance to object, Ruth darted off by herself. In fact, her house was some distance away and she walked there as fast as she could, head down, face contorted, her mind filled with searing memories of her ordeal. When she finally reached home, she hurried up the drive and fumbled for her key, eager to hide her shame and wash off the stink of her attacker. She needed three attempts to get the key in the lock. When the door opened, she staggered into the hall. Her mother came waddling out of the living room to greet her but her welcoming smile vanished when she saw how dishevelled Ruth was. Miriam Stein's questions came out in a breathless stream.

'What's happened, Ruth?' she asked, appalled at what she saw. 'Where have you been? Why is your coat torn? Who damaged your hat? Why have you come back on your own? Where's your father? Why hasn't be brought you home? Is he all right? How did you get here? Can't you speak? Is there something wrong with you? Why don't you answer me? *Tell* me, Ruth – what's going on?'

It was all too much for her daughter. Faced with the well-meant interrogation, she fainted on the spot.

By the time the detectives had driven to Jermyn Street, the fire brigade had the blaze under control and had prevented it from spreading to adjacent buildings. A sizeable crowd had gathered on the opposite pavement, watching the flames finally succumbing and hissing in protest. Acrid smoke filled the night air, causing some onlookers to cough or put their hands to their eyes. Pulsing heat was still coming from the shop. There was little sympathy for the owner. He had a German name. That was enough.

Harvey Marmion spoke to the officer in charge of the operation. Sergeant Joe Keedy, meanwhile, talked to the three policemen on duty to see if they'd managed to collect any witness statements. Keedy was a tall, wiry, good-looking man in his thirties with his hat set at a rakish angle. Though he earned less than the inspector, he spent much more on his clothing and appearance. Marmion was a family man. Keedy was a bachelor.

'What does he say?' asked Keedy when the inspector came across to him. 'Can anything be salvaged?'

'I'm afraid not, Joe. The whole building is gutted.'

'It's a pity. Jacob Stein made good suits. Not that I could ever afford one, mark you,' he said with a wry grin. 'My wage doesn't stretch to high-quality bespoke tailors.'

'You'll have to wait until you become commissioner,' said Marmion with a chuckle. 'Sir Edward was a regular customer here. That's why he gave this incident priority. As for the fire,' he went on, 'it's done its worst. It's eaten its way through some of the ceiling joists, so the floors in the upper rooms are unsafe. They're going to get a man inside there, if they can, to take a closer look at the body. It's in the room at the front.'

'Poor devil didn't get out in time. My guess is that he died of smoke inhalation. Once that stuff gets in your lungs, you've got no chance. I've seen lots of people who've died that way – and just about every other way, for that matter. Call it an occupational hazard.'

Before he joined the police force, Keedy had worked briefly in the family firm of undertakers but he lacked the temperament for a funeral director. His lively sense of humour was considered distasteful in a world of professional solemnity. The irony was that his work as a detective involved dead bodies as well, with the added challenge of finding out who had actually committed the murders.

'What about witnesses?' asked Marmion.

'They're few and far between. According to the constable who was first on the scene, there were over forty people scrambling around inside the shop. When the fire took hold, they got out quickly with whatever they'd managed to grab.'

'Were any arrests made?'

'Only two,' said Keedy. 'It was like bedlam here, apparently. The constable was lucky to nab the two men that he got.'

'I'll make a point of talking to both of them.'

'One of them was caught with a suit he'd stolen. Why bother to take it? It's not as if he could wear the blooming thing. He's a plumber by trade. Can you imagine him going to work in a Jacob Stein suit?'

'I daresay he wanted a souvenir.'

'He's got one, Inspector – a visit to the magistrates' court.'

They shared a laugh then surveyed the crowd. While Keedy picked out the pretty faces of young women, Marmion was studying the expressions on the faces of the men.

'Some of them are here, Joe,' he said. 'Some of the people who did this have come back to see their handiwork. They know they're safe. When a crowd is on the rampage, it's almost impossible to pick out individuals. They're here to gloat.'

'What about the women?'

'In their case, it's mostly idle curiosity.'

'I don't know about that,' said Keedy. 'Did you read about what happened in Liverpool yesterday? When they ran riot there, one of the ringleaders was a sixty-year-old woman.'

'I saw the article. She helped to set fire to a garage owned by someone with a German name. Her son was a carpenter on the *Lusitania.* He's feared dead.'

'What she did was understandable.'

Marmion was firm. 'That doesn't make it right, Joe.'

'No, no, I suppose not.'

There was a buzz of interest from the crowd when they saw the fire engine moving closer so that its ladder could be brought into use. Hoses had stopped playing on the upper floor and were concentrating their aim on the glowing embers in the shop. A fireman removed his helmet to wipe the sweat from his brow. After receiving orders from a superior, he gave a nod and put the helmet on again. There was no glass left in the upper windows and smoke was still curling out of them. When the ladder was in position, the fireman went slowly up it.

'Better him than me,' said Keedy. 'I can feel the heat from here.'

'It's what they're trained to do, Joe.'

'They've had plenty of practice since the *Lusitania* sank.'

'I'll be glad when this mania dies down. It's costing too many lives. All right,' said Marmion, 'they may have German names but they've all been naturalised. If they hadn't been, they'd be interned by now. They're British citizens who chose to live here because they believed they could have a better life in our country. They work hard, set up businesses, pay their taxes and keep out of trouble.' He gestured towards the shop. 'Then *this* happens. It's sickening.'

'It's the prevailing mood, Inspector. Nothing we can do about that except to pick up the pieces afterwards. Hang on,' said Keedy, looking up. 'I think he's going inside.'

They watched with interest as the fireman at the top of the ladder used his axe to hack away the charred remains of the window frame. Putting the axe away in his belt, he cocked a leg over the sill then switched on his torch. The next moment, he ducked his head and climbed gingerly into the room to test its floorboards and joists. Marmion and Keedy waited for what seemed like an age for the man to reappear. When he finally did so, he came back through the window then descended the ladder. His superior was waiting for him.

The detectives remained patient as the fireman removed his helmet before delivering his report. Though he could hear none of the words spoken, Marmion could see that it was an animated discussion. When the officer pointed upwards, the fireman shook his head decisively. At length his superior gave the man a congratulatory pat then looked around for the detectives. Marmion and Keedy stepped forward to meet him.

'Well,' said Marmion, 'what did he find?'

'There *is* a body there, Inspector,' replied the officer, 'but he was unable to reach it because part of the floor had given way. We'll have to wait until we can approach it from below.'

'How long will that take?'

'Your guess is as good as mine – hours at least.'

'What state was the body in?' asked Keedy.

'Oh,' said Marmion, introducing his colleague, 'this is Sergeant Keedy. He's not asking his question out of ghoulish curiosity. He used to work for an undertaker and has seen many victims of fires.'

'They've usually been overcome by smoke,' noted Keedy.

'Not in this instance,' said the officer, grimacing. 'My man couldn't reach him but he got close enough to see the knife sticking out of his chest. There was something else he noticed, Inspector. The safe door was wide open.' He shook his head in disgust. 'You're not just dealing with arson and theft, I'm afraid. You've got a murder case on your hands.'

CHAPTER FOUR

Ruth stayed in the bath even though the water was getting cold. She felt dirty all over. She was still stunned at the way that her body had been invaded by a complete stranger. Until her terrifying encounter in the alley, she'd had only a fuzzy idea of what sexual intercourse involved. All that her mother had told her was that she had to 'save yourself for your husband'. That was impossible now. The thing she was supposed to save had been cruelly wrested from her. What potential husband would even consider her now? He'd regard her as tainted. And if she hid the awful truth from him, he'd be bound to discover it on their wedding night. Ruth's virginity had gone for ever. In its place, her assailant had left her with pain, fear and revulsion. The thought that he might also have left her pregnant made her tremble uncontrollably.

They would all blame her but not as much as she blamed herself. What had she done wrong? Why didn't she call for help? Should she have pleaded with them? Should she have run back to her father? Why did she slap one of them across the face? Was that her mistake? Would they have let her go if she'd simply given them a kiss? Who would believe what she had suffered and who could possibly understand? Ruth felt defenceless and horribly alone.

Her mother had tried to send for the doctor but Ruth had begged her not to do so. She claimed that she would be fine after a bath and locked herself in the bathroom. Water was hopelessly inadequate. It might cleanse her body but it could not remove the ugly stain of her torment. That would always be at the back of her mind. Ten minutes in an alleyway had ruined her life. It was unfair.

Her mother banged on the door.

'Ruth!' she called. 'Are you all right in there?'

'Yes, Mother,' replied her daughter, meekly.

'You don't sound all right. You've been in there over an hour.'

'I'll be out soon, I promise.'

'I want you to come out now,' said Miriam, 'and I still think that the doctor should have a look at you. It's not right for a healthy girl of your age to faint like that. You frightened me.'

'I'm sorry, Mother. I didn't mean to.'

'Your Uncle Herman agrees with me. I spoke to him on the telephone. He thinks we should call the doctor. I told him what had happened and he was very worried. He said that it was unlike you to desert your father like that.'

'He told me to go,' bleated Ruth. 'Father told me to go.'

'Your Uncle Herman was shocked.'

It was something else for which she'd be blamed. Ruth winced.

'Can you hear me?' said Miriam, raising her voice. 'Your Uncle Herman was shocked. He's driven off to the West End to find out what happened to your father. He feels that you should have stayed with him. You're our daughter. It was your duty.'

'I've said that I'm sorry.'

'It's so uncharacteristic. Whatever possessed you?'

There was a long silence. It served only to provoke Miriam. Pounding on the door with a fist, she delivered her ultimatum.

'Get out of that bath,' she ordered. 'If you don't do as you're told, I'll fetch the doctor this instant. Get out of that bath and let me in. I won't ask you again, Ruth.'

There was no escape. Ruth decided that she would sooner face an angry mother than an embarrassing examination from a doctor. She heaved herself up into a standing position.

'I'll be there in a moment,' she said.

'So I should hope.'

Ruth clambered out of the bath and reached for the towel. When she'd wrapped herself up in it, she turned the key and unlocked the door. Her mother stepped in with an accusatory stare.

'What on earth's got into you, Ruth?' she demanded.

'I feel much better now.'

'I'm your mother. You don't need to lock me out.'

'I'm sorry.'

'And look at the way you've dropped everything on the floor,' said Miriam, bending over the pile of clothes. 'You're always so careful about hanging things up. What's got into you?'

She picked up the clothes and was about to put them on a chair when her eye fell on a stocking. Miriam gaped at the large bloodstain.

Herman Stein bore a close resemblance to his elder brother. He had the same paunch, the same rounded shoulders and the same facial features. He'd kept much more of his hair than the tailor but that was the only marked difference between the two men. Having driven to the West End, he parked his car and hurried to Jermyn Street. The fire engine was still outside the smoking shop owned by his brother but some of the crowd had melted away. When he spoke to the senior officer, he was told that the incident was in the hands of Scotland Yard detectives. Marmion and Keedy were pointed out to him. Face clouded with foreboding, he went straight across to them.

'My name is Herbert Stone,' he said. 'Jacob Stein is my brother.'

Marmion didn't need to ask why the man had anglicised his surname. It was a precaution that many people of German origin had taken after the war had broken out. He introduced himself and the sergeant then chose his words with care.

'Your brother's premises were attacked by a mob,' he explained. 'We've reason to believe that he was trapped by the fire in an upstairs room.'

'That's where he'd have been, Inspector,' said Stone. 'Earlier this evening, he was up there with my niece, going through the books. I hear that she came home alone in a terrible state but there was no sign of Jacob. His car is still in its usual parking place. I left mine beside it.'

'Nothing is certain, sir. We're only working on assumptions.'

'It must be Jacob – who else could it be?'

'I have no idea, Mr Stone.'

'Can't they get the body out?'

'Not until it's safe to do so,' said Keedy. 'Much of the floor in that room has collapsed and the staircase has been burnt down. They'll need to prop up the remaining part of the floor before they can climb up there, and they can't do that until they can clear enough of the debris from the ground floor.'

'What kind of scum did this?' asked Stone, staring angrily at the wreckage. 'It's unforgivable. How did the police let this happen? Aren't you supposed to protect property?'

'We can't stand vigil over *every* shop, sir. Our manpower is limited. When there was an appeal for volunteers to join the army, we lost a lot of policemen.'

'That's no excuse, Sergeant.'

'It's a fact of life.'

'What are you doing about this outrage now?'

'We have two of the culprits in custody,' said Marmion, 'and there'll be other arrests before too long. First of all, of course, we need to establish if it *is* your brother in there. Given the circumstances, that may not be easy.'

'I'd recognise Jacob in any condition,' asserted Stone. 'Even if he's been badly burnt, I'll know if it's him.'

'We're very grateful for your assistance, sir. You say that your niece was here earlier this evening?'

'Yes – she joined her father after the shop was closed.'

'Then she may well have been on the premises when the window was smashed and the fire started. We'll need to interview her. She should be able to give us valuable information.'

'Ruth has been acting very strangely since she got back.'

'That's not surprising,' said Keedy. 'She'd still be in shock. It would have been a gruesome experience for anyone.'

'Needless to say,' added Marmion, 'we'll exercise discretion. If her father *is* dead, she'll need time to adjust to the tragedy. We won't bother her until she's ready to help us.' He glanced up at the shop.

'I understand that there was a safe in that room. Do you happen to know what your brother kept in it, Mr Stone?'

'Of course,' said the other. 'The safe contained documents relevant to the business – invoices, receipts, designs, account books, details of current orders and so on.'

'What about money?'

'He always kept a substantial amount in there, Inspector. Apart from anything else, there was the wages bill at the end of each week. He employed a full-time staff of four and one part-timer.' His chest swelled with pride. 'As a gentleman's outfitter, my brother was a match for anyone.'

'I see that *you're* wearing a Jacob Stein suit, sir,' noted Keedy.

'I'm not just doing so out of family loyalty, Sergeant. I like the best and that's what he always provided.' His irritation sharpened. 'How much longer do they have to wait until they can go in there?'

'Only the fire brigade can tell you that, sir.'

'Then I'll see if I can hurry them up.'

Turning on his heel, Stone went off to accost the senior officer, leaving the detectives on their own. Keedy watched him go.

'I didn't see much sign of grief,' he commented. 'If it was my brother up there in that room, I'd be heartbroken.'

'His anger is masking his grief,' said Marmion. 'Underneath that bluster, I'm sure that he's already in mourning. What we're seeing is a natural fury that the shop has gone up in smoke simply because it had a German name over it.'

'Why didn't you tell him the full story, Inspector?'

'What do you mean?'

'His brother was stabbed to death,' Keedy reminded him.

'First, we're not absolutely sure that it *is* Jacob Stein. Second, even if it is, we need to establish the exact cause and likely time of death before we give those details to any relatives. Police work is sometimes about holding back information, Joe.'

'Supposing one of the firemen tells him?'

'I made it clear that they were to say nothing. There are a couple of reporters hanging about. If they get a sniff of murder, it will be all over the newspapers tomorrow. I want to conduct this investigation at *our* pace and not that of the British press.'

'Fair enough – what do we do now?'

'Nothing much is going to happen here for a while,' decided Marmion, 'so I'll slip off and interview the two people in custody.'

'Do you want me to come with you?'

'No thanks, Joe. You stay here. And if any reporters try to pester you, don't give anything away.' Marmion was about to leave when he remembered something. 'By the way, that was very clever of you. How did you know that Mr Stone had a Jacob Stein suit?'

'That was easy,' explained Keedy. 'I can pick out the work of all the best outfitters in London. Their styles are so individual. Then there's the other clue, of course.'

'What other clue?'

'You've met Stone. He likes to dress well and he's the kind of man who'd always patronise someone who gave him a big discount. Nobody else but his brother would do that.'

Marmion grinned. 'You ought to be a detective, Joe Keedy.'

Ruth was in a world of her own. Wearing a dressing gown, she sat on the edge of the sofa with her arms wrapped protectively across her chest. Her mother had replaced annoyance with sympathy. All her instincts told her that her daughter had been through a devastating experience and was in need of love and comfort. She made Ruth a hot drink but the girl would not even touch it. Miriam sat beside her, stroking her back gently.

'You're home now, Ruth,' she said, softly. 'You're safe. Nobody can touch you here.' She picked up the cup. 'Why don't you take a sip of this?' The girl shook her head. 'It will do you good.'

Ruth could not imagine that anything on earth could do her good. She was utterly beyond help. In spite of what her mother said, Ruth was not safe in her home. He'd followed her there. She could still smell his foul breath and feel his weight pressing down on her. She could still recall the intense pain he'd inflicted in pursuit of his pleasure. Her breasts were still sore after their kneading. Her mouth still tasted of him. Her vagina was smarting.

Miriam put the cup back in the saucer and moved in closer.

'What happened?' she whispered.

'Nothing . . .'

'Something must have upset you. What was it?'

'There was nothing.'

'I'm not blind, Ruth. I saw that blood and it's not the right time of the month for that. It's not the only stain I saw on your stocking. I'm bound to wonder, darling. Every mother has those fears for her daughter. I'm no different.' She put an arm around Ruth's shoulders. 'Tell me the truth. It will have to come out sooner or later. Why hold it back? *Whatever* has happened, I'll still love you – we all will. But we can't help you if you don't tell us how. Do you see that?'

'Yes, Mother,' said Ruth, quietly.

'Then please – *please* – tell me what this is all about.'

There was a long pause. Her mother was right. Ruth could not stay silent indefinitely. The truth could not be hidden. When she tried to speak, however, Ruth almost choked on the words. She began to retch. Miriam pulled her close and rocked her gently to and fro until Ruth recovered. Then she kissed her daughter on the forehead.

'Take your time,' she advised. 'There's no hurry.'

Taking a deep breath, Ruth summoned up her courage.

'It was my fault,' she said, blankly. 'It was all my fault.'

The first man interviewed by Marmion at the police station was of little help. Roused from a drunken stupor, he admitted that he'd joined the mob when it marched past the pub where he'd been drinking because he was hoping for some excitement. When the window of the shop in Jermyn Street had been broken, he'd clambered inside and helped to smash the place up until someone set it on fire. As he tried to flee, he was arrested by a policeman. Marmion was satisfied that he was telling the truth and that he'd been acting alone. He clearly had no idea who had been leading the mob or who had started the fire.

The second man who was cooling his heels in a police cell was a different proposition. Brian Coley was a surly plumber in his late twenties, a solid man with tattooed forearms and an ugly face twisted into a permanent scowl. When Marmion started to question him, the prisoner became truculent.

'You got no reason to keep me here,' he protested.

'From what I hear, Mr Coley, we have *every* reason. According to the arresting officer, you were part of a gang that broke into the shop and vandalised it. When you were leaving, you had a suit in your possession.'

'It weren't mine.'

'I gathered that.'

'I mean, *I* didn't steal it. What happened was this, see? Some other bloke give it me. When he saw that copper waiting to pounce on him, he shoves the suit in my hands then hops it. So the copper arrests me instead, when I was just an innocent bystander.'

'You were actually seen inside the shop area.'

'Who says so?'

'It was the policeman who arrested you.'

'Then he's lying his bleeding head off.'

'Now why should he do that, Mr Coley?'

'Coppers are all the same,' said the plumber, curling his lip. 'They're liars. I never went into that shop.'

'But you admit that you were in Jermyn Street?'

'Yeah . . . I sort of . . . happened to be passing.'

'Really?' said Marmion, raising a cynical eyebrow. 'I checked your address before I came in here. How does someone who lives in Shoreditch happen to be passing a gentleman's outfitters in the West End?'

Coley folded his arms. 'Can't remember.'

'You were in that vicinity with the express purpose of damaging private property. Why not be honest about it? You entered that shop and stole a suit.'

'It's not true.'

'Let me ask you something else,' said Marmion, changing his tack. 'What do you think of the Germans?'

Coley snorted. 'I hate the whole lot of them.'

'Why is that?'

'They're fighting a war against us, of course – and they sunk the *Lusitania* off the coast of Ireland. Germans are vicious animals.'

'That's a term that might be used of the mob in Jermyn Street this evening. The attack was certainly vicious – and all because the shop was owned by a man named Jacob Stein.'

'He deserved it.'

'Why?'

'He's one of them German bastards.'

'He was a naturalised British citizen,' affirmed Marmion. 'That means he has as much right to live in this country as you or me. If you're so keen to punish Germans, why don't you have the guts to join the army? You could fight them on equal terms then.'

Coley glowered at him. 'I got my job to look after.'

'Thousands of other able-bodied men have already volunteered.'

'That's their business.'

Marmion regarded him with a mixture of interest and contempt. He'd met a lot of people like the plumber, resentful men with a hatred of any authority and a particular dislike of the police. From the way that Coley seemed at ease in custody, Marmion deduced that he'd been in trouble before. One thing was certain. Coley had not been alone. He knew others who'd been party to the attack on the shop. He had the names that could be useful in the inquiry.

'Who else was with you?' asked Marmion.

Coley shrugged. 'I was on my own.'

'What about the man you claim handed you that suit?'

'Never set eyes on him before.'

'I don't believe that he existed. Your friends, however, do exist. You run with a pack. You wouldn't have the courage to do anything like that on your own. A man who's too afraid to fight for his king and country needs someone else to hide behind.'

'I'm not afraid of anything!' yelled Coley.

'Not even a long prison sentence?'

'You can't send me to prison. I done nothing wrong.'

'That's not what the jury will think,' warned Marmion. 'You were part of a mob involved in arson, trespass, theft, wilful destruction of private property and – directly or indirectly – in the death of the owner of the shop. Mr Stein was upstairs at the time.'

Coley swallowed hard. 'I never touched him.'

'That may be true but you might know someone who did. At the very least, you know other people who were there and they, in turn, can give us additional names.' Marmion put his face close to him and spoke with quiet menace. 'However long it takes, I'm going to track down every single person who was involved in that disgraceful attack and bring them to justice. The one I'm most anxious to meet is the man who started that fire then threw petrol on to it. Was it you or one of your friends, sir?' Coley shook his head vigorously. 'I'll leave you to think it over. When I come back again, I'll expect you to remember the names and addresses of those who brought you all the way from Shoreditch so that you could vent your spleen on an innocent man.'

'I had nothing to do with that fire,' asserted the prisoner.

'Then who did?'

Coley eyed him warily. All his defiance had gone. The one thing on his mind was self-preservation. The scale of the notional charges against him was unnerving. When he'd been arrested before, he'd always managed to get away with a fine. Not this time. Inspector Marmion had rattled him. The prospect of a prison sentence suddenly seemed a real one. Coley tried to win favour.

'I saw someone carrying a petrol can,' he confessed.

It was a start. Marmion was content.

CHAPTER FIVE

To relieve the boredom of the long wait, Joe Keedy chatted to one of the policemen. Having spent years in uniform himself, Keedy had compassion for the men who patrolled the streets on their beat in all weathers. They were a visible deterrent to criminals and a sign of reassurance to the law-abiding public. Since the war started, the scope of their duties had widened considerably and they worked assiduously to discharge them. Notwithstanding their best efforts, however, they sometimes came in for harsh criticism. Herbert Stone was their latest detractor. He was pulsing with exasperation.

'It's maddening,' he complained as he came over to Keedy. 'The fire brigade is almost as bad as the police force.'

'They're only doing their job, sir,' said Keedy.

'Then why don't they do it properly? The same goes for the police. You knew that trouble was expected. After what happened to the *Lusitania*, there were bound to be repercussions. Why weren't more of you on duty?'

'We can't police every street in London.'

'People like my brother deserved preferential treatment,' insisted Stone. 'He was a man of standing in the West End. I'll raise the matter with the commissioner himself – and I'll also have stern words to say about the fire brigade.'

'Why is that?'

'I've been insulted, Sergeant. The officer in charge of the operation has just told me that, if I don't stop badgering him, he'll have me removed by the police.'

'He doesn't want to be impeded, sir.'

'I'm not impeding anyone,' argued Stone, pointing at the shop. 'My brother is dead in there. I'm entitled to know why they're taking such an eternity to bring him out.'

'It's still too dangerous to go in,' said Keedy, seeing a chance to get rid of him. 'My information is that it may be past midnight before they've cleared the debris. There's really no point in hanging on until then, sir. You can't make a formal identification here. That will have to be done at the morgue.'

'I want to see my brother.'

'Perhaps you should consider his family, Mr Stone. His wife will be worried sick and you mentioned a daughter earlier. She's bound to be very anxious. In the event of bad news, they need to be prepared.'

It took Stone a few moments to regain his composure.

'Yes,' he conceded, anger subsiding, 'you're right, Sergeant. My sister-in-law will fear the worst and so will Ruth. They must be told the truth.' After consulting a pocket watch, he reached a decision. 'I'll drive back to Golders Green. This is not something that I can do over the telephone. I need to be there in person.'

'That's very considerate of you, sir.'

Stone wagged a finger. 'But I'll want to know the moment the body has been moved.'

'We'll contact you at once.'

'Here's my card.' Slipping the watch back into his waistcoat pocket, he took out his wallet and extracted a business card. He handed it to Keedy. 'Ring that number any time of night. I'll be up.'

'Leave it with me, sir.'

'Out of respect to my brother, I feel that I ought to stay,' said Stone with a final glance at the shop, 'but you're right – my place is with his family. Goodbye, Sergeant.'

'Goodbye, sir.'

'We don't want to impede the fire brigade any more, do we?'

On that sarcastic note, Stone wheeled round and headed off towards the street where he'd parked his car. Aggressive as the man's manner had been, Keedy nevertheless felt sorry for him. Losing a brother was a severe blow and Stone now had to pass on the bad tidings to his family. Keedy did not envy him the task. In the course of his work, he'd had to impart bad news to people and most had been unable to bear it. He hated being the one to spread grief and despair.

Now that the fire had been extinguished, the firemen were working heroically to clear up the mess so that they could shore up the vestiges of the ceiling. Because a famous British vessel had been sunk, a business that had taken many years to build up had been burnt out of existence in little more than two hours. Its proud owner, it seemed, had been murdered and his safe plundered. It was not simply a case of mob violence. They were looking for a killer.

A car approached and pulled up nearby. Marmion got out and surveyed the scene before strolling over to Keedy.

'I don't see Mr Stone anywhere,' said Marmion.

'I sent him home, Inspector. He was making a nuisance of himself to the fire brigade and he was far from complimentary about the police. I pointed out that his brother's family would be desperate for news and implied that he was the best person to deliver it.'

'Well done, Joe. He has my greatest sympathy but the truth is that he was only in the way.'

'It was a double triumph,' boasted Keedy. 'I not only got rid of him, I saved us the awkward job of being the bearers of bad tidings.' His grin warned Marmion that there was a joke coming. 'You might say that I killed two birds with one Stone.'

Marmion groaned. 'I'm glad you didn't tell him that.'

'How did you get on at Vine Street?'

'Oh, it was worth the visit. One of the men arrested had nothing of value to say but the other was quite helpful once I'd persuaded him of the dire position he was in. He gave me the names and addresses of three friends involved in the incident, so we'll be able to pay them a visit. He also told me that he saw someone carrying a can of petrol.'

'You thought something was used to speed up the fire.'

'With luck the can will have been discarded,' said Marmion. 'It may be somewhere under that rubble. Oh,' he went on, 'there was another snippet of information I picked up at Vine Street. The station sergeant told me that Jacob Stein's daughter called in there to report the fire. She was very agitated. In fact, she was in such obvious distress that the sergeant asked one of his men to take her home on the Tube. I feel for the girl,' said Marmion with a sigh. 'Ruth Stein is going to be even more distressed when she learns what happened to her father.'

Still wearing her dressing gown, Ruth was curled up on the sofa in her mother's arms. She had not been pressed for details or forced to relive the horrors of her ordeal. Somehow her mother understood what her daughter must be going through and spared her any questioning. Miriam uttered no words of condemnation, nor had she summoned the doctor. That could wait until morning. What her daughter needed most was the uncritical love and sympathy of a mother and that is what she was given. It helped to still Ruth's fears and enable her to count her blessings. She'd come through a terrible crisis but she was still alive. She still had a home where she was adored. Overshadowed as it might be, she still had a future. That was not the case with her father. Jacob Stein had still been in the building when it was set alight. Had he escaped, he would surely have come back to the house by now or, at the very least, have made contact by telephone.

They heard the sound of car tyres scrunching on the gravel in the drive. An engine was turned off. Ruth felt her mother's grip tighten in trepidation for a few seconds, then the two of them got up and went into the hall. When Miriam opened the front door, her brother-in-law was getting out of the car. The expression on his face told them what had happened. Ruth burst into tears, her mother enfolded her in her arms and Stone ushered the two of them gently back into the house.

Harvey Marmion hated having to visit the morgue. It brought back unhappy memories of the time when he'd been called upon to identify the corpse of his father. It had been a harrowing experience. As he looked at the body of Jacob Stein, he was relieved that his father had not been reduced to such a hideous condition. Fire had burnt off the clothes of the dead man, singeing his hair and eyebrows, then eating hungrily into his flesh. Marmion could hardly bear to look at the blackened figure but Joe Keedy was studying it with interest, noting the ugly gash in the chest. When they had been able to reach the body, the detectives had it removed under cover so that it escaped the prying eyes of the press. Marmion would have to make a statement in due course but only after the body had been formally identified by a close family member. There was the commissioner to consider as well. He would need to be told that his tailor had been murdered.

'Shall I ring Mr Stone?' asked Keedy.

'No,' said Marmion. 'I'll do that, Joe.'

'Are you going to tell him about the murder weapon?'

'Not until he gets here.'

'You'll need this.' Keedy handed over Stone's business card. 'He said that we could ring, no matter how late it is.'

Marmion glanced at the clock on the wall. 'Look at the time,' he said. 'Ellen will think I've run off with another woman.'

'Your wife knows you too well to think that.'

'Police work plays havoc with family life.'

'That's why I never married,' said Keedy, smiling. 'Well, that's one of the reasons, anyway.'

'We all know the main one, Joe, but I don't think this is the place to discuss your lively private life. Let's get out of here, shall we?' They left the morgue and stepped into the corridor outside. Marmion inhaled deeply. 'That's better – we can breathe properly now.'

'I used to see dead bodies every day in the family business.'

'*I* could never work in a place like this, I know that. But I'm grateful that someone can. A post-mortem always yields some useful clues. Well,' he added, 'you might as well sign off for the night.'

'Don't you want me to hang on until Mr Stone arrives?'

'No, thanks – I can cope with him. You get your beauty sleep.'

Keedy grinned. 'Who says I'm going to sleep?'

'I do,' warned Marmion. 'I want you wide awake and turning up on time. We've got a busy day ahead of us tomorrow – and the same goes for the days ahead. This will be a very complex investigation.'

'The killer was one of dozens of people who got into that shop. Talk about safety in numbers. Do you think we have any chance at all of catching him, Inspector?'

'Oh, we'll catch him, Joe,' said Marmion, eyes glinting. 'I can guarantee it.'

Alice Marmion crept downstairs in the dark so that she would not wake her mother. Wearing a dressing gown and a pair of fur-lined slippers, she was a relatively tall, lean, lithe young woman in her twenties with an attractive face and dimpled cheeks. When she got to the hall, she was surprised to see a light under the kitchen door. She opened the door gently and saw her mother, dozing in a chair with her knitting resting on her lap. Ellen Marmion was an older and plumper version of her daughter. Her hair was grey and her face lined. Alice smiled affectionately. She was uncertain whether to rouse her mother or to slip gently away. In the event, the decision was taken out of her hands. Ellen came awake with a start.

'Oh!' she exclaimed, seeing Alice. 'What are you doing here?'

'I might ask you the same thing, Mummy. There's no point in staying up for Daddy. He might be hours yet.'

'I'm not tired.'

'Then why did you fall asleep?'

'I just dozed off for a few minutes.'

'I couldn't get off at all,' said Alice. 'I've got too many things on my mind. In the end, I thought I'd sneak down here and finish the marking. The children will expect their books back tomorrow.'

Ellen was concerned. 'I think I can guess what's on your mind.'

'Vera Dowling and I talked about it at school yesterday. If I will, then Vera will. She just needs me to take the lead.'

'You know what your father and I think, Alice. We're against the idea. You've got a good job – an important job. Why do you need to run off and join the Women's Emergency Corps?'

'We want to help in the war effort.'

'But, in a sense, you're already doing that. You're taking the children's minds off the horrible things that are happening on the front. A lot of them have fathers who are fighting over there in the trenches. Your pupils must be so worried.'

'They are,' agreed Alice. 'Most of them are too young to realise the full implications but, deep down, they're very afraid. So are the mothers, of course. You can see it in their faces when they drop the kids off. Some, of course, have already lost their husbands. I feel so sorry for them. This war seems to be about nothing else but loss.'

'That doesn't mean you have to give up your job.'

'I could always return to teaching later.'

'I can't bear the thought of you in uniform, Alice.'

'Paul is in uniform.'

'That's different,' argued Ellen. 'Your brother is a man. He felt that it was his duty to enlist.'

'Joining the WEC doesn't mean that I'll be in any danger,' said Alice. 'I'd still be based in this country – in London, probably. There's a whole range of jobs that need doing.'

'Teaching is one of them,' Ellen reminded her.

She stifled a yawn and put her knitting on the kitchen table. It was too late to reopen an argument that she'd been having with her daughter for some weeks now. Ellen's position was simple. She was proud that Alice was a schoolteacher. Having been denied a proper education herself, she wanted her daughter to pursue her studies and gain qualifications. It had involved dedication and many sacrifices. She could not understand why Alice was ready to turn her back on a job she'd striven so hard to get.

'One more uniform in the family won't make any difference,' said Alice with a teasing smile.

'What do you mean?'

'I was thinking about Uncle Raymond. He's been wearing a uniform for years in the Salvation Army. And he has to put up with far more hostility than I'd have to face in the WEC.'

'I know,' said Ellen, ruefully. 'He's been called names and pelted with stones time and again. He's only trying to help people. I don't agree with everything he believes in but I think your Uncle Raymond is a very brave man.'

'Perhaps I should talk it over with him.'

Ellen was firm. 'This is a matter between you and your parents, Alice. We don't want to drag your uncle into this. Now why don't you forget all about that marking and try to get some sleep.'

Alice touched her mother's arm gently. 'Let's go up together.'

'Your father can't be all that long now.'

'Daddy can't expect you to wait up for ever,' said Alice, helping her mother to her feet. 'You leave your knitting and I'll leave my marking. Off we go, Mummy.'

Feeling another yawn coming, Ellen put a hand to her mouth. Then she let herself be led out of the kitchen, leaving the light on. When they got to the bottom of the stairs, she grasped Alice's wrist.

'I want you to promise me something,' she said.

'I can't promise not to join the WEC.'

'That's not what I'm asking, Alice. Your father and I have been very happy and I wouldn't change him for the world. But I don't want the same life for you. Promise me that you'll never marry a policeman.'

Herbert Stone looked so dejected that Marmion took pity on him. Opening a drawer in his desk, the detective took out two glasses and a bottle of brandy. He poured a tot into each glass then offered one to his visitor. With a nod of thanks, Stone took it from him and had a restorative sip. It was late at night. After a visit to the morgue, they were in Marmion's office. It had been trying enough for Stone to identify the corpse but there was an additional burden for him to carry now. He'd been told that foul play was involved. As well as coping with his own grief, it fell to him to inform the rest of the family that his brother had been stabbed to death.

Taking another sip of brandy, he mastered his sorrow.

'When can we have the body?' he asked.

'That's a matter for the coroner to decide,' said Marmion, softly. 'He'll want a full post-mortem.'

Stone was dismayed. 'Does my brother *have* to be cut to pieces, Inspector? Surely, he's suffered enough indignity already.'

'It's standard procedure in the case of unnatural death, sir.'

'Our religion enjoins us to bury the deceased as soon as possible. There are strict rituals to observe. Ideally, we'd like to reclaim the body today.'

'That's very unlikely, I'm afraid, Mr Stone. The body has far too much to tell us and that takes time. You'll have to be patient.'

Stone's anger surfaced again. 'This wouldn't have happened if the police had been protecting my brother's shop, as they should have done. How could you allow such a tragedy to occur?' he demanded. 'My brother has led a blameless life. He didn't deserve to die like this. What kind of police force permits a drunken mob to charge through the streets of London and murder someone with impunity?'

'The killer will be punished,' said Marmion with conviction. 'That's one thing of which you may rest assured.'

'How on earth will you find him? It was the random act of someone who hates all Germans. He was one of a crowd. You'll never pick him out.'

'I disagree, sir. This was no random murder.'

'What else could it be, man?'

'I think it's the work of someone who took advantage of the situation, using the mob as his cover. He must have known that the shop was a likely target and – more to the point – that your brother might actually be on the premises at the time. There was calculation at work here,' decided Marmion. 'That means we're not looking for an anonymous figure caught up in the attack. We'll be searching for someone who *knew* Mr Stein and who had reason to wish him dead.'

'Are you saying that the murder was planned?'

'That's my feeling, sir.'

'What evidence do you have?'

'Very little at the moment,' admitted Marmion, 'so I'm relying to some extent on intuition. But ask yourself this. If you're simply intent on breaking into a shop and looting it, why would you carry a knife?'

'I never thought of that,' said Stone.

'We're looking for a killer who had some kind of grudge against your brother – and it may have nothing to do with the fact that he has a German background. Think carefully, sir,' he urged. 'You may be able to suggest some names. Did your brother have any enemies?'

Before he spoke, Stone drained the glass of brandy.

'Of course,' he said, resignedly. 'Jacob was a Jew – we always have enemies.'

CHAPTER SIX

When Alice came downstairs for breakfast, she found her mother in the kitchen. Fried bacon was already waiting on a plate in the gas oven and eggs were sizzling in the pan with some tomatoes. Toast was slowly turning brown under the grill.

'What time did Daddy get back last night?' wondered Alice.

'I don't know. I was fast asleep.'

'You were quite right to go to bed.'

'Then why do I feel so guilty about it?' asked Ellen. 'I felt it was my duty to be here for him.'

Alice was crisp. 'Daddy is the detective – not you. If he has to work long hours, it doesn't mean that you have to as well.' She grinned. 'After all, you don't get paid for overtime like him.'

Ellen laughed. 'That's one way of putting it.'

She continued to make the breakfast before sharing it out on three separate plates. By the time that Marmion arrived in his shirtsleeves, the meal was on the table for him with a cup of tea beside it. He gave Ellen a kiss of gratitude then sat beside her. Alice was opposite him.

'Good morning, teacher,' he said.

Alice smiled. 'You may not be able to call me that much longer.'

'Don't tell me they've sacked you.'

'No – but I may be handing in my resignation.'

Realising what she meant, Marmion stiffened. He hoped that he'd talked his daughter out of her plan to join the Women's Emergency Corps. Clearly, it was still a live issue. Before he could speak, Ellen jumped in quickly to avert an argument.

'Let's not discuss it over a meal,' she suggested. 'We don't want a row this early in the day.'

'I'm entitled to pass an opinion, love,' said Marmion.

'Alice already knows what it is, dear.'

'And you both know *my* opinion,' said Alice, 'so let's leave it at that.' She put sugar in her tea and stirred it with a spoon. 'I didn't hear you come in last night, Daddy. Where had you been?'

'Joe Keedy and I found an illegal gambling den,' joked Marmion, 'and we lost a month's wages on the roulette wheel.' He shook his head. 'Actually, it was a lot more serious than that. A mob raided a gents' outfitters in Jermyn Street. They burnt it down and the owner was murdered.'

'What a dreadful thing to happen!'

'Do you have any suspects?' asked Ellen.

'At the moment, we have too many of them – forty or more.' He looked quizzically at his daughter. 'What do you do with your pupils, Alice? When one of them does something naughty and nobody owns up, how do you handle the situation?'

'I threaten to keep them all in after school.'

'Does the threat work?'

'Every time – the children all stare at the culprit.'

'Unfortunately, that option is not open to Joe and me.'

Ellen swallowed some bacon. 'How is Joe Keedy?'

'He's in fine form.'

'We haven't seen him for ages. You should ask him round.'

'Yes,' said Alice, fondly. 'That would be nice. Invite him to tea.'

'There won't be time for luxuries like tea for quite a while,' said Marmion. 'Joe and I are going to be working at full stretch.'

'He can always drop in for a drink one evening,' suggested Ellen. 'I like him. Joe Keedy is good company. He's got a sensible head on his shoulders.' She shot a glance at Alice. 'He might even be able to persuade a certain someone to abandon this urge to join the WEC.'

'I thought we weren't going to talk about that,' protested Alice. 'Besides, Joe might be on my side. The last time he was here, he told me I should think about joining the Women's Police Service.'

Marmion pulled a face. 'Oh no you don't.'

'One police officer is enough in any family,' said Ellen, stoutly.

'In any case,' said her husband, 'it was only formed last year. It still hasn't sorted out exactly what it's supposed to do. In essence, I think it's a good idea but that's not a view shared by some of my older colleagues. They feel that policing is a man's job.'

'Everything was a man's job until the war broke out,' noted Alice. 'Then women proved that they could mend cars and drive ambulances and make shells in munitions factories and do just about anything else that a man can do. It may be one of the best things to come out of the war.'

'I'm not convinced of that,' said Ellen.

'Good things do come out of bad ones, Mummy.'

'How can you call having women car mechanics a good thing?'

'Alice makes a fair point, love,' said Marmion, chewing some toast. 'Every cloud has a silver lining. Look at this business with the *Lusitania*, for instance. I bet the captain of that submarine thought he'd struck a blow for Germany when he ordered that torpedo to be fired. It's led to some bad results, of course – I was dealing with one last night – but there was also a gain. Enlistment has picked up amazingly. When I went past the recruiting centre yesterday, there was a queue halfway down Whitehall. So the loss of the *Lusitania* was not a total disaster.'

Irene Bayard was one of the first of the survivors to return to England. Rescued by a fishing boat, she'd been taken to Queenstown where she was given food, shelter and limitless sympathy. As soon as a ship departed for Liverpool, however, she was on it with Ernie Gill and a number of other survivors. She was keenly aware of how fortunate she'd been and was upset to learn that almost all the passengers she'd looked after on the *Lusitania* had perished. Irene had no desire ever to go to sea again but there was no other way to reach Liverpool, so she steeled herself for the short voyage. Though irritating at times, Gill helped her to keep up her spirits.

Neither of them was prepared for the welcome they received in Liverpool docks. It was overwhelming. The pier was thronged with relatives and friends of those who'd survived the sinking, their numbers swelled by well-wishers. But it was the number of newspaper reporters that surprised Irene. There were dozens of them. She was ambushed the moment she stepped off the ship. Irene tried to pretend that she had nothing to do with the *Lusitania* but her uniform gave her away. She was still wearing the distinctive garb of a stewardess that she'd had on when she jumped into the sea. The seemingly endless questions were both painful and intrusive. Irene wanted to forget the tragedy, not be forced to reconstruct it for the benefit of an article in a newspaper. She was glad to escape from the harassment.

Ernie Gill, by contrast, had enjoyed all the attention.

'They even took my photograph,' he boasted. 'Well, I'll see you around, Irene. Will you be staying here for a while?'

'I don't know, Ernie.'

'I will. The only trouble is that I've got here too late.'

She was puzzled. 'Too late for what?'

'Too late for the fun,' he explained. 'I wanted to help them chase every bleeding Hun out of Liverpool. There was a pork butcher from Lubeck at the end of our street. If I'd been here, I'd have sliced the ugly bugger up with his own meat cleaver.'

Irene let him give her a farewell kiss then she went off to catch her tram. Gill's violent streak disturbed her. She was happy with the thought that she'd probably never see him again. She would certainly never be part of a crew with him. That phase of her life was decidedly over. When she reached the house where she rented a couple of upstairs rooms, the first thing she had to do was to calm her tearful landlady down and assure her that she felt no ill effects. Then she filled the boiler so that she could heat enough water to have a bath. Once that was done, she put on fresh clothes and threw her uniform into the bin. Her break with the past was complete.

Next morning, Irene caught the early train to London.

When the commissioner faced Herbert Stone across his desk in Scotland Yard, both of them were wearing Jacob Stein suits. It was the morning after the crimes in Jermyn Street and his visitor's ire had increased rather than subsided. Sir Edward Henry kept a respectful silence while

Stone ranted on about the shortcomings of the police and the fire brigade. It was only when he began to criticise Harvey Marmion that the commissioner interrupted him.

'You're being too censorious, Mr Stone,' he said. 'Inspector Marmion is one of my best detectives.'

'That's not the impression I got.'

'Then you've been badly misled.'

'The inspector doesn't inspire me,' complained Stone.

'He's not paid to give inspiration, sir. He's there to catch criminals. I like to make a prompt start to the working day,' said Sir Edward, 'but when I got here first thing, Inspector Marmion was already in his office, preparing a report on last night's tragic events. If you knew his background, you might have more faith in him.'

'I have little enough at the moment, Sir Edward.'

'Then let me tell you something about him. Harvey Marmion started his career in the civil service, which is exactly what I did, albeit in India. Marmion's father was a policeman who was shot dead in the line of duty. I don't need to tell you what it feels like to be closely related to a murder victim.'

'No,' said Stone, grimly, 'you certainly don't.'

'The killer fled abroad to France and two detectives went after him. He kept eluding them. Marmion couldn't bear the thought of the man getting away with it so he gave up his job, raised money from friends and family then used it to fund his own search.'

'What happened?'

'It took him less than a week to find the man and hand him over. In short, he showed far more skill and tenacity than the two detectives assigned to the case. The very fact that he went in pursuit of an armed villain says much about his character.'

'What he did was admirable,' conceded Stone.

'There's more to it than that, sir,' said Sir Edward. 'When he got back home, he sold his story to a newspaper and used his fee to reimburse every person who'd contributed to his fund. They all got their money back and had the deep satisfaction of seeing the killer convicted and hanged. Harvey Marmion is an exceptional man.'

'I'll have to take your word for it.'

Stone was impressed by what he'd heard about the inspector but could still not warm to him. His dislike of Marmion arose partly from the fact that – in Stone's view – he showed insufficient deference. As a successful businessman, Stone employed a large number of people and was accustomed to having his orders instantly obeyed. Clearly, that would not happen with the inspector. He was his own man. No matter how much Stone railed against him, Marmion would not be taken off the investigation. He was in charge. Stone realised that he had to accept that.

As if on cue, there was a tap on the door and it opened to reveal Harvey Marmion. The commissioner beckoned him in. Marmion exchanged a greeting with Stone then took a seat beside him.

'I was just telling Mr Stone how you came to join the police force,' said Sir Edward. 'You followed in your father's footsteps.'

'It was against his wishes, Sir Edward,' said Marmion. 'He always wanted me to choose a less dangerous occupation.'

'You thrive on danger.'

'I suppose that I do.'

'It's not only policemen who face danger,' argued Stone. 'Look at my brother. You'd have thought that being a gentlemen's outfitter would keep him out of harm's way. Then there's me. When the war broke out, I immediately changed my name to hide the fact that our parents emigrated from Germany. That didn't stop someone from burning down one of my warehouses. I regret to say,' he added, pointedly, 'that the police never caught the man responsible.'

'I'll find the arsonist from last night,' said Marmion, confidently.

'How?'

'We'll do it by a variety of means, sir. I think I told you that two of those involved were in custody. Three other members of that mob will be arrested and questioned this morning. I've no doubt that we'll be able to squeeze other names out of them.'

'All that will take time, Inspector.'

'An investigation like this can't be rushed,' said Sir Edward.

'I want results.'

'We all share that desire, sir.'

'We have to separate out the different elements in the case,' said Marmion. 'Several people were guilty of wilful destruction of property and looting but there are also individuals responsible for arson and murder. The perpetrators of all those crimes will be brought to book.'

Stone fell silent. His head lowered and his shoulders sagged. He seemed at once hurt and embarrassed. He ran his tongue across dry lips. Marmion and the commissioner put the sudden change of manner down to his grief at the death of his brother but that was not the case. Stone was thinking about Ruth Stein. It needed a conscious effort to force the words out.

'There's another crime to add to your list, Inspector,' he said.

'Oh?' Marmion's ears pricked up.

'At the time when the shop was starting to burn down . . .' He paused, gritted his teeth then blurted out the information. 'My niece was being raped in the alley at the rear of the property.'

* * *

When they reported to their barracks that morning, they changed into their uniforms and joined the rest of the regiment in the square. Their equipment was checked by an eagle-eyed sergeant, then they climbed into an army lorry that would take them to the railway station. The general banter of their companions gave them no chance for a private conversation. In fact, it was not until they boarded a ferry in Dover that they had an opportunity to speak alone. As the two of them stood in the stern and watched the white cliffs slowly receding behind them, remorse stirred in the shorter man.

'It was wrong, Ol,' he said, squirming with regret. 'What we did last night was very wrong.'

His friend sniggered. 'It felt right to me.'

'She was only a young girl.'

'That's how I like them.'

'I can't stop thinking about her.'

'Why? I was the one who shagged her. You were too shit-scared to take your pants down. I juiced her up nicely for you and you ran away.'

'I felt sorry for her.'

'It was her own stupid fault. She should have given us a kiss.'

'It was cruel, Ol.'

'Forget it, will you? It's over and done with now.'

'Suppose she reports us to the police.'

'Let her,' said the taller man, spitting into the sea. 'What use will that do? She's got no idea who we are. The coppers would never find us in a month of Sundays. Besides,' he went on, 'the pair of us could be dead soon. I was determined to have at least one good shag before that happens. You should have done the same.'

'I couldn't,' confessed the other. 'I just couldn't somehow.'

'What was the trouble – brewer's droop?'

'I thought it was wrong. And – no matter what you say – I still believe we might pay for it one day.'

His friend laughed derisively. 'Not a chance, Gatty – we're in the clear, I tell you. If we do ever get back to Blighty, it will all have blown over.' He slapped him on the back. 'Now stop worrying about it, will you? Think about shooting Huns instead.'

Given the circumstances, Marmion was amazed that Miriam Stein was prepared to be interviewed about the crime. Ruth was completely unequal to the task but her mother was determined that mourning her husband would not prevent her from seeking justice for the rape of her daughter. When he reached the Stein home, Marmion found that Stone had got there before him and taken charge. His wife and two daughters were also there, as were the rabbi and some family friends who'd come to offer solace. As he entered the house, Marmion removed his hat and was conducted along a passageway by Stone. Beside every door was a symbol that it was a Jewish household. The inspector was shown into a room at the far end.

'Wait here, please,' said Stone. 'I'll fetch Mimi.'

Left alone for a couple of minutes, Marmion was able to take his bearings. He was in what had obviously been Jacob Stein's office. The man was scrupulously tidy. Everything on the desk was in neat piles and the books were arranged carefully on the bookshelves that covered two walls. A framed photograph of the Jermyn Street shop hung above the desk, flanked by photos of Stein's son and daughter. Seeing the smiling innocence on Ruth's face, Marmion felt a mingled sadness and anger when he thought of the ordeal she must have suffered. His own daughter came into his mind. Had Alice been the victim of rape, he could imagine how enraged he would be.

Stone eventually returned and introduced his sister-in-law. Though Miriam had clearly shed tears, she was bearing up well under the double tragedy. She sat on the little settee beside Stone. Marmion lowered himself onto the upright chair opposite them. He was not certain if Stone was there to offer moral support to his sister-in-law or simply to keep a watchful eye on him. Since the man was determined to stay, however, there was nothing that Marmion could do about it.

'Allow me to offer my condolences, Mrs Stein,' he began. 'It's very good of you to speak to me at such a trying time.'

'What happened to Ruth was appalling,' she said. 'Somebody must be called to account for it.'

'Both you and she have my sympathy. I have a daughter of my own. I can appreciate the anguish this must have brought you.'

'We're not talking about *your* daughter,' said Stone.

'Indeed not, sir.' He took out a pad and pencil. 'When you feel ready, Mrs Stein, perhaps you could give me the details.'

'There are precious few to give,' she said. 'I had to tease them out of Ruth one by one. She was trying to block the whole thing out of her mind but I told her that she must face it. I also made sure that the doctor examined her this morning. Ruth feels somehow that she's in disgrace but I keep telling her that she's not. She was a victim.'

'What exactly happened?'

Miriam bit her lip then launched into her tale. It was necessarily short. She described why and when Ruth had left the shop and whom she'd encountered in the alley. Of the two young men, only one had actually committed the rape. They had told Ruth that they were going abroad with their regiment next day. Miriam explained how Ruth had behaved on her return and how the bloodstain on her stockings had aroused suspicion. After her daughter's protracted stay in the bath, her mother knew that something was seriously amiss. Marmion waited until she had finished. Having to recount such unsavoury details had put great strain on Miriam. Stone patted her arm to show his approval then he flicked his gaze to Marmion.

'We want this kept out of the papers, Inspector.'

'Oh, yes,' said Miriam. 'I promised Ruth that there'd be no publicity. She'd die if that happened. You know the sort of lurid headlines that they use.'

'There'll have to be a mention when the case comes to court,' said Marmion, apologetically, 'but the interest should have died down by then and your daughter, hopefully, will feel strong enough to identify the two men.' He looked at his notes. 'She gave only the sketchiest descriptions. Did she say anything else about them? Their height, weight, skin complexion, for instance? What were they wearing at the time?'

'Ruth didn't notice that. They were just . . . drunken young men.'

'People with beer inside them tend to talk a lot. What sort of accents did they have? Were they from London or another part of the country?'

'She didn't say, Inspector.'

'They must have called each other something.'

'Oh, yes,' said Miriam, 'they did. Ruth remembered that. One was called Ol – short for Oliver, I presume. And he referred to the other as Gatty.'

Marmion put his pad away. 'That's enough to go on.'

'It doesn't sound as if it is to me,' argued Stone.

'I can soon find out which regiments were shipped to France today, sir. Oliver is not that common a name. I'll use a process of elimination.

As for his accomplice, Gatty must be a diminutive of some sort. A thorough search will uncover his real name.' He rose to his feet. 'Thank you, Mrs Stein. I'll intrude no longer. What you've told me has been extremely useful. We'll have to see if it's related in any way to the other crimes that took place or if it was a separate incident.'

'What can we tell Ruth?' asked Miriam.

'Tell her that her attackers made a fatal mistake in mentioning that they're in the army. I know where to look for them now. Being a member of the British Expeditionary Force doesn't make them immune from arrest – as they'll find out in due course. Goodbye to both of you.'

'Goodbye, Inspector,' said Miriam.

'I'll show you out,' said Stone, getting up and opening the door. 'And I want to thank you,' he added when they were alone in the passageway. 'Miriam's emotions are very fragile at the moment, as you can well understand. You handled that interview with sensitivity.'

It was unexpected praise from an unlikely source. Marmion had the feeling that he might win over Herbert Stone after all. But he knew that there was a long way to go before he did that.

Dorothy Holdstock was peeling potatoes in the kitchen when she heard a knock at her front door. After running her hands under the tap for a moment, she dried them on her pinafore and went out. When she opened the door, she was taken completely by surprise. Standing in the porch with a suitcase in her hand was her sister.

'Irene!' she exclaimed. 'You're still alive!'

Throwing their arms around each other, they cried with joy.

CHAPTER SEVEN

Joe Keedy enjoyed questioning suspects. The process was a battle of wills that he usually won. Marmion had taught him a valuable lesson. Divide and rule. When more than one person was involved, it was important to split them up to avoid collusion. As a result of the names gleaned from Brian Coley, three men from Shoreditch were arrested at their places of work and brought in separately. Keedy interrogated each of them in turn. The first was the easiest to break. After an initial denial, he soon buckled and confessed that he had been in Jermyn Street the night before. A chimney sweep by trade, he claimed that he was accidentally caught up in the attack and had not actually entered the shop. When Keedy pointed out that items stolen from the property had been found at his home, he wilted completely.

The second man was a street trader, a fast-talking cockney who swore that he'd been nowhere near the West End at the time. His girlfriend would vouch for him. After ten minutes of verbal jousting, Keedy exposed his claim as an arrant lie and charged him. It was the third man who gave the sergeant the most trouble. Sidney Timpson was a wily character in his twenties who worked as a glazier. Keedy seized on the man's occupation.

'So you came to the West End touting for trade, did you?'

Timpson frowned. 'What you on about?'

'That shop window you smashed in Jermyn Street,' said Keedy. 'It's a clever way to get business, Sidney. You break someone's window then offer to mend it.'

'Is that supposed to be a joke, Sergeant?'

'I was never more serious. You were seen outside the premises of Jacob Stein yesterday evening.'

'I've never even heard of the bloke.'

'Do you deny it, then?'

'Of course I bloody well do. I was out with friends in Shoreditch. You ask the landlord of the Lamb & Flag. He'll tell you that we were drinking there until closing time.'

'That was well after the incident in Jermyn Street.'

'We were there all evening.'

'Do you know a man named Brian Coley?'

Timpson became defensive. 'Not really – why do you ask?'

'What about Tommy Rudge, the barrow boy?'

'Yes, I know old Tommy. He was boozing with me at the Lamb & Flag. Tommy will speak up for me.'

'I don't think so, Sidney. According to him, he spent the evening with his girlfriend. That was before I got him to admit the lie. Then he named you as being with him and the rest of that mob.'

'Don't listen to Tommy,' said the other, contemptuously. 'He makes things up.'

'Then the pair of you have something in common. Right,' said Keedy, rubbing his hands, 'where are we? You don't really know Brian Coley and Tommy Rudge is a liar. Is that what you're saying?'

Timpson glared at him. 'Yeah, it is.'

'Then there must be some mistake in our records.'

'Eh?'

'You've been a bad boy, Sidney, haven't you? Our records show that you've been arrested on three occasions for being drunk and disorderly. And the person who was arrested with you,' said Keedy, reading from the sheet of paper in front of him, 'was the man you don't really know – Brian Coley. In my experience, you can get to know someone pretty well when you spend a night in a police cell with him. In any case,' he continued, 'you and Coley live in the same street. Can the pair of you really be such strangers?'

Timpson was adamant. 'I was at the Lamb & Flag.'

'Nobody disputes that. You went there with Rudge and Len Harper – *after* you'd looted that shop in Jermyn Street. Both of them confirm that.'

'What's Lenny Harper been saying?'

'It sounded like the truth to me.'

'I know nothing about any mob in the West End.'

'Then how come I have three witnesses who place you there, three close friends of yours who realise just how much trouble they're in and who decided to come clean?' He leant across the table. 'Do you know what I think, Sidney? *You* were their leader. Coley, Rudge and Harper all look up to you. I think it was your idea to go on the rampage yesterday.'

'No, it wasn't.'

'You actually led the mob.'

'Piss off!'

'When they'd had enough to drink, you stirred them up into a rage then took them off to attack a shop with a German name over it. You probably threw that brick through the window.'

'No, I never!' howled Timpson.

'I bet you were the first to clamber in, weren't you – the first to grab what you wanted? It was your privilege as the leader.'

'I wasn't even there.'

'Then why do three people swear otherwise?' asked Keedy.

'Ask them.'

'It's no good lying, Sidney. You were *seen*. That's how I know that you were the one who poured petrol onto that fire.'

'That wasn't me!' shouted Timpson, unnerved by the charge. 'It was that bloke in the dungarees. He brought the can with him.'

When he heard what he'd just said, he put his hands to his face and groaned inwardly. The game was up. Under pressure from Keedy, he'd just confessed the truth. There was no way out.

'Good,' said Keedy, beaming. 'I'm glad that we sorted that out. Let's start all over again, shall we?'

Dorothy Holdstock was both relieved and delighted to see her sister again. Having had no official confirmation that Irene had survived the disaster, she'd been on tenterhooks as she waited for news. It had come in the best possible way – her sister's arrival on her doorstep. Over a cup of tea, Irene explained how she'd managed to escape drowning. Playing down the role she took in helping others to get safely off the ship, she talked about the chair that she clung to as she waited to be rescued by a boat.

'It sounds to me as if you owe a lot to your friend,' said Dorothy.

'Ernie has always looked out for me.'

'How long have you known him?'

'Years and years, Dot.'

'Is he the one who proposed to you?'

'Yes, he is.'

'Why did you turn him down?'

'There were lots of reasons,' said Irene, pensively. 'First of all, I don't want another husband. I had a wonderful marriage with Arthur and no man could ever replace him. Second, I discovered that I wasn't the only female member of the crew that Ernie Gill had proposed to.' Dorothy was scandalised. 'And third, much as I like him, he really upsets me sometimes.'

'How does he do that?'

'Well, he has a bit of a temper and uses bad language. I think he could turn violent if he was crossed.'

Her sister clicked her tongue. 'You don't want that,' she said. 'On the other hand, a proposal is a proposal. A woman can't afford to be too fussy.'

There was deep sadness in Dorothy's voice because she had never received a proposal of marriage. Irene had been the pretty sister. None of the boys had been interested in Dorothy. Now in her forties, she was a tubby and rather unprepossessing woman who'd given up all hope of finding a husband and settled for being a pillar of the local church, an occasional babysitter and the manageress of a shoe shop. She lived in the little house that she and Irene had jointly inherited at the death of their parents and staved off loneliness by renting out a room to a blind old lady named Miss James.

'How long can you stay, Irene?'

'If it's all the same to you, I'll stay indefinitely.'

'What about your job?'

'I've finished with the sea, Dot. It's had one go at trying to kill me and that's one too many. I want to keep my feet on dry land from now on.'

'I don't blame you,' said Dorothy. 'Though I do wish that I'd had all those adventures you enjoyed – sailing on a famous liner, going to America all those times, getting proposals. I mean, it's so romantic.'

'That's not how it felt at the time. If truth be told, it was too much like hard work.'

'So what will you do now?'

'Look around for a job in London,' said Irene. 'I hope you don't mind having me back.'

'No – of course I don't. It's a real treat for me. Besides, you own half the house.'

'Do you still have Miss James here?'

'Yes, she's no bother – keeps herself to herself.'

'When did she first move in?'

'It must be almost five years ago.'

Irene smiled. 'You live with someone for almost five years and you still don't call her by her Christian name?'

'No, she'll always be Miss James to me.'

'And does she still call you Miss Holdstock?'

'Of course,' said Dorothy with mock propriety. 'I don't allow any familiarity under this roof.' They traded a laugh. 'Oh, it's so wonderful to have you back again, Irene. When I heard the awful news about the *Lusitania*, I nearly had a heart attack. I went to church every day to pray for you – and it worked. Thank God you came home on my day off so that I was here when you knocked. I can't tell you how marvellous it was to see you in the flesh again.' They heard the tinkle of a small bell. 'That will be Miss James. I'll go and see what she wants.'

Dorothy got up from the table and went off, leaving her sister to look around the kitchen and see how little it had changed in the past decade. Irene was pleased to be back in the house where she'd been born and brought up. It made her feel safe and wanted. Yet she was not simply returning to her roots. Moving to London would be the start of a new phase of her life, she told herself, and that was an exciting prospect.

By the time he'd finished interviewing the suspects from Shoreditch, Joe Keedy had elicited two additional names of people who took part in the looting of the shop in Jermyn Street. One was a member of the bar staff of the pub where the mob had been drinking beforehand. Another was a newspaper vendor with a regular pitch near Piccadilly Circus. Keedy sent off men to arrest the pair of them. The other three, meanwhile, had been charged and released on bail. They went off arguing furiously, each accusing the others of betraying him.

When Keedy went to Marmion's office to compare notes with him, he found the inspector poring over a sheaf of papers on his desk.

'Hello, Joe,' said Marmion, 'how did you get on?'

'I had them singing like canaries in the end.'

'What did they tell you?'

Keedy gave him an attenuated version of the three interviews. The most important development, he felt, was that all of the suspects had described the man with the petrol can and actually seen him pour the liquid out before using his cigarette to ignite it. None of them had known the man's name but all said that he worked somewhere in the West End and knew the area intimately.

'I've had the report from the fire brigade,' explained Marmion. 'They found the petrol can amid the debris but there was no way of identifying where it was bought. The intense heat had melted it and caused it to buckle.'

'We've drawn a blank there, then,' said Keedy.

'My guess is that it was sold by a garage nearby. Nobody wants to carry a full can of petrol any distance. It would be too heavy. I've sent men off to check at any garages in the locality.'

'That's very wise, Inspector.'

'Wisdom is like sciatica, Joe – it comes with age.'

'You're still a young man at heart.'

'I don't feel young. When I look at our Alice and realise how old she is now, I feel quite ancient.'

'How is Alice?'

'I'd like to say that she's very well but she's got this weird idea into her head that she'd like to join the WEC.'

'What's so weird about it?'

Marmion sighed. 'Alice worked her socks off to get qualifications to teach, Joe. I don't want her to throw all that effort away. In any case, the WEC is not short of recruits, whereas schools are certainly short of good teachers like my daughter.'

'It's her decision and she is over twenty-one.'

'We accept that, Joe. At the end of the day, we'll support her in whatever she does – as long as she doesn't join the Women's Police Service, that is. Apparently, that's what you advised her to do.'

'I did,' said Keedy. 'I think she'd make a good policewoman. Alice is bright, hard-working and she's got a natural authority. I know there's a lot of opposition to the Women's Force but I think girls like Alice could do certain things much better than we can.'

'That's exactly what I thought when I visited the Stein house,' recalled Marmion. 'I was following up that rape allegation. I never actually spoke to the victim herself – she was still in shock – but I felt very awkward as I talked to her mother. It was exactly the sort of situation where a woman would have come into her own.'

'You should have taken Alice with you.'

'She is *not* going to join the police.'

It was Marmion's turn to recount details of an interview. He told Keedy how struck he was by Miriam Stein's dignity and by her steely determination to seek justice for her daughter. At a time when she was coping with one family catastrophe, she had the strength to deal with another one. She'd been able to pass on two significant details about Ruth's attackers. Keedy was interested to hear of them.

'It took one phone call to find out what I wanted,' he said. 'The only soldiers who embarked for the Continent today were members of the East Surrey Regiment. They're going to Ypres as reinforcements.'

'Then they're brave men. Ypres is a real hellhole.'

'The two people we're after are not brave, Joe. They're cruel, heartless bastards and their names are somewhere on this list.' He indicated the sheaf of papers in front of him. 'I had this sent over from the War Office. They were very reluctant at first, then I threatened to set the commissioner onto them. That did the trick.'

'Have you discovered who the two men are?'

'Not yet, I haven't. Bring that other chair over and help me.'

Keedy picked up an upright chair, placed it behind the desk and sat beside the inspector. Marmion spread the pages out.

'How far have you got?' asked Keedy.

'I've had a first glance through the names and there are four Olivers in the regiment. One is a major, so I think we can discount him immediately. We're looking for two uncouth characters. They'll be somewhere in the ranks.'

'What was the other name Mrs Stein mentioned?'

'Gatty.'

'Could that be short for Gareth or something?'

'If it is, we're stumped. There's no Gareth on the list.'

'Let me see.'

Keedy pulled the pages closer so that he could scan them. When he'd been through the Christian names of all the men, he went quickly through the list again and concentrated on the surnames. Finding what he was after, he jabbed a triumphant finger at the name.

'That's him,' he decided. 'John Gatliffe. I'd put money on him being called Gatty.'

'You could be right, Joe.'

'I am right. There's no other surname like it.'

'If Gatliffe is our man, we can soon unmask his friend, Oliver.'

'How can you do that, Inspector?'

'By comparing addresses,' said Marmion, opening a folder to take out another list. 'Friends usually live close to each other. Let's see where our three Olivers live, shall we?' It took him less than a minute to identify the man. 'Here he is – Oliver Cochran. He lives in Ewell and so, by a strange coincidence, does John Gatliffe. It *has* to be him, Joe. Oliver Cochran was the one who actually carried out the rape. Gatliffe held the girl down.'

'Then they're both culpable.'

Marmion gathered up the pages. 'I promised to have these sent back at once to the War Office. They've fulfilled their purpose.'

'What's the next step, Inspector?'

'The commissioner will have to go into battle for us.'

'Do you think there'll be opposition?'

'I'm certain of it, Joe. The army won't want any of its men subject to a police investigation. They need every soldier they can get. Sir Edward will have to use his full weight,' said Marmion. 'We must have warrants for the arrest of those men and documents that give us access to them. Apart from the rape, they may have also been guilty of looting the shop.' His jaw tightened. 'Gatliffe and Cochran are in for a big surprise.'

They had never been abroad before and the sheer novelty of France diverted their minds from the uncertainties that lay ahead. Private John Gatliffe and Private Oliver Cochran of the East Surrey Regiment were amazed by the long straight roads lined with trees and by the quaint villages through which they were driven to the cheers of the locals. When the procession stopped for refreshment and everyone hopped out of their respective lorries, the friends were able to have a quiet chat together. Gatliffe lit a cigarette then used its tip to light the one he'd just given to Cochran. After inhaling deeply, they blew out smoke in unison.

'It's so *different*, Ol, isn't it?' said Gatliffe.

'Yes,' said Cochran, gloomily. 'We're heading for a war zone.'

'I was talking about the countryside and the people.'

'The countryside is all right but I don't like the look of the people. All we've seen so far are scrawny old men and ugly peasant women. I loathe the French.'

'But they're our allies.'

'That doesn't mean I have to like them.'

'I'm hoping to learn some French while I'm here.'

Cochran was mystified. 'Whatever for?'

'So I can talk to them in their own language.'

'That's stupid, Gatty. If they want to talk to us, let them learn English. The only time we might need French is if we go on leave and find a brothel. Two words will do – "How much?" That's unless we can get it free, of course.'

Gatliffe was uncomfortably reminded of the incident on their final night in England but he did not bring it up again. Cochran had told him to forget all about it and that was what his friend was trying and failing to do. After another pull on his cigarette, Gatliffe looked ahead.

'What do you think it will be like, Ol?'

'Where?'

'At the front.'

'I've got no idea.'

'You hear such terrible stories.'

'I just ignore them,' said Cochran, airily.

'Aren't you afraid of the Germans?'

'No, Gatty, I'm more afraid of the bloody Frenchies. They'll let us down. They can't even defend their own borders. If it wasn't for us, the Germans would have occupied Paris by now.'

'Why did you join up?'

'You know why.'

'I know you got that white feather – so did I. But was that the real reason? I enlisted because my cousin was badly wounded at Mons. They shipped back what was left of him and he hung on until this year before he died.' Gatliffe hunched his shoulders. 'Pete was just nineteen. When he first came home, I couldn't bear to look at him. He'd lost both legs and an eye. I wanted to hit back at the Germans who'd done that to him.' He went off into a reverie for a few minutes. When he jerked himself out of it, he turned to Cochran. 'What about you, Ol?'

His friend blew out a smoke ring. 'I was bored, Gatty.'

'What – bored with living in Ewell?'

'I was bored with everything. I was bored with my job, for a start. Mending roofs all day is no fun, I can tell you. I was bored with living at home and arguing with Dad time and time again. Most of all, I was bored with being asked by people why I hadn't joined the army and gone off to fight for my country. In the end, I just wanted a bit of adventure so, when you decided to enlist, I did so as well.'

'Weren't you scared of the danger?'

'No,' said Cochran, emphatically. 'You're used to danger if you work as a roofer. I've seen two men badly injured after falling from a ladder and one killed when he slipped off a church roof. It can't be much more dangerous than that at the front.'

'Nothing ever seems to frighten you, does it?' said Gatliffe, enviously. 'I wish I was like that.' A memory stabbed him like the thrust of a bayonet and he winced. 'I also wish that we hadn't bumped into that girl in London.'

'Are you still worrying about that?'

'I keep seeing her face, Ol.'

Cochran laughed. 'I keep feeling her body and tasting her lips and remembering how I shot my spunk into her. It was terrific, Gatty, every second of it. You don't know what you missed.'

Ruth Stein sat on the edge of the bath with the box of tablets in her hand. In her febrile mind, they seemed to offer an escape from the ruins of her life. She opened the packet, put a tablet in the palm of her hand and stared at it.

CHAPTER EIGHT

David Cohen was on the verge of tears as he stood outside what had once been his place of work. All that was left of the shop now was an empty smoke-blackened shell. A waist-high fence had been erected to keep anyone from actually entering the premises but, since there was nothing left to steal, it was largely redundant. Acting as a second line of defence was a solitary policeman. Cohen was bound to wonder why he and his colleagues had not been on duty there the day before to safeguard the premises.

Harvey Marmion had agreed to meet him in Jermyn Street rather than at Scotland Yard because he wanted to view the full extent of the damage in daylight. The two men stood side by side on the opposite pavement.

'Mr Stein didn't stand a chance,' said Cohen, sorrowfully. 'He was trapped upstairs by the fire.'

'That's not what happened,' said Marmion, gently. 'According to the pathologist conducting the post-mortem, your employer might have been dead before the fire even reached him. I've issued a statement to the press to the effect that Jacob Stein was murdered.'

Cohen was horror-struck. 'Murdered – but *how*?'

'He was stabbed through the heart, sir.'

The news was like a hammer blow to Cohen. He needed minutes to recover from the shock. Dabbing at his eyes with a handkerchief he plucked from the sleeve of his jacket, he looked up to heaven in supplication. Cohen was the manager of the shop, the person entrusted to run it and handle any initial enquiries for the high-quality bespoke tailoring on offer. Since the man had worked there for well over fifteen years, Marmion deduced that he was good at his job. Otherwise Stein would not have kept him. Cohen was a slim, sinewy man of medium height in a superbly cut suit. Marmion put him somewhere in his early fifties.

'What sort of an employer was he?' asked Marmion.

'You couldn't wish to work for a better man,' said Cohen, loyally. 'It was a pleasure to be a member of his staff. He expected us to work hard, of course, but he set us all a perfect example.'

'Did Mr Stein follow a set routine?'

'Yes, Inspector – he was always the first to arrive and the last to leave. When the shop was closed, he'd take any cash and cheques from the till and put them in the safe upstairs. He was very conscious of security. That's why all the doors had special locks.'

'So when he went upstairs yesterday evening, he would have locked the door to the shop behind him.'

'There's no question about that.'

'What about his other employees? I gather that apart from you, there were three full-time tailors and one man who worked part-time. Would they have had keys to all the doors?'

'Oh, no,' said Cohen, anxious to stress his seniority. 'Only Mr Stein and I had a full set.'

'What about the key to the safe?'

'Mr Stein had that, Inspector. He kept a duplicate at home in case of loss. However, the key alone wouldn't have opened the safe. You'd need to know the combination as well.'

'Did anyone apart from Mr Stein know the combination?'

'Nobody on the staff was told.'

'What happened to the day's takings if Mr Stein was not there and you had no access to his safe?'

'It was only very rarely that he was absent during business hours. On such occasions,' said Cohen, 'I'd put everything in the night safe at the bank. He was such a kind man,' he continued, wiping away a last tear, 'and generous to a fault. Who could possibly have wanted to kill him?'

'I'm hoping that *you* might point us in the right direction, sir.'

Cohen was nonplussed. 'How can I do that?'

'By providing more detail about him,' said Marmion. 'Mr Stein was clearly well known but success usually breeds envy. Is there anyone who might have nursed resentment against him?'

'I can't think of anybody.'

'What about his business rivals?'

'Well, yes, there were one or two people who felt overshadowed by him. That's in the nature of things. But surely none of them would go to the length of killing him,' argued Cohen. 'When the shop was burnt down, we'd effectively have been put out of business for a long time. Wasn't that enough?'

'I'd like the names of any particular rivals.'

Cohen was circumspect. 'I'm not accusing anyone, Inspector.'

'That's not what I'm asking you to do, sir,' said Marmion. 'I just want an insight into the closed world of gentlemen's tailoring. Nobody is universally admired and none of us look benevolently upon all our fellow human beings. We tend to like or loathe. Is there anyone about whom Mr Stein spoke harshly?'

'Yes,' admitted the other, 'there were a few people whom he regarded with . . .' He searched for the right word. 'Well, let's call it suspicion rather than contempt.'

'I'd appreciate their names, Mr Cohen.'

'Very well – but you're looking in the wrong direction.'

'I'd also like the names of any employees who might have left under a cloud. Have any been dismissed in the last year?'

'There was one,' said Cohen, uneasily, 'and another left of his own accord shortly afterwards. Not because of any bad treatment from Mr Stein, I hasten to add. They were simply . . . not suitable employees.'

'Yet he must have thought so when he took them on.'

'We all make errors of judgement, Inspector.'

'So Mr Stein was not the paragon you portray him as,' observed Marmion, taking out a pad and pencil. 'Before I have those names from you, answer me this, if you will. I take it that you know Mr Stein's brother quite well.'

'Yes, I do,' said the other, guardedly.

'How did the two of them get on?'

David Cohen was too honest a man to tell a direct lie. At the same time, he did not wish to divulge confidential information and so he retreated into silence and gave an expressive shrug.

Marmion read the message in his eyes.

'Very well,' he said, 'let's have those names, shall we?'

* * *

Detective Sergeant Joe Keedy had conducted countless interviews during his time as a policeman but none had resembled the one in which he took part that evening. Visiting the pub where members of the destructive mob had reportedly been drinking before they made for Jermyn Street, Keedy sought out Douglas Emmott, who worked there behind the bar. Emmott was a short, slender, ebullient man in his thirties with a swarthy complexion and shiny dark hair that gave him an almost Mediterranean look. When Keedy explained who he was and why he was there, Emmott took a combative stance.

'Yes, I was there,' he confessed, freely, 'and, if you want the truth, I'm damned glad that I was.'

Anticipating lies and evasion, Keedy was taken aback by the man's defiant honesty. Emmott put his hands on his hips.

'Given the chance,' he said, 'I'd do the same thing again.'

'Oh – so you feel proud that you broke the law?'

'I feel proud that I struck a blow for the downtrodden masses. I belong to them, see?' He pointed an accusatory finger. 'Have you ever seen the prices of the suits in that shop?'

'I have, as a matter of fact,' said Keedy.

'They cost more than I earn in a whole year. That's *indecent*, Sergeant. Why should anyone pay all that money for a suit when there are people starving in this city?'

'That's not the point at issue, sir.'

'It is for me. I believe that society should have a moral basis. Let me explain what I mean,' said Emmott, warming to his theme. 'I started work in this pub last January and I got here very early in the morning on my first day. Do you know what I found?'

'No,' said Keedy, 'what was it?'

'I found an old man, curled up in the doorway, frozen to death.

Imagine it, Sergeant. He'd crawled in there like an unwanted dog and spent his last hours on earth shivering throughout a cold winter's night. How could that be allowed to happen in a civilised society?'

'I don't have the answer to that, sir. What I can tell you is that, unfortunately, the incident is not an isolated case.'

'He was dressed in rags and wrapped in newspaper,' said Emmott with vehemence. 'Compare that poor devil to the overpaid toffs who buy their expensive suits and thick overcoats from people like Jacob Stein. It's wrong, Sergeant. Why should some prosper while others live and die in absolute penury? It's all wrong.'

'I'm inclined to agree with you there.'

'Then why aren't you doing something about it?'

'I don't accept that looting and destroying someone's shop is a legitimate way of righting social inequalities,' said Keedy, forcefully. 'It's sheer vandalism and it's a crime.'

'Jacob Stein was a symbol of class dominance.'

'He was a man who made the most of his exceptional abilities. As such, he's entitled to the respect of the general public and the protection of the law.'

'Don't talk to me about the law,' said Emmott, frothing. 'It's been devised by the rich for the benefit of the rich. Our police are nothing but the lackeys of the ruling class. You should be ashamed to be part of them, Sergeant.'

'We serve people from all ranks of society, Mr Emmott.'

'That's rubbish!'

'We do, sir.'

'Where were you when that old man froze to death?'

'Where were *you* when Jacob Stein was murdered?' asked Keedy, tiring of the barman's rant. Emmott was stunned. 'You didn't know about that, did you? While you were striking your blow for the downtrodden masses, somebody was stabbing Mr Stein to death.'

The barman paled. 'Is that true?'

'That murder was probably hatched in this very pub.'

'There was no talk of murder when we set out,' pleaded Emmott. 'Most people just wanted to show what they thought of Germans, whereas me and Archie were there on behalf of the deserving poor. We got principles, see? We fight against oppression.'

'I'm sure that you think your motives are laudable,' said Keedy with an edge, 'but they won't stop you being arrested. The same goes for this other person, Archie whatever-his-name-is. We were told that he sells newspapers in Piccadilly Circus. Is that correct?'

'Yes, he's my best friend.'

'And he holds the same political views, by the sound of it.'

'It's the only reason we joined that march,' said Emmott. 'Me and Archie were not like the others. They wanted to avenge the sinking of the *Lusitania*, yet only a thousand or so people died as a result of that.' Drawing himself up to his full height, he struck a pose. 'We were there on behalf of the millions – yes, millions – of British subjects who are drowning in a sea of destitution.'

'Who else was part of that mob?' asked Keedy. 'Apart from you, Archie and your high moral principles, who else set out to destroy Mr Stein's shop once they'd come in here for some Dutch courage?'

But there was no reply. Questioned about his own involvement, Emmott was frankness itself but he refused to incriminate anyone else. The information that a murder had taken place in Jermyn Street altered his whole view of the enterprise. He would happily admit that he and his friend stormed the premises of Jacob Stein but he would not identify his companions. Keedy knew instinctively that he would get nothing further out of Douglas Emmott. The barman had clammed up completely. Keedy suspected that the newspaper vendor would react in the same way. Convinced that they were political martyrs, the two friends would endure their own punishment while saying nothing about others who'd been part of the mob.

Keedy arrested the barman and took him off. On their way to Vine Street police station, they picked up a newspaper vendor from Piccadilly Circus. Two more members of the mob would face charges.

When her husband broke the news to her that evening, Ellen Marmion was astounded. It was a possibility that had never crossed her mind.

'You're going to *France*?' she gasped, staring in disbelief.

'If it can be arranged, love,' said Marmion. 'Then we'll cross the border into Belgium. It's where their regiment is heading.'

'You won't go near the front, surely.'

'We'll go wherever necessary to arrest the two men.'

Hand to her chest, she sat on the arm of the sofa. 'You've taken my breath away, Harvey. I mean, it's such a long way to go.'

'Scotland would be much further.'

'It would be a lot safer as well. So many of our soldiers are being killed in Belgium, I find it hard to read the papers anymore. Well, you saw Paul's last letter. He's stationed further south, thank heaven, but he'd heard awful things about the battle raging around Ypres.'

'Joe and I may not need to get anywhere near the town itself.'

'All the same,' she said, nervously, 'I don't like it.'

'We can't let them get away with it, Ellen.'

'Well, no . . .'

'Think how you'd feel if Alice had been assaulted like that,' he suggested. 'You'd want me to pursue them to the ends of the earth.'

Giving her a hug, he kissed the chevron of anxiety on her brow. 'Don't worry, love. I did go to France once before in pursuit of a criminal, remember, and I didn't know a word of French that time. I'll be a lot better prepared now.'

'Can't you send someone else?'

'It's my responsibility. The commissioner put me in charge of this case, so this is not something I feel that I can delegate.'

'Why can't Joe Keedy go there by himself?'

'One detective can't arrest two suspects,' said Marmion, 'and he certainly couldn't bring them back alone. When they realise the sentence they're facing, they'll seize any chance to escape.'

'In that case, *you* could be in danger.'

'Stop getting so upset, love. You've never been like this before.'

'You've never been to Belgium before.'

He spread his arms. 'It's not an ideal situation, I grant you, but I want these two men behind bars. I'll do whatever it takes to put them there. It's all part of the inquiry into the looting and burning of Mr Stein's shop.'

Ellen made no reply. She took a close interest in her husband's work and – though he kept any unpleasant details to himself – he found it helpful to use her as a sounding board. As a rule, she simply listened and made a few comments on what she'd been told about an investigation. This time, however, she was raising objections.

'When will you go?' she asked.

'We have to wait for clearance first. Sir Edward is taking care of that. It could take a day or two.'

'And will you and Joe be entirely on your own?'

'Hardly,' he told her. 'We'll cross the Channel on a troopship. We'll probably have the protection of a battalion or two of infantry. There's certain to be reinforcements and supplies going to the front.'

'Will you travel with them in France?'

'Yes – we'll have bodyguards all the way, love.'

She was mollified. 'Oh, well, that sounds a little better.'

'The pity is that I won't get a chance to see Paul while I'm there,' he said, 'but his regiment is somewhere near the Somme. We won't exactly be on a pleasure trip, so we can't just move around at will. It's a shame – I'd love to see our son again.'

'I'd love you to make sure that he's safe and well.'

Paul Marmion had been part of a collective enlistment. When it was announced that those who signed up together would serve together, groups of young men had rushed to the recruitment centres. Paul played for a football team that had volunteered as a complete unit. Knowing that their son was among friends gave Marmion and his wife a degree of reassurance at first. However, as the lists of British casualties on the Western Front steadily lengthened, they had serious concerns for Paul's safety.

Ellen stood up and Marmion embraced her again. It had been a long day but he had got home in time for the evening meal. The sound of bubbling hot water took his wife into the kitchen to turn down the gas underneath a saucepan. Marmion followed her and sniffed.

'Something smells tasty.'

'It'll be another ten minutes yet,' she warned him. 'Tell me about the rest of the investigation. Have you made any progress?'

'We think so. Joe Keedy interviewed three suspects and got two more names of people who were there at the time. He went off earlier to arrest both of them. I'll be interested to hear what he managed to winkle out of the pair.'

'Have you caught the man who started the fire?'

'There were two, apparently. Witnesses talk of seeing smoke not long after the looting began. Then a second man emptied a can of petrol at the rear of the shop and – boom – the fire really blazed.'

'It's such an appalling thing to do.'

'We'll get him eventually,' he said, determinedly. 'We managed to find the garage where he bought the petrol and the owner remembered him well enough to give us a good description of him. It tallies with what some of the others told us. I issued the description to the press when I made a statement about the murder. That will be tomorrow's headline.'

'What about the rape?'

'We're keeping quiet about that, Ellen. It's what the family wants. They also want the body, of course. I had Mr Stein's rabbi hassling me this afternoon.'

'When can it be released?'

'Later this evening, with luck,' he said. 'The post-mortem is almost complete. It's been given top priority.' He heard a door open upstairs. Feet then descended the stairs. 'Here comes Alice.'

'She's been marking books up in her room.'

'Has she said anything else about the WEC?'

'Not a word, Harvey.'

'Then I won't bring it up.' He turned to greet his daughter as she came into the kitchen. 'Hello, teacher – how are you?'

'Very well, Inspector,' she replied, turning a cheek to accept a welcoming kiss from him. 'You're back earlier than usual.'

'Is that a complaint?'

'No, Daddy, it's quite the reverse. It's a nice surprise.'

'Your father has to go to France,' said Ellen.

Alice blanched. 'Going to France in the middle of a war?'

'It's all part of the investigation,' he said.

Marmion gave her a brief explanation. Pleased that the two men accused of rape were being pursued, she was naturally worried about her father's safety. He did his best to allay her fears.

'What if they're actually fighting at the front?' she asked.

'I think that's unlikely,' he replied. 'They only set sail today. However, if they are in the trenches when we get there, Joe and I will have to put on a helmet and go in search of them.' He laughed at the expressions of horror on their faces. 'I was only joking.'

'That kind of joke is not funny,' chided Ellen. 'I worry about Paul every day. Now I'll have you to worry about as well.'

'So Joe Keedy is going with you, is he?' said Alice.

'I couldn't stop him. You know Joe. He loves action.'

'Make sure you bring him back in one piece.'

'He can look after himself, I promise you.'

Alice pondered. 'What are your chances of getting a conviction?'

'Why do you ask that?'

'Well,' she said, seriously, 'we all know how difficult it is to get a successful prosecution for rape. It's one of the reasons some women won't even report the crime.'

'That's a fair point,' he remarked.

'It would be a terrible shame for you to go to all that trouble to arrest these two men, only to see them walk scot-free from court.'

'That won't happen, Alice.'

'Are you sure?'

'No,' he admitted. 'When a case goes to court, you can never be one hundred per cent certain of the outcome. Juries have minds of their own. They sometimes come up with unexpected verdicts.'

'That could happen in this case,' said Ellen, siding with her daughter.

'Don't misunderstand me. What those two men did was dreadful and they should be imprisoned for it. I'm just thinking how it would look in court. On one side, you've got two soldiers, fighting for their country and putting their lives at risk. On the other, you've got a teenage girl who's bound to be a bundle of nerves. It will be her word against theirs.'

'Are you suggesting that we don't bother to go to France?'

'No, Harvey, I'm just saying that it could be a waste of time.'

'We won't simply be arresting them for what they did to Ruth Stein,' Marmion pointed out. 'Several other crimes were committed. We'll want to question them about their possible involvement in the attack on the shop. They may have a lot to answer for.'

'I never thought of that.'

'Mummy's comment is very apt,' Alice reflected. 'What will happen in court? Everything turns on the evidence of the victim. To be cross-examined about what the attackers did to her would be a humiliating experience for any woman. How will this girl stand up to it?'

'I don't know,' said Marmion.

'Is she the sort of person who'd convince a jury?'

'I can't say, Alice. The truth is that I've never met Ruth Stein.'

Staring ahead of her, Ruth sat upright in bed. Her face was drawn and her eyes were pools of despair. Miriam Stein sat on a chair beside the bed, holding her daughter's hand and trying to temper her criticism with tenderness. Ruth had lost her nerve. Having taken enough of the pills to make her feel ill, she'd abandoned her suicide attempt and turned in a panic to her mother. After treatment in hospital, Ruth had been sent back home again.

'Suicide is a criminal act,' said Miriam, quietly. 'Judaism is very clear on that. Someone who commits suicide is considered to be a murderer. Is that how *you* wished to be remembered?'

'No, Mother,' whispered Ruth. 'I'm sorry.'

'You'd have brought such shame upon the family.'

'I did it because of my own shame.'

'Remember your teaching. You must think of your soul.'

Ruth nodded and tears began to form. She was sick, distraught and helpless. Conscious that suicide was anathema in her religion, she had nevertheless been unable to resist the impulse to end her life. She would now have to face further guilt and misery. Her life had become even more unbearable.

Miriam waited a short while then rose to her feet.

'I'll send in Rabbi Hirsch,' she said, moving to the door. 'After you've spoken with him, your Uncle Herman wants to see you.'

Ruth was frightened. Closing her eyes, she started to pray.

CHAPTER NINE

One day in her sister's company convinced Irene Bayard that she'd made the right decision in coming to live in London. There was a dimension of peace and security there. Dorothy Holdstock led an uncomplicated life. She had a full-time job, a small circle of friends and she shared her home with an undemanding old lady. Miss James occupied the downstairs front room behind thick lace curtains. In spite of her disability, she remained active. She would visit friends on most days and her younger brother would come up from Brighton once a fortnight to take her out for lunch. Much of the time, Dorothy was unaware of her presence. It was only when Miss James emerged to visit the bathroom or to make use of the kitchen that the two women had a proper conversation. A copper bell was the link between them. When it was rung three times, it was a signal for Dorothy to enter her lodger's domain.

'Does she still clean her own room?' asked Irene.

'Oh, yes,' said Dorothy. 'I offered to do it when I clean the rest of the house but Miss James wouldn't hear of it. She doesn't like anyone else in there and she's quite able to spruce the place up.'

'How old is she?'

'I daren't ask and she wouldn't, in any case, tell me. She gave up having birthdays many years ago.'

'I admire her independence.'

'Oh, it's nothing compared to yours, Irene.'

'What do you mean?' said Irene, surprised by the envy in her sister's voice. 'I've never been really independent.'

'Yes, you have,' countered Dorothy. 'When most women lose a husband so young, as you did, they're likely to shrink back into their shell. You came out of yours. I couldn't believe it when you told me that you were going to sail thousands of miles a year across the ocean on a Cunard liner. If that's not independence – what is?'

'It's not as wonderful as it sounds,' warned Irene. 'I was a member of the crew and I had no independence at all on board. If I'd been a passenger, of course, it would have been a different matter.'

'Weren't you afraid when you sailed from New York this time?'

'No, Dot, I wasn't.'

'But there were threats to all shipping from the Germans.'

'I ignored them and got on with my job.'

'What would you do if the same situation arose again?'

Irene was brisk. 'It won't arise,' she said. 'I never wish to go to sea again. My home is here now. All I need to do is to find a new job.'

'There's no hurry – you've earned a rest.'

'I'm not the restful type.'

Dorothy laughed. 'I discovered that years ago,' she said. 'You're always on the go. I could never keep up with you.'

It was late evening and the two of them were sitting in the living room with a glass of cheap sherry apiece. As she looked around, Irene saw that the wallpaper was fading and that the paintings chosen by their parents were still on the wall. Time had stood still in the house. It was at once comforting and saddening. If she was to live there on a permanent basis, Irene thought, she would insist on redecoration. But that could wait. All she wished to do now was to ease back into an old existence.

Dorothy glanced at the evening paper on the arm of the sofa.

'Did you find anything that tempted you?'

'Yes and no,' said Irene. 'There are plenty of jobs advertised but I'd like to know a bit more about them before I commit myself.'

'What did you have in mind?'

'I wanted something that gets me out and about. I'd like a job that helps me to meet new people all the time.'

'Then you should work in our shop,' said Dorothy, chuckling. 'We have all sorts coming through the door.'

'I'm not sure it would suit me, Dot.'

'Then what would?'

'Well,' said Irene, reaching for the newspaper, 'one of the adverts that caught my eye was to do with trams.'

'You mean, working as a conductress?'

'I might start as that but I'd really want to be a driver. Apart from anything else, they earn more money. The tram that brought me here had a woman driver.' Having opened the paper to the correct page, she passed it to her sister. 'There you are – down at the bottom. I put a circle round it.'

'There are four or five circles.'

'Those are other jobs I might go after.'

'Here we are,' said Dorothy, finding the advertisement and reading the details. 'Well, why not? A job on the trams would give you continuity.'

'What do you mean?'

'It's another form of transport. You start off on ships then you move on to trams. You'd certainly meet lots of people that way.' There was a twinkle in Dorothy's eye. 'You might even get a proposal of marriage out of one of them.'

Irene smiled wanly. 'No, thank you. That's all behind me.'

'You never know.'

'Oh yes I do. My future is here with you and Miss James.'

'She was thrilled when I told her you were back.'

'Good – it feels so *right*, Dot.'

'Let's celebrate with another glass, shall we?'

Putting the newspaper aside, Dorothy topped up their glasses from the sherry bottle. It was such a long time since she'd been able to share a companionable drink with anyone. Indeed, very few people were even invited into the house. Such as it was, Dorothy's social life took place elsewhere. She regarded her sister through narrowed lids.

'What was he like, Irene?'

'Who?'

'I'm talking about the chap who fell madly in love with you.'

Irene gave a half-laugh. 'I don't know about falling in love,' she said. 'Ernie wasn't romantic in that way. He just wanted a woman and I happened to be the one on hand.'

'There must have been more to it than that.'

After thinking it over, Irene gave an affirmative nod.

'There was, Dot.'

'Well?'

'It no longer seems to matter. Ernie Gill belongs to a past life before the ship went down. Everything is different now. I've no regrets about what I did. I just don't want to dwell on it.'

'In other words, I'm to mind my own business.'

'I'd just like you to give me more time to . . . settle down.'

'I understand,' said Dorothy, sweetly. 'You want to forget.'

'This sherry will help me to do that.'

They clinked their glasses then sipped their drinks. After they chatted for another hour, Dorothy looked at the clock on the mantelpiece and saw how late it was.

'I have to leave early in the morning,' she said, 'but you deserve a long lie-in. You can spend the whole day in bed, if you like.'

'I wouldn't dream of it,' said Irene. 'I'll be up at the crack of dawn. When you go off, I'll probably come with you. I may have a lot of doors to knock on tomorrow.'

It took two days to gather all the documentation together. Before they departed, Sir Edward Henry insisted on speaking to Marmion and Keedy in his office. He handed over passports, warrants and a letter from the War Office.

'I can't tell you what a struggle I had to get authorisation,' he said, clenching his teeth. 'I had to contend with some blunt speaking at the War Office. One man went so far as to claim that any young unattended woman out at night is more or less asking to be molested and that Miss Stein had effectively provoked the rape.'

'That's a revolting suggestion,' said Marmion, angrily.

'There was worse to come, Inspector. The same fellow had the gall to ask me which was the more important – a deflowered Jewish virgin of no consequence or a pair of gallant soldiers ready to lay down their lives for their country? I gave him a flea in his ear.'

'That was very restrained of you, Sir Edward.'

The commissioner nodded. 'In retrospect, I think it was,' he agreed, 'but I got my way in the end. However, let's put that aside, shall we? We must consider practicalities. What will happen while you're away?'

'The investigation will continue along the lines we've set down,' said Marmion. 'I've briefed my team. They'll search for other people involved in the incident but the main focus will be on identifying the killer.'

'Mr Stone keeps ringing me to ask about progress.'

'What do you say?'

'I'm suitably vague but mildly encouraging.'

'Have you told him about our trip to France?'

'Yes, Inspector – it's the one thing of which he approved. He voiced his disapproval of just about everything else.'

'I'm surprised that he has time to hound you, Sir Edward,' said Keedy. 'His brother's body has been released to the family. I would have thought he'd be preoccupied with the funeral arrangements.'

'Mr Stone seems to think that he has to bark at our heels to get any results.' The commissioner gave a forbearing smile. 'Given what happened to his brother and to his niece, the fellow is under intense pressure. We must make allowances for that.'

He looked down at the report in front of him and flicked through the pages. It had been prepared by Marmion and gave details of all arrests, interviews and names relevant to the investigation. Marmion and Keedy had spoken to everyone who worked for Jacob Stein, as well as to some of his rival tailors. They'd built up a much fuller picture of the deceased. What they had not so far been able to do was to track down the man who had been dismissed and the one who left Stein's employ of his own accord. Nor had they managed to identify and arrest the arsonist with the can of petrol. Newspapers had carried a detailed description of the individual and a number of names were put forward by members of the public. Though they were all checked, none of them belonged to the man in question and so he remained at large.

'Who was the ringleader?' said Sir Edward. 'That's what I really want to know. Was he also the killer?'

'That's possible,' said Marmion, 'but none of the witnesses picked out one particular person. All they remembered seeing was a chanting mob coming along the street.'

'One of whom had a petrol can,' added Keedy.

The commissioner pursed his lips and shook his head sadly.

'Murder, rape and arson,' he said, ruefully. 'It's not what we expect of the West End. Were the crimes related?'

'We won't know until we've interviewed the two soldiers,' said Marmion. 'One of them was certainly guilty of rape and might also have been responsible for the fire. But I think we can absolve the pair of them of the murder.'

'On what grounds do you say that, Inspector?'

'I'm going on what the victim told us – or, at least, on what her mother was able to tell us on the girl's behalf. Ruth Stein left her father upstairs and went off to raise the alarm. The two men pounced on her in the alley. They could have come from the shop, of course,' reasoned Marmion, 'but they definitely did not come from the upstairs room where Mr Stein was murdered. After the rape, they went off in the opposite direction. The fire had taken hold on the shop by then.'

'Somebody else killed him,' concluded Keedy.

The commissioner sat back in his chair, steepling his fingers.

'Do you have any theories about who that might be?'

'We do, Sir Edward.' Keedy glanced at Marmion. 'As it happens, the inspector and I have slightly conflicting theories.'

'What's yours, Sergeant?'

'Well,' said Keedy, seizing his chance to impress, 'we know for a fact that the property was attacked because it had a German name over it and obscenities were being chanted against all Germans. However, that may not be the explanation for the murder. I have a feeling – and it's no more than a feeling, mark you – that Jacob Stein was killed because he was a Jew, and not because of any association with the enemy.'

'What leads you to think that?'

'I've been looking at some of the riots in the East End where they've been far more prevalent. The main targets were shops and houses owned by people of German origin. But they were not the only victims,' said Keedy. 'Some people took advantage of the situation to attack Jewish immigrants in general, especially those from Russia.'

'You'll no doubt remember the activities of the British Brothers' League,' said Marmion. 'They organised constant demonstrations against Jewish immigration at the start of the century.'

'I remember it vividly,' said the commissioner. 'They made a lot of noise until they got what they wanted – the Aliens Act. But that was ten years ago,' he went on. 'I thought the BBL more or less disappeared after 1905.'

'So did I, Sir Edward,' said Keedy, 'but some of its members formed much smaller groups under other names. Jews continue to be their scapegoats. They blame them for everything. I'm wondering if Jacob Stein was killed by a member of one of these rabid anti-Semitic groups.'

'It's an interesting theory. What do you think, Inspector?'

'It's a line of inquiry that needs pursuing,' said Marmion, 'and I have men doing just that. But I still hold to the view that there's a personal aspect to this case. Stein was murdered by someone who knew him and his routine at the shop. It was someone with an axe to grind, someone with a score to settle. Above all else, it was someone who knew where that safe was kept.'

'That points to a present or former employee, then.'

'We can discount the present ones, Sir Edward.'

'What about former ones?'

'There are two who've aroused our interest. One was middle-aged and left after a long time with the firm. The other was much younger and was – according to Mr Cohen, the manager – very angry at being dismissed. We're urgently seeking both of them.'

'You say that one was middle-aged, Inspector. Would this man have been physically capable of stabbing Mr Stein to death?'

'Possibly not, Sir Edward.'

'Then how can he be held culpable?'

'Because he stage-managed it,' said Marmion with growing certainty. 'He knew the confusion that would be created by the attack on the shop and he hired someone to take full advantage of it. Jacob Stein was not killed accidentally, Sir Edward. His death was plotted and paid for in advance. In my opinion,' he decided, 'what confronts us is a bespoke murder.'

There had been a heady excitement when they first joined the army. They were treated as heroes by their families and friends. When they marched in uniform through the streets, they were cheered to the echo by large crowds. That was all in the past. There was no cheering now, only the distant boom and whizz of artillery. Oliver Cochran and John Gatliffe found a moment to have a cigarette together. They were camped with their regiment to the west of Ypres where hostilities were continuing apace. Gatliffe had seen some of the wounded British soldiers being stretchered from the front.

'It turned my stomach, Ol,' he said with a grimace. 'Keep away from that field hospital unless you want to spew up your dinner. I saw men with arms and legs missing and others who'd been blinded. One was crying because they'd shot his bollocks off.' He shuddered at the memory. 'I don't know how the stretcher-bearers can do their job.'

'We do far worse to the Germans,' insisted Cochran.

'It's not what I expected at all.'

'War is war, Gatty. We're not here to play ping-pong.'

'The noise never stops – and I hate that terrible stink in the air.'

'You'll get used to it.'

'There was something else,' said Gatliffe, 'and it really scared me. They're using poisonous gas, Ol. The Germans are attacking us with gas bombs.'

'So? We'll probably have gas masks to wear.'

'I'd hate to be poisoned to death.'

'Stop getting so upset, will you?' said Cochran, irritably. 'A fine bloody soldier you are – giving up before we've even started. We've already fought one battle at Ypres. That was last year and we won it.'

'Yet look at how many thousands of our men were killed in the battle. And they were regular soldiers, blokes who'd fought in the Boer War and that. They were professionals, Ol. We're just raw recruits.'

'I'm not raw. I'm as good as any fucking Hun.'

Snatching up his rifle, he jabbed at an imaginary enemy then pulled out his bayonet before stabbing a second one. As he showed off his proficiency with rifle and bayonet, there was a zestful fury about Cochran that lifted his friend's spirits. Gatliffe, too, picked up his weapon and went through some of the moves they'd learnt during bayonet drill. It felt good to have a rifle in his hands. Confidence returned. He looked forward to the time when he could fire at the enemy. With Cochran beside him, he was ready for the fight.

Tossing his cigarette butt to the ground, Cochran sliced it apart with a thrust of his bayonet. Like Gatliffe, he was having misgivings about his decision to join the army. While his friend was honest about his fears, however, Cochran suppressed his apprehension beneath a mixture of boasting and bravado. He would never show a hint of trepidation to Gatliffe because it would undermine his strong hold over his friend. Cochran was the acknowledged leader and he was determined to retain his leadership.

'Know what, Ol?' said Gatliffe. 'You ought to be a corporal, even a sergeant.'

'Nah!' retorted Cochran with a sneer. 'It's a stupid idea.'

'You'd be really good at it.'

'NCOs are all wankers, especially the ones we've got.'

'I could just see you with three stripes on your arm.'

'You're off your bleeding head, Gatty. There's only one thing worse than being a sergeant and that's being a fucking officer. Look at the idiots we got in command. You wouldn't catch me mixing with silly sods like that. They all talk as if they got a plum in their gobs.'

Gatliffe scratched his head. 'It was only a thought.'

'Well, don't bleeding think it again,' said Cochran. 'I'm where I want to be and I'll stay right here, OK?' A slow smile spread across his face. 'If you want something to think about, remember what we did on that last night in London. She was an ugly little thing but she had a good body, I'll give her that. I had a great ride on her and you could have done the same.'

Gatliffe was reflective. 'I'm beginning to wish I had now.'

'You got cold feet, Gatty, that's your trouble.'

'I was afraid that somebody would come and catch us.'

'You didn't want it enough, did you? Whereas I did,' bragged Cochran, 'and so I bloody well had it. That's the thing about women. You got to grab them when you get the chance.' His smirk broadened. 'And there's something special about virgins like her. It means I was the *first*. She'll always remember me.'

Ruth Stein felt imprisoned in her own house. They never left her alone. When her mother was not watching her, she was kept under surveillance by her Uncle Herman or by a member of his family. She was not even allowed to sleep by herself. One of her cousins shared the same bedroom. Nobody ever mentioned her suicide attempt in so many words but it was neither forgotten nor forgiven. Everything they did was informed by it. At one and the same time, she was being punished for her crime and smothered by their collective love. It was agonising. Her father's funeral was over now and they had entered a seven-day period of bereavement called shiva when Ruth and the other chief mourners did not leave the house. It all served to heighten her sense of incarceration. When she joined the others in the thrice-daily recitation of Kaddish, she could barely mumble the words.

Armed with their documentation, and carrying a pair of handcuffs apiece, Harvey Marmion and Joe Keedy took a train to Dover and boarded a ferry. Standing on deck, they were the only passengers not in uniform. Inevitably, Marmion thought about his son who had crossed to France with his regiment the previous year. Since then they'd only seen him once on leave. Paul Marmion's letters from the front were eagerly seized on by every member of the family. They were not always comfortable reading. Joe Keedy had many friends who had enlisted in the army, several of them from the police force. But they were not in his thoughts at the moment. What interested him was the large number of horses on the vessel.

'Is there still a place for a cavalry regiment?' he wondered.

'Somebody clearly thinks so, Joe,' said Marmion.

'I wouldn't fancy charging at the German lines with nothing but a lance or a sabre. The enemy have got machine guns and rifles. What use are horses when bullets are flying about?'

'They get our soldiers to the point of attack much quicker. It's one of the things Paul is always complaining about – how painfully slow you are, trying to run across a field with mud up to your ankles.'

'I keep remembering that poem we learnt at school.'

Marmion grinned. 'I never took you for the poetic type.'

'I'm not, Harv,' said Keedy, speaking more familiarly now that they were off duty. 'I used to hate having to learn all those verses. But this one stuck in my mind somehow. It was about the Crimean War.'

'I know it,' said Marmion. '*The Charge of the Light Brigade* – it's about the battle of Balaclava.'

'They didn't stand a chance against the Russian cannon. No wonder it was called the "Valley of Death". I would have thought the days of a cavalry charge were over after that.'

'Apparently, they're not.'

'You wouldn't get me galloping at the enemy on a horse. I could be blown to pieces by a shell before I got anywhere near them.'

'The same goes for the infantry,' observed Marmion. 'That's why there's so little movement in the war zone now. Soldiers on both sides are hiding in trenches for protection. Paul hates it.'

'I can imagine.'

'He joined up to see some action, not to be stuck in a hole in the ground with rats for company. Paul enlisted after the retreat from Mons. I was glad he missed that bloodbath.'

'What about the rest of his soccer team? They all joined up together, didn't they? How many of them are still alive?'

'Seven,' said Marmion, grimly, 'though two had to be invalided home when they were badly injured in a mortar attack. According to Paul, neither of them will be able to kick a football again.'

War had suddenly become more of a reality for Harvey Marmion. Momentous events were taking place on the Continent but – while he was in London – they seemed to be a long way away. He'd had to rely on letters from his son and newspaper reports to give him some idea of what was actually going on. He was now travelling on a troopship with men who would be flung into action against a German army that had already made territorial advances on a number of fronts. Because of its strategic value, Ypres was being staunchly defended against German attack. If it fell, the enemy could move on to capture the vital Channel ports of Calais and Boulogne. Marmion realised what a catastrophe that would be. Latest reports indicated that British and French soldiers were putting up strong resistance in the second battle of Ypres. They were holding their own. Marmion was interested to see exactly how they were getting on.

It was left to Keedy to point out one possibility.

'What if we get there too late, Harv?' he asked.

'Too late?'

'Cochran and Gatliffe are soldiers. By the time we reach them, they could be fighting in the front line. What if they're already dead?'

'Then I'll feel terribly cheated,' said Marmion, bristling with anger. 'They committed a heinous crime and must be punished for it. Getting themselves killed in action would help them to escape justice and I'd hate that to happen. I *want* these men, Joe,' he emphasised. 'I want the pair of them behind bars where the bastards belong.'

CHAPTER TEN

War had profound social effects in Britain. When it first broke out in August 1914, the general assumption was that it would all be over by Christmas. The carnage of Mons shattered that illusion and the prime minister was soon calling for 500,000 soldiers. Women had at first confined themselves to urging men to enlist or – in some cases – sending them white feathers if they failed to do so. As more and more men joined up and went overseas, there was a crisis in the labour market. It was met by enterprising women who took over work that had hitherto been essentially a male preserve. For many of them, it was a liberating experience, allowing them to travel to places they would not otherwise have visited and to take up occupations that gave them both an income and the satisfaction of helping in the war effort.

In the course of a day, Irene Bayard found an endless sequence of jobs on offer. The problem lay in choosing the one that most attracted her. Calm and methodical, she made no instant decisions. Going from place to place, she made a mental note of over a dozen potential jobs that covered everything from nursing to operating a lathe in a factory. It was all a far cry from being a stewardess on the *Lusitania* and that was its appeal.

She took the opportunity to call at the shop managed by her sister and was given a cup of tea in a small room stacked high with shoeboxes. Irene had lunch alone in a café. Sitting in the window, she watched a number of women going past, many of them in uniforms of one kind or another. London streets had changed visibly. With recruitment at its height, there was a comparative dearth of young men counterbalanced by an increase in the number of working women. Things were different now.

It was late afternoon when she returned to the house and she planned to put her feet up for an hour. After so much walking, she was quite fatigued. The moment she let herself in, however, she heard the tinkle of Miss James's bell. Tapping on the lodger's door, she opened it tentatively.

'Good afternoon, Miss James.'

'Good afternoon,' said the old lady from the comfort of her armchair. 'This is the first chance I've had of speaking to you, Mrs Bayard.'

'Oh, you'll have plenty of chance from now on,' Irene told her. 'I'll be living under the same roof.'

'So I understand, dear, and I'm very happy to hear it. Your sister gets very lonely at times. Having you here will be a tonic.'

Miss James seemed smaller and frailer than when Irene had last seen her. Her face still had a faded prettiness and her white hair was as well groomed as ever, but she'd lost weight and colour. She was not idle. As she talked, the knitting needles in her hand clicked away.

'What are you knitting?' asked Irene.

'That depends on whether or not you can keep a secret.'

Irene understood. 'Oh, it's something for Dorothy, is it?'

'Yes, it's a new scarf – but please don't tell her.'

'I won't breathe a word, Miss James.' She smiled invitingly. 'Is there anything I can get you?'

'No, thank you, dear.'

'I just wondered why you'd rung your bell.'

'Well, I wanted to tell you how pleased I am to see you back,' said Miss James, 'but I also needed to pass on a message. While you were out, a gentleman called.'

Irene was surprised. 'Was he looking for me?'

'Yes. I can't really describe him because my eyesight is all but gone. But he had a nice voice and I could tell from his manner that he was fond of you.'

'Did he give you his name?'

'Of course,' said the old lady. 'I made a point of asking. His name was Mr Gill – Mr Ernest Gill.'

Irene's heart sank.

They were miles from their destination when they first heard the continuous thunder of artillery. As they got closer, the sound grew steadily in volume. The British Expeditionary Force was undergoing a constant bombardment and retaliating accordingly. Stopping well short of Ypres itself, they established that the regiment they sought had its headquarters in an old farmhouse. The first person they encountered was a peremptory captain who treated their request with barely concealed hostility, arguing that Scotland Yard detectives had no jurisdiction over members of the BEF and that their journey had therefore been futile. Refusing to be turned away, Marmion waved the letter from the War Office under his nose and the man eventually gave them some grudging cooperation. He introduced them to Major Nicholas Birchfield, a portly man with a neat moustache, bulging blue eyes and a peppery disposition. When he'd heard them out, Birchfield clasped his hands behind his back and spoke with clipped politeness.

'That's all very well, Inspector,' he began, 'but your arrival is deuced awkward. As I'm sure you appreciate, we need every man we have. We can't release two of our soldiers on the basis of what may turn out to be a wholly false accusation.'

'There's nothing false about it, Major,' said Marmion. 'The young lady in question was raped. A doctor confirmed it.'

'He may have confirmed that she had intercourse but that's hardly proof of rape. We are all men of the world, are we not?' he went on with a ripe chuckle. 'This situation is as old as the hills. A young woman drinks too much then gives herself willingly to a chance acquaintance. Later, when she comes to her senses, the only way that she can account for the loss of her virginity is to cry rape. It's happened before a hundred times.'

'Well, it's not the case with Miss Stein.'

'How do you know? Have you spoken to her about it?'

'No,' admitted Marmion, 'but I talked with her mother. She was able to pass on the relevant details.'

'Oh, so this is the mother's doing, is it?' said Birchfield, amused. 'That settles it in my mind. What mother believes that her darling daughter would sacrifice herself before marriage? She simply *has* to claim that rape took place. It's maternal instinct.'

'We're not only concerned with the charge of rape,' said Keedy, annoyed by the man's tone. 'Murder, arson and theft are among the related crimes. In all probability, Gatliffe and Cochran may be guilty on other counts as well.'

'Do you have any evidence to that effect, Sergeant?'

'We know that they were at the rear of the premises at the time, Major. That's evidence enough to make them suspects.'

'And who provided that evidence?'

'The young lady,' said Marmion. 'Miss Ruth Stein.'

'Doing so by proxy, I gather.'

'She was under immense stress. You have clearly never dealt with rape victims before, Major. Sergeant Keedy and I have, and we know how hard it is to get them to come forward. In all my years in the police force,' he went on, 'I've never heard one false accusation, because women know the kind of punitive cross-examination they'll face in court, not to mention the cruel and unfair assumptions that people like you will invariably make.'

Biting back a reply, Birchfield walked behind the table that was serving as his desk. The room he was using as his office was small and low-ceilinged. It had undulating paving slabs on the floor and peeling walls. Judging by the pungent aroma, it had once been used to store cheese and other dairy products. Weighing his words, the major returned to the attack.

'Do you know what is happening at the moment?' he asked.

'You're fighting a fierce battle,' replied Marmion.

'It's more than that, Inspector. This is the second time Ypres has been in the thick of the action and Brother Bosch has decided to assault us with a new weapon – poison gas. It's already taken its toll.'

'This is hardly relevant to the matter in hand.'

'I think it's extremely relevant, because it goes to the heart of the matter. Priorities – that's what we're talking about, isn't it? What takes priority? Is it the word of some girl who let her emotions get the better of her, or is it two members of an overstretched army fighting against a deadly enemy? Private Cochran and Private Gatliffe are no use to us if they're carted off to London. We need them here. They'll be in the trenches very soon, where they'll run the risk of being shot, shelled, forced to cough up their lungs by chlorine gas or made to cry their eyes out by a swinish German lachrymator, benzyl bromide. In short, they are brave soldiers acting out of patriotic impulse.'

Marmion was scathing. 'I don't consider rape to be brave or patriotic, Major,' he said with asperity, 'nor do I find the idea of two drunken men setting upon a defenceless young woman anything but repulsive. You should be ashamed that Cochran and Gatliffe are wearing army uniforms. They are a disgrace to your regiment.'

'That's for us to judge,' said Birchfield, stung by his words. 'All that I've heard so far are unsubstantiated allegations.'

'They are supported by two arrest warrants.'

'What if it's a case of mistaken identity?'

'Then the two men will be released without charge.'

'From the information that we have,' said Keedy, 'that seems unlikely. The victim was able to supply us with the names of the two men and the fact that they were leaving for France on the following day. That led us to *your* regiment, Major.'

Birchfield scowled. He sat down behind his makeshift desk and weighed up the possibilities. Reluctant to hand the two men over, he searched for ways to send the detectives packing. Marmion seemed to read his mind and jumped in smartly.

'I can see that we are wasting each other's time, Major,' he said, briskly. 'You clearly don't have the authority to make a decision on the matter. We would therefore ask to speak to your commanding officer, Lieutenant Colonel Knox. Unlike you, he will doubtless understand the importance of arrest warrants and a letter from the War Office.'

'*I* was assigned to deal with this,' said Birchfield, haughtily.

'Then please do so without prevarication. Yes,' said Marmion, stifling a protest with a raised hand, 'I know that there's a war on. My own son is stationed south of here with his regiment. And in case you think Miss Stein would surrender herself to a drunken stranger in an alley, I should tell you that she comes from a respectable middle-class family and that her brother, Daniel, is fighting on the Mesopotamian Front under the command of Sir John Nixon. Now then,' he added, crisply, 'are you going to comply with our request or do we need to discuss your obstructive behaviour with your commanding officer?'

Eyeing the inspector with distaste, Birchfield capitulated.

'I'll have these men sent for,' he said, coldly.

Alice Marmion got back from school to find her mother on her knees as she cleaned the grate in the living room. When she looked around, Alice saw that the whole place was spick and span. Her mother had even burnished the copper plates that stood on the mantelpiece. There was no need to clean the grate. It might be months before they needed to have another fire. And there was no call for vigorous housework in a room that was already spotless. Alice understood. Her mother was eager to keep herself busy so that she did not brood on Marmion's visit to the Western Front. The worried look on Ellen's face showed that the strategy had comprehensively failed.

'Hello, dear,' she said, hauling herself to her feet. 'I was just sprucing the place up a bit.'

'It doesn't *need* sprucing up, Mummy. Come here.'

Alice took her by the arm, led her to the sofa and lowered her onto it. Putting her bag aside, she sat beside her and held her hand.

'Daddy is fine,' she said. 'There's no point in worrying.'

'I'm bound to have some fears, Alice.'

'Why? He'll be nowhere near the actual fighting – much to Joe Keedy's disappointment, I daresay. The person we need to worry about is Paul, not Daddy. Paul is in the trenches yet you don't let anxiety about him weigh you down.'

'I did when he first joined up,' said Ellen. 'I stayed awake for nights on end. As time passed, it somehow got easier to bear.'

Alice squeezed her mother's hand then rose to her feet.

'I know what you need.'

'I'll make the tea, Alice.'

'Oh no you won't,' said her daughter, easing her back down on the sofa as she tried to get up. 'Stay here – that's an order.'

Ellen gave a grateful laugh. Going into the kitchen, Alice filled the kettle, set it on the stove and lit a gas ring. Evidently, her mother had spent a lot of time there because every surface gleamed and every item was in its rightful place. In the time that Alice had been at school, her mother had also done the washing and ironing. The windows had been cleaned on the outside and the inside. When she glanced into the back garden, Alice saw that a lot of effort had been expended on tidying that up as well.

Having made the tea, she took it back into the living room on a tray and set it down on the low table beside the sofa. Alice perched on the edge of an armchair.

'I've just seen how much work you've done today,' she said. 'If this is what being married involves, I'm going to stay single.'

'I have to keep the place looking nice, Alice.'

'Then clean it once a week at most.'

'Believe it or not, I like housework.'

'Well, I don't. I find it soul-destroying.'

After waiting a short while, Alice put milk into the two cups then removed the tea cosy. As she poured from the teapot, she used the strainer to catch the leaves. Her mother added sugar and stirred her cup. Alice spurned the sugar. Grabbing one of the biscuits, she wolfed it down.

'I didn't have time for a proper lunch,' she explained.

'Why not?'

'Well, I still can't make up my mind about whether or not to join the Women's Emergency Corps. You and Daddy are against the idea so I decided to get some independent advice.'

'What do you mean?'

'I went over to see Uncle Raymond.'

'I told you to keep him out of this discussion.'

'He's family. His opinions count. So I walked over there.'

'That was a long way to go.'

'I didn't mind. I felt that he'd listen without hectoring me. He's so patient and he never makes you feel that you're stupid.'

Ellen frowned guiltily. 'Is that what *we* do, Alice?'

'Not exactly,' said Alice, 'but I don't always feel that I get a fair hearing. I was able to talk at length to Uncle Raymond without any interruption.'

'And what was his advice?'

'He said that I should follow my instincts. After all, that's what he did when he joined the Salvation Army against the wishes of just about everyone in the family.'

'I'm surprised that he didn't try to recruit *you*.'

'As a matter of fact, he did,' said Alice, grinning, 'though it was partly in fun. Anyway, he gave me food for thought but nothing that I could actually eat.'

She munched a second biscuit. Looking at her daughter, Ellen could not believe that someone so attractive and patently intelligent had not met her partner in life yet. Ellen had been years younger when she'd met and married Harvey Marmion and she tended to use that fact as a yardstick. The thought that Alice might end up as a spinster was deeply unsettling. After a mouthful of tea, Ellen tried to sound casual.

'It's high time you had a chap of your own, you know.'

'I don't *want* one, Mummy.'

'You have such a limited social life.'

'That's not true. I go to dances occasionally and I sing in a choir. I just haven't met the right man yet.'

'I'm not sure that you've been looking, Alice.'

'I've had more important things to do.'

'Nothing is more important than marrying and having a family.'

'That's a matter of opinion. At the moment, I'm enjoying my freedom while I can. There'll be little chance of doing that if and when I do eventually have a husband.'

'Haven't you met *any* young man you really liked?'

'I've met several,' said Alice, 'but they already have girlfriends. Either that, or they've gone off to join the army. I don't want my choice to be limited to a small number of chaps, Mummy.'

'What sort of person would attract you?'

'I want one who is fabulously rich and who'll indulge my every whim.' They both laughed. 'Failing that, I'm looking for someone who is . . . very special.'

'Does he have to be handsome?'

'He has to have pleasant features, certainly.'

'Will he be older than you or a similar age?'

'Oh, he must be older, that's definite.'

'Why do you say that?'

'Men take much longer to grow up,' said Alice, mischievously. 'That's been my experience, anyway. Every chap I went out with was very nice until he had a drink inside him. All of a sudden, they became giggling schoolboys and I have enough of those at work.'

'So you want somebody more adult? What about character?'

'He must be honest, reliable and have a sense of adventure.'

'Is there anything else?'

Alice was pensive. 'I'm not sure,' she said. 'Except that I'd want him to treat me as his equal, of course.' Ellen grinned. 'Did I say something funny?'

'No,' replied her mother. 'It's just an odd coincidence, that's all.'

Alice was befuddled. 'Coincidence?'

'Your ideal man has to be very special, handsome, older than you, honest, reliable and with a sense of adventure. Oh, and he must treat you as an equal. Is that a fair summary?'

'Yes, it is.'

'Then you've given me a perfect description of Joe Keedy.'

Alice came extremely close to blushing.

Divide and rule. The detectives adopted their usual policy. While Marmion interviewed John Gatliffe, Keedy was given the task of confronting Oliver Cochran. They made sure that the two men were summoned separately so that they had no time to concoct an alibi together. Keedy had the use of a room so small that its only furniture was a table and two chairs. He made sure that he sat down between Cochran and the door. Taking out his pad and pencil, he looked the suspect up and down. He could see instantly that he would meet with resistance. When he was told who Keedy was and why he had come into a theatre of war, Cochran was at first flabbergasted. He quickly recovered and stoutly denied the allegation of rape.

According to the soldier, he'd been drinking in a Soho pub on the evening in question and could call on several friends to vouch for him. He had no idea where Jermyn Street was, he insisted, and would have had no reason to be there.

'How do you explain the fact that the young lady knew your names?' asked Keedy.

Cochran looked blank. 'What young lady?'

'The one who remembers you well enough to identify you.'

'She's making it all up.'

'Why on earth should she do that, Private Cochran? What woman in her position wants to admit that she was sexually assaulted by two men in the alley at the rear of her father's shop? It's highly embarrassing for her. Why would she do it?'

'Ask her.'

Keedy aimed several more questions at him but Cochran had erected a brick wall that the detective could not penetrate. Now that he was in the army, the soldier felt safe. A touch of arrogance crept in. Keedy changed the angle of attack and asked him something that caught him off guard.

'Did you murder Jacob Stein?' he demanded.

Cochran blenched. 'What are you on about?'

'During the time that you and John Gatliffe were close to the scene of the crime, the owner of that shop was stabbed to death. Was that your doing, by any chance?'

'We weren't even there.'

'Think carefully before you give another glib answer,' warned Keedy. 'Rape is a serious offence but murder carries the death penalty. If you fight in the trenches, you stand a chance of being killed by a bullet or a shell. It will probably be a quick death. That's not the case on the gallows. When you and Gatliffe are found guilty of murder, it will be a slow and deliberate end to your useless lives.'

Though he was certain that Cochran was not involved in the death of Jacob Stein, Keedy saw no harm in using the accusation as a prod. It quietened the suspect completely. Instead of trying to brazen it out, Cochran lapsed into silence. He realised that he was in serious trouble. He also knew that there was a strong possibility that Gatliffe would crack under pressure and give them both away. Cochran was determined to avoid a prison sentence. Somehow he had to escape. His head fell to his chest and his arms were slack. He pretended to have given up. Gathering his strength for attack, he suddenly made his bid for freedom.

He stood up, turned the table on its side and used it to knock Keedy from his chair and ram him against the door. When he tried to scramble over the detective's body, however, Cochran felt a hand taking a firm grip on his ankle before yanking him off his feet. With both of them on the floor, there was a frantic fight and Keedy was always going to be the victor. He was quicker, stronger and more agile. His first punch caught Cochran on the nose, splitting it open and sending blood dribbling down his chin. A relay of heavy punches to the body stunned the soldier. Before he could counter, Cochran found himself expertly turned over so that the handcuffs could be snapped onto his wrists. Keedy stood up, righted the chair and table then lifted his assailant from the floor by the scruff of his neck.

'I fancy that that amounts to a confession, Private Cochran,' he said, breathing hard. 'You will also face the additional charges of resisting arrest and assaulting a police officer in the execution of his duties.' He took out a handkerchief and held it beneath Cochran's nose to stem the bleeding. 'It's easy to overpower a frightened young woman like Miss Stein, isn't it? When you take on someone your own size, it's a different matter.'

Cochran glared malevolently at him.

Harvey Marmion sized the man up before inviting him to take a seat. John Gatliffe was on the defensive at once. They were in the room that Major Birchfield used as his office. Remaining on his feet, Marmion explained why he was there and asked for Gatliffe's response to the charge of rape.

'I didn't do it, Inspector,' said the soldier, urgently.

'We know that. The man who raped her was your friend, Oliver Cochran, but you assisted him by holding the girl down, didn't you?'

'No – I wasn't even there. Nor was Olly – we're innocent.'

'I very much doubt that, Private Gatliffe.'

'I've never heard of this Ruth Stein.'

'That's only because you never took the trouble to have any formal introductions,' said Marmion with light sarcasm. 'You were both drunk, a young woman comes out of the shop, so you felt that she was fair game.'

'It's a lie,' wailed Gatliffe. 'It wasn't us, Inspector, I swear it.'

Marmion sat opposite him and looked deep into his eyes. What he saw was fear and desperation. There was also a hint of remorse. He surmised that it had not been Gatliffe's idea to set upon Ruth Stein. He had simply done what he was told by a friend who was a stronger character. That did not, however, entitle him to Marmion's sympathy. Gatliffe was an accessory. Even though it might have been against his will, he had committed a crime and merited severe punishment.

'There are two ways to proceed,' said Marmion.

'It wasn't us!' repeated Gatliffe. 'There's been a mistake.'

'Listen to me, please. You're not a bad man, are you? In fact, I suspect that you have more than an ounce of decency in you. That's why you spared the girl a second ordeal.'

'I don't know what you're talking about.'

'That's the first way to proceed,' explained Marmion. 'I make allegations and you respond with a tissue of lies. We could go on like that all day, Private Gatliffe. The problem with that strategy is that it will bring about your downfall. My colleague, Detective Sergeant Keedy, is interviewing Private Cochran and will meet with the same blanket denial that I'm getting. Your friend will invent an alibi which will differ substantially in detail from the one *you're* trying to think up. In other words, we'll know that you're lying through your teeth.'

He fixed Gatliffe with a stare. 'Are you going to tell the same lies under oath in a court of law?'

Gatliffe quailed. 'It wasn't me and Ol,' he said, weakly.

'The second way is the one that I'd recommend. It will not only save time, it will earn you some favour with the judge and jury. I'm talking about a confession,' said Marmion. 'I'm talking about having the courage to admit that you did something terribly wrong and that you're prepared to face the consequences. We didn't come all this way to let you slip through our fingers, Private Gatliffe. Back in London, a young woman is tormented by what you and your friend did to her. It's a permanent wound that will never heal. The one thing that might act as balm to that wound is the knowledge that her attackers have been imprisoned. That's why Sergeant Keedy and I are here.'

'I need to speak to Olly,' said Gatliffe, close to panic.

'That won't be possible, I'm afraid.'

'We got rights, Inspector.'

'I'm more concerned with Miss Stein's rights. She's the victim here, not you and Private Cochran.'

'We're in the army now – you can't touch us.'

'I'm afraid that you've been misinformed on that point.'

Gatliffe was cornered. His eyes darted and sweat broke out on his brow. His friend's assurances that they were in the clear had proved groundless. Detectives had pursued them to the front and called them to account. He knew that Cochran would rebut any charges hotly but Gatliffe did not have his friend's limitless capacity for telling lies. When their respective statements to the police were compared, they would be caught out. The girl would identify them in court. Gatliffe trembled. Instead of returning home as a war hero, he would be dragged back to London under arrest to face trial. Those fevered minutes with a terrified girl had been their ruination.

'Well?' said Marmion, watching him. 'What have you decided?'

'I need to think,' said Gatliffe, morosely.

'Let me remind you what else happened that evening. A mob, of which you may well have been part, attacked the shop owned by Jacob Stein in Jermyn Street. The window was smashed, the place was looted and someone set fire to the premises. Mr Stein – whose daughter was being raped nearby – was murdered. It remains to be seen if you and Cochran were implicated in these other crimes.'

'We know nothing about murder,' protested Gatliffe.

'What about the fire? Did you start it?'

'No, we never went inside the shop.'

Marmion smiled. 'Ah, so you *were* there, after all,' he said, making a note in his pad. 'We're making progress at last. Why don't you tell me the full story, Private Gatliffe? Do you know what I think? I fancy that you'd like to get it off your chest. Am I right?'

After a lengthy pause, Gatliffe nodded his head.

CHAPTER ELEVEN

How had he found her? That was what Irene Bayard kept asking herself. She had never given Ernie Gill her sister's address in London, nor had she told him about her intention to go there on her return from Ireland. Gill was essentially a friend and work colleague to her, someone with whom to pass the time while they were sailing on the *Lusitania* together but, on her side, there was no deeper commitment. Irene had never even told him where she lodged in Liverpool. How, therefore, had he managed to turn up on Dorothy's doorstep? It was disturbing. As far as Irene was concerned, Gill was unwanted and unwelcome, a link with a past she was determined to sever.

He would be back. That much was certain. Gill was nothing if not persistent. She'd had ample evidence of that on board the liner. Rejection only seemed to intensify his interest in her. Since he'd come back in search of her, she needed to have an excuse to get rid of him without even inviting him into the house. Irene rehearsed various possibilities in her mind. Whatever happened, she did not want Gill to meet her sister because it would lead to a flurry of awkward questions from Dorothy. If Irene wanted to preserve the serenity of the house, Gill had to be kept at bay. In her new life, he simply did not belong.

After a second day in search of employment, Irene made her way back home. As she walked down the street towards it, she wondered if he had called again and if Miss James would be waiting to tell her about it. But there was no bell summoning her. All she could hear from the front room was the rhythmical click of knitting needles. She was grateful there had been no second visit from Gill. It gave her a breathing space. While waiting for her sister to get back, Irene sat at the kitchen table and went through the list of jobs on offer. She narrowed the choice down to three. Hearing the sound of a key in the front door, she lit the gas under the kettle then gave Dorothy a smile as her sister entered the room.

'A busy day?' she enquired.

'It's always busy,' said Dorothy, wearily, 'though there's more trying on than actually buying. We had one woman in this morning who tried on eight pairs of shoes before she decided that she didn't really need any of them.'

'I wouldn't have the patience to deal with someone like that.'

'It can be frustrating at times, Irene. We've had people who dart into the shop to escape a sudden downpour and who pretend they came in search of shoes. All they really want is a place to sit down in the dry.' She removed her hat. 'But what about you – have you made up your mind yet?'

'More or less,' said Irene.

'Does that mean you've accepted a job?'

'No, it means that I've got three to choose from, Dot. I'm still thinking it over. My guess is that I'll finish up on the trams or in that toy factory, but there's a third possibility as well.'

'What is it?'

'Well, I was accosted by a lady this afternoon,' recalled Irene. 'She noticed me looking at a job advert and asked if I'd ever thought of joining the WEC – that's the Women's Emergency Corps.'

Dorothy wrinkled her nose. 'They're all suffragettes, aren't they?'

'That's not true, Dot. Besides,' said Irene, 'it wouldn't worry me if they were. She was such a nice well-spoken lady. I had no idea of the range of the work that the WEC do. For instance, they have a kitchen department that's aided by the National Food Fund. And they join with another organisation to train unemployed girls for domestic service and so on. They also help refugees from abroad by having women who can speak French waiting at railway stations and at the docks to advise them about accommodation and that.'

'You don't speak French, do you?'

'No, but that's not the point. The service is there. When they see a need, the WEC moves in to meet it.'

'I think you're better off on the trams,' said Dorothy. 'I'm sure these other people do good work but they're too strident for my liking. They're always demanding this and campaigning for that.'

'Don't you believe in women getting the vote, Dot?'

'I believe in a quiet life.'

'If we were able to vote, we might even use it to get equal pay one day. Surely, you'd want that.'

'I get by.'

While her sister took off her coat and slipped it over the back of a chair, Irene began to get the tea things ready. She did not want an argument with Dorothy, who had always been subservient towards men. In Irene's view, it was a major reason why her sister had never married. She was too deferential. The few men in Dorothy's life had sought obedience in a future wife but not when it verged on a kind of obsequiousness. It was best to keep off the subject of the WEC for the time being. Irene was about to launch into another topic of conversation when there was a loud knock on the front door.

'Who can that be?' wondered Dorothy.

'I'll go,' said Irene, pulling her by the arm to stop her going out. 'You make the tea, Dot.'

As she went out of the kitchen and into the little passageway, Irene made a point of closing the kitchen door behind her. It was Ernie Gill, she was sure of that. It was just the kind of authoritative knock that he would use. Even if it meant being rude to his face, she would have to get rid of him somehow. His pursuit of her had to be nipped in the bud. Bracing herself for the reunion, Irene put a hand on the knob and opened the front door.

'I'm sorry, Ernie,' she said, 'but I can't speak to you now.'

The man at the door blinked in astonishment. It was not Gill at all but a dapper individual in his fifties with a well-trimmed beard. Raising his hat, he gave a diffident smile.

'Good evening,' he said, politely. 'I've come for Miss James.'

The main problem was to keep them apart. On the return journey, Marmion and Keedy had to make sure that their prisoners did not get close to each other. Their fear was that, given the chance, Cochran would attack his former friend. Now that Gatliffe had given a full confession, Cochran's denials were meaningless. The only way that he could assuage his anger was by giving Gatliffe a beating but he was never allowed to get close enough to do that. He was either handcuffed to Keedy or, when they boarded a ship at Calais, confined on his own. It was a joyless voyage. Apart from the detectives and the prisoners, the passengers were almost exclusively wounded soldiers being sent home. Their war was over. Many of them had suffered hideous injuries and were in constant pain.

It was a sobering experience for Harvey Marmion. When his son had first joined up, he had been proud of him and sent him off gladly to France, expecting him to be part of a relieving British army that supported French forces in driving out the Germans. Nine months later, the nature of the conflict had been transformed. Casualties on both sides were mounting rapidly and new weapons were doing unspeakable things to the human body. As he looked at some of the amputees lying on deck, Marmion wondered how he and Ellen would cope if their son came home without a leg or an arm. And even if he survived injury, what impact would the horrors he had witnessed have on Paul's mind? It was bound to change his whole attitude to life.

Keedy strolled across to join his superior at the rail.

'It's a pack of lies, Harv,' he said.

'Have you been talking to Cochran again?'

'No, I was thinking about the newspapers. They're not telling us the truth. We've seen what it's like at the front and it's not being reported properly in the press. They say nothing whatsoever about the pitiable scenes in the clearing stations, and they never mention the awful smell of death and decay.'

'They don't want to scare people, Joe.'

'Why not?' asked Keedy. 'It's not going to put off new recruits. I reckon that it will do the reverse. If people really know what the

Germans are doing to our lads, they'll want to wipe them off the face of the earth.' He looked at a wounded man nearby, both legs missing and a bloodstained bandage across his eyes. 'What sort of life is that poor fellow going to have?'

'I dread to think,' said Marmion.

'Aren't you glad that Paul's regiment is not in Ypres?'

'Yes, Joe, I am.'

Keedy gestured with an arm to take in the whole deck.

'Are you going to tell Ellen about this? Are you going to describe some of the things we saw and heard at the front?'

'There's no point in upsetting her unnecessarily.'

'What about Alice?'

'She's more likely to press for details,' said Marmion, 'and I won't deceive her. Our daughter is not squeamish. She doesn't get upset easily.'

'I know,' said Keedy, fondly. 'Alice has an inner strength. I think she must get that from you, Harv.'

Marmion's laugh was hollow. 'I don't have much inner strength at the moment. I just feel depressed and humbled by it all.' He pulled himself together and managed a smile. 'But we didn't cross the Channel to act as war reporters, Joe. We had a mission and it was successful. Two men will now be tried for the rape of Ruth Stein. The only disappointment,' he added, 'is that they were unable to give us any information regarding the other crimes committed that evening. I believe what Gatliffe told me. They never went inside the shop.'

'We have to start all over again, then.'

'It's not that bad. I'm hoping that some new ground has been broken while we've been away and that we'll get back to find there's been some definite progress.'

'We need to track down Jacob Stein's two former employees,' said Keedy. 'The fact that they've disappeared so conveniently could be significant.'

'We shall see, Joe,' said Marmion. 'The main thing is that we have good news to report to the commissioner. Cochran and Gatliffe have been arrested and there's absolutely no doubt about their guilt. Sir Edward will be able to get Herbert Stone off his back now.'

Ruth Stein sat in the living room with her mother, her aunt and two of her cousins. They had been receiving condolences from a string of friends who called in, one of whom was David Cohen, erstwhile manager of the shop. Ruth was too numb to do anything more than offer a pale smile of thanks to the various visitors. She was still locked in her private suffering, convinced that everyone now knew about her attempt at killing herself and condemned her for it. There had been long and painful conversations with Rabbi Hirsch and with her Uncle Herman. Her mother spared her any more questioning and tried to bathe her in a soothing love. It gave Ruth some much-needed relief but failed to disperse her corroding sense of worthlessness.

There was a tap on the door and Herbert Stone popped his head into the room. When he asked to speak to Ruth, she felt the familiar sickness stirring. He was going to take her to task once more, she thought, and it would be gruelling. Stone escorted her to the room that her father had used as his office and he closed the door behind them. When they were both seated, he put a hand on her arm.

'I have some news for you,' he said.

'What is it, Uncle Herman?'

'I've just taken a phone call from Scotland Yard.'

‘Oh!’ She drew back instinctively.

‘It’s good news, Ruth. You should be glad. Inspector Marmion is in charge of the case. Thanks to the information you provided, he was able to identify the two men who attacked you. They were arrested in Flanders, where they’d gone with their regiment. Both of them are now back here in custody. Can you hear what I’m telling you?’ he asked, squeezing her arm. ‘The crime has been solved.’

Ruth was unsure what to make of the news. The sheer mention of Scotland Yard had brought the whole incident flooding back into her mind. It seemed extraordinary to her that something which had happened in an alley in London had sent detectives abroad in pursuit of the men responsible. Somehow she did not wish to hear any more. She wanted to put her hands over her ears and block out sound.

‘Aren’t you pleased?’ asked Stone.

‘I don’t know.’

‘But they’ll be punished for what they did to you.’

‘Will they?’

‘When they’re convicted, that is. One of the men has already confessed, I gather, but the other is maintaining his innocence. You’ll be asked to identify him in court.’

Ruth’s brain was suddenly ablaze. The notion that she had to confront the man who raped her threw her into confusion. She never wanted to get anywhere near him again. He’d robbed her of something she could never get back and, in doing so, had shattered her confidence. She’d tried with all her might to put the whole incident out of her mind but it was back there with vivid immediacy. There was a choking sensation in her throat and her eyes began to mist over. It was too much to bear.

Her uncle was very disappointed in her response. Expecting a sign of pleasure at his news, he shook her arm hard as if to force it out of her. It produced a very different result. Putting her head back and opening her mouth wide, Ruth emitted a long, hysterical, high-pitched cry and began to shake convulsively.

After listening to his report, Sir Edward Henry congratulated Marmion on his success. As soon as they'd reached Dover, the inspector had telephoned him to say that the two suspects had been arrested, thus enabling the commissioner to pass on the tidings to Herbert Stone. Marmion had now given a much fuller account of what had occurred in the farmhouse near Ypres.

'It's a pity we can't trumpet this in the press,' said Sir Edward, 'but the family has begged us not to give it publicity for the sake of Miss Stein. I suggested to Mr Stone that we could release details of the arrest while keeping the name of the victim anonymous but he was not happy with that idea.'

'Her name will have to be mentioned when the case comes to court,' said Marmion, 'unless we can persuade Cochran to plead guilty and save everyone a lot of trouble.'

'What are the chances of that?'

'They're rather slim, Sir Edward. He's a bloody-minded fellow.'

'We see far too many of those in our line of work,' said the commissioner, dryly. 'All the more reason to ensure that he's exposed in court in his true light.'

'Gatliffe's confession makes his friend's position untenable but there are some people who, even if caught red-handed, will never admit guilt. It's an article of faith with them. Oliver Cochran falls into that category,' said Marmion.

'What – even after his assault on Sergeant Keedy?'

'That never took place, apparently. Cochran is now claiming that *he* was the victim of an unprovoked attack.'

'That's palpably absurd!'

'But I take your point about publicity, Sir Edward,' continued Marmion. 'Rape convictions are so rare that it would be good to send the message that we take the crime seriously. With so many soldiers on leave in London, looking for a good night out, it's more than likely that there'll be other young women like Ruth Stein who are in the wrong place at the wrong time.'

'Sadly, I must endorse that prediction.'

When Marmion went on to ask what had been happening in their absence, the commissioner was glad to report that there had been no more incidents of mob violence in the West End and that the many roaming gangs in the East End seemed to have died away. It was a pattern repeated in other cities. In the immediate aftermath of the sinking of the *Lusitania*, summary justice had been sought by people with an anti-German bloodlust. It had peaked in ports like Liverpool, then slowly subsided. Police and other authorities were still involved in cleaning up the gigantic mess left behind. What they could not tidy away was the aggressive impulse latent in so many British people and liable to be aroused by the next enemy outrage.

'Needless to say,' explained Sir Edward, 'there's been universal condemnation of the sinking. America is especially critical, of course, because so many of the victims were American citizens.'

'What have the Germans said in response?'

'Their argument is that the ship was carrying armaments and that it was therefore an acceptable target for their submarine fleet.'

'*Were* there armaments aboard?' asked Marmion. 'It seems highly unlikely.'

'The Germans are basing their claim on the fact that only one torpedo was fired, yet there were two explosions. According to their propaganda, the second blast could only have been caused by the presence of explosive materials in the hold.'

'What response has there been from Cunard?'

'A firm denial,' said the commissioner.

'Then the German excuse can be dismissed out of hand.'

'That's my feeling, Inspector.'

'Had there been intelligence in advance to the effect that the vessel *was* carrying material destined for the war front, then every U-boat in the blockade would have been ready to ambush the *Lusitania*. Yet that isn't what happened,' argued Marmion. 'She was hit by a solitary torpedo when she was assumed to be a passenger ship with no armaments aboard. That's a violation of maritime neutrality.'

'There'll be more repercussions to come, I suspect.'

'More disorder in our streets, you mean?'

'I was thinking about international responses,' said Sir Edward, 'but there'll be further work for the Metropolitan Police, I've no doubt.'

'You told me that everything had quietened down.'

'That could be a temporary respite, Inspector. There's still so much danger in the air,' said the commissioner, sucking his teeth. 'We've not done with this business yet.'

St Saviour's church gave Irene Bayard a warm welcome when she attended morning service there on Sunday. She was introduced to the vicar, the churchwardens and to a number of her sister's friends. When they discovered she was a survivor of the *Lusitania* disaster, people crowded round to offer their sympathy and to ask for details of the event. It served to give Irene an eminence she neither sought nor relished. After the service, Dorothy, as its secretary, needed to discuss the next meeting of the Parochial Church Council. Leaving her sister behind, Irene slipped out and made her way back to the house alone. In spite of the attention she was given, she was glad that she had gone to church. It was as if she had touched a spiritual base that had been lacking in her life for some time. She felt restored.

Her sense of well-being only lasted until she turned the corner into her street. Coming towards her was the unmistakable figure of Ernie Gill, wearing his best suit and strutting jauntily along. When he spotted her, he whisked off his hat to wave at her. Irene stopped in her tracks. He was the last person she wanted to meet but, for old times' sake, she steeled herself to be pleasant to him.

'There you are,' he said, rushing towards her and kissing her on the cheek before replacing his hat. 'Miss James said that you went to church with your sister.'

'That's right, Ernie.'

'Where is she?'

'Oh, Dorothy had something to sort out with the churchwarden.'

'I was looking forward to meeting her.'

'That . . . won't be possible,' she said, guardedly.

'I bet you're wondering how I found you,' he said, grinning at his cleverness. 'When we parted in Liverpool, I knew I'd want to see you again and so I followed you back to your digs. I saw you go in and thought I'd let you recover for a day or two before I turned up again.'

'Mrs Hoskins gave you this address, didn't she?' guessed Irene.

'Yes – your landlady took a bit of persuading, mind you, but she told me you'd come to London. She was used to forwarding letters and things when you were staying with your sister.' He looked over his shoulder. 'It's a nice little house.'

'Yes, it is.'

'Aren't you going to invite me in?'

'No, Ernie, it's . . . not convenient.'

'But I was hoping to meet your sister.'

'Dorothy won't be here for ages and I have lots to do. I'm sorry but this is a bad time for you to call.'

'That's no problem, Irene,' he said, cheerily. 'I'll come back another time. Just you name the day.'

It was the moment when she ought to have told him that she didn't really wish to see him again but the words simply wouldn't come out. Instead, Irene stood there and gesticulated nervously. Sensing rejection, Gill spoke with subdued anger.

'You're ashamed of me, is that it?' he challenged.

'No, no, it's not that, Ernie.'

'I'm not good enough to meet your precious sister.'

'You've got hold of the wrong end of the stick.'

'Then why aren't you pleased to see me?'

'I am – in a way,' she lied.

'I'm not Miss James,' he retorted. 'I'm not blind like that old biddy. I can see it in your face, Irene. You don't even want to speak to your old shipmate, do you?'

'Of course I do, Ernie.'

His anger was surging. 'Then why are you giving me the cold shoulder? I've got rights, after all, and I don't just mean that we sailed together so often. Have you forgotten what happened when we jumped overboard?' he said, wagging a finger. 'I didn't have to come to your rescue, you know. I could have thought only of myself. But I didn't, Irene. I looked around for you then swam over. I saved your life. Is this all the thanks I get? Don't you think you *owe* me something?'

There was hurt as well as accusation in his voice and it melted her resolve. Gill *had* come to her aid in the water. She would always remember that. After all they'd been through together, it was both wrong and unfair to antagonise him. Irene accepted that now. Reaching out a consoling arm, she touched his shoulder.

'I would like to see you sometime, Ernie,' she said with a degree of enthusiasm, 'only it can't be today and it can't be here.'

His chirpiness returned. 'That suits me,' he said. 'Let's make a date, shall we? Give me a time and place and I'll be there.'

Joe Keedy was delighted to be invited to tea with the Marmion family. Ordinarily, he would have spent Sunday afternoon with the nurse he'd been courting for some months but she had decided her skills were needed on the Western Front and had volunteered for army service. Sad to see her go, Keedy had admired the impulse that took her across the Channel but they'd made no arrangement to meet up again on her return. The romance was over. In practical terms, it meant that what might have been a pleasant day with his girlfriend had now turned into a yawning chasm. A visit to the Marmion household was the ideal way to fill it.

They had clearly made efforts on his behalf. The place had been thoroughly cleaned, the meal was excellent and the conversation never flagged. Keedy always enjoyed seeing his colleague in his domestic setting where Marmion could relax, smoke his pipe and put the world to rights from his armchair beside the fireplace. Ellen and Alice were so hospitable that he almost felt like a member of the family. There was one proviso to the visit. Ellen insisted that it was a social occasion and that the detectives were not allowed to talk about their work. It was a condition to which both men readily acceded.

When the meal was over and the hours had rolled by, Alice offered to do the washing-up and Keedy insisted on helping her. Alone with him in the kitchen, Alice broke the embargo.

'What was it like when you went after those two men?'

'I thought we weren't supposed to talk about work.'

'That was Mummy's idea,' she said, 'not mine.'

'Hasn't your father already told you?'

'He's told me bits of what happened, Joe, but I had the sense that he was holding a lot back. What he did mention was the fight you had with one of the men.'

He was modest. 'It was over so quickly, Alice.'

'I don't believe that. Tell me what happened.'

While she washed the dishes and he wiped them dry, Keedy gave her an abbreviated but straightforward account of their visit to Ypres. He admitted how shocked he was by what he saw at the front and how he feared for the lives of some friends who were fighting there. One particular man came to mind.

'I wondered if Palm Tree was still alive,' he said.

'Who?'

'His real name was Detective Constable Ralph Palmer but we called him Palm Tree because he was so tall and skinny. The day that war was declared, he resigned his job and joined the 5th Field Company, Royal Engineers. They're real heroes, Alice.'

'Are they?' she asked.

'They were the unit that dug our army out of Mons then provided them with trenches during the long retreat. They blew up bridges to hinder any pursuit, then they had to rebuild them when the Germans drew back and our lads were able to reclaim territory that they'd just given up. And all this, remember,' said Keedy, taking another wet plate from her, 'was done in full view of the enemy infantry. Palm Tree and his company deserve medals.'

'Where are the Royal Engineers now?'

'They're where we left them, Alice – in Flanders. They dug those trenches in Ypres.'

'Did you never have the urge to join up yourself?'

'Of course,' he said, 'but I'd just been promoted and I felt there was important work to be done on the home front. Well, the current investigation is a case in point.'

'You'll never catch *all* the people in that mob.'

'That won't stop us from trying.'

'What about the killer?'

He was adamant. 'Oh, that's one crime we *will* solve.'

'How can you be so categorical?'

'I'm working with your father,' he said, grinning. 'And Inspector Marmion has never failed yet. You should know that.'

As they chatted happily, their shoulders touched and both of them enjoyed the proximity. Keedy had always been attracted to Alice but had held back from seeking a closer acquaintance with her because of the age gap between them and because he felt that her father would disapprove. For her part, Alice was very fond of him, though she had never entertained serious thoughts about a closer relationship. Working side by side with him, however, she was increasingly drawn to Keedy and hoped that the pleasure was mutual. It was not the most romantic setting. With her hands in a bowl of water, she could never be seen at her best, and he was hardly at his most dashing while buffing plates with a tea towel. Yet it was companionship of the most satisfying kind. They were at ease with each other.

'Have you decided to join the WEC yet?' he asked.

She pulled a face. 'I can't make up my mind, Joe.'

'That doesn't sound like you. Your father says that you're the most decisive woman he's ever met.'

'What that amounts to is that I argue with him a lot.'

'It's good to have a mind of your own.'

'Not every man thinks that about a woman. A lot of them prefer quiet and submissive types who wouldn't say boo to a goose.' She handed him the last saucer. 'What about you, Joe?'

'Oh, I could never be interested in any woman afraid to stand up to me,' he said, drying the saucer before putting it on the pile. 'An occasional argument adds spice to a friendship.'

'It always ended the friendships that I've had with men,' she admitted.

'Then perhaps you chose the wrong kind of men.'

Facing each other as he spoke, they were only inches apart and each felt the urge to reach out and embrace the other. Keedy gave her a dazzling smile and her eyes twinkled in response. There was far more than companionship now. There was affection and need. Before either of them could make the first move, however, the door opened and Marmion put his head into the kitchen.

'Come on, you two,' he said, pipe still in his mouth. 'We've got the cards out. It's time to play.'

CHAPTER TWELVE

She met him for lunch in a small café recommended by her sister. Gill had suggested a drink at a pub but Irene preferred to keep him away from alcohol because it melted his inhibitions in a way that she found rather alarming. A chat over a wholesome meal and a cup of tea was much safer. Irene was smartly dressed and Gill had his best suit on once more. He'd even acquired a flower for his lapel and looked quite raffish. She made it clear from the start that she intended to pay half of the bill, thus liberating her from any feeling of obligation. After some token protests, Gill agreed.

'What brought you to London?' she asked.

'*You* did, Irene,' he replied with a chortle.

'Don't be silly.'

'It's partly true. I've got men friends here – I'm staying with one at the moment, as it happens – but, knowing that *you'd* moved to London helped me to make my decision. I'd be able to see you again. That doesn't mean I'm going to pester you,' he added, raising his palms in a placatory gesture. 'You're entitled to your privacy. I know that. I just hoped that we could . . . well, meet up now and then to talk about old times.'

'As long as that's all it is, Ernie,' she said, levelly.

He put a hand to his heart. 'On my word of honour.'

Not wishing to start an argument, Irene forbore to point out that she'd heard him make and break such solemn vows before. She let it pass, feeling that she had made her position clear and resolving that any future meetings with him would be few in number. Gill would not be allowed to upset the equilibrium of her new existence.

'No thought of going back to sea, then?' she asked.

'Not a hope,' he said. 'My sailing days are over. There's always work for a barber ashore. In fact, I'm going to see someone about a job this afternoon.'

'Why didn't you stay in Liverpool?'

'It was time for a change, Irene.'

'But you had family there.'

'A brother and two sisters,' he confirmed. 'I never got on with any of them, to be honest. So I thought I'd give the Big Smoke a chance and see what it had to offer – apart from you, that is.'

'Now, now, Ernie,' she scolded. 'Control yourself.'

'It was meant as a compliment.'

'You're a bit too ready with your compliments – and I'm not the only woman who's aware of that. You scattered them about like confetti on the *Lusitania*.'

He smirked. 'I've always had a soft spot for a pretty face.'

'Let's go back to Liverpool,' she said. 'You once told me it was the best city in the world and that you'd never leave it. What changed your mind?'

'Oh, it was lots of things.'

'What did you do after we parted company at the docks?'

'First of all, I followed you,' he recalled, 'then I went back to my digs and dumped all my stuff there. After that I walked to the pub where my friends go and spent the evening having pints bought for me. They all wanted to know what happened when the ship went down. I was treated like a hero.'

'That's what you are, Ernie.'

'I don't feel it. I was lucky, that's all.'

'We both were,' she said, soulfully.

'Anyway,' he went on, 'when I had enough beer inside me, I was raring to go. They told me that most of the Germans had been either burnt out or chased out but I knew of a family that'd sort of slipped through the net. They'd been there for donkey's years, you see, and changed their name so long ago that people forgot they were still foreigners. I knew the truth,' he said, tapping his chest, 'and I wasn't going to let them get away.'

'What did you do?'

'We paid them a visit, Irene.'

'I hope there was no violence.'

'Let's say that we did what needed to be done,' he told her. 'They won't be able to hide behind the Union Jack anymore. Britain belongs to the British. Huns are not wanted.'

'There's been far too much senseless brutality.'

'What about that blinking torpedo?' he retorted, banging the table. 'That's what *I* call senseless brutality. Think of all those dead bodies floating in the sea – men, women and children murdered on the orders of some cruel German admiral. So don't you criticise me, Irene. At least we gave people a chance to defend themselves.'

She was uneasy. 'What exactly happened?'

'It doesn't matter.'

'Go on – tell me. When I left you in Liverpool, you were spoiling for a fight. Where did you find these people?'

'Forget them,' he said, evasively. 'They're not even worth talking about. I've got bigger fish to fry. Talking of which,' he continued as he speared a chip with his fork, 'I don't think much of this cod. We had far better grub on the ship.' He nudged her arm. 'In fact, we had far better *everything*.'

'Those days are over, Ernie.'

'A man can have his memories.'

'Provided he knows that they *are* only memories,' she said.

He cackled. 'I'll win you over one day, Irene.'

'Don't you even dare to try.'

'Oh, come on – is this the kind of life you *really* want?'

'Yes, it is,' she affirmed, chin out.

'What – sharing a house with your spinster sister and a blind woman with one foot in the grave? You were born for better things than that. My guess is that you'll be bored stiff within a week.'

'Then your guess will be wrong.'

'What the hell are you going to do all day?'

'Have no qualms on that score. I'll soon be working in a toy factory. That will keep me out of mischief.'

'I love mischief,' he said, laughing. 'Whenever I get the chance, I enjoy causing trouble. I went to a meeting last night of people who think like me – good, honest, British citizens who are fed up with being told what to do by the government and are ready to stir things up on their own. We hit and run – just like I did in Liverpool.'

'What do you mean?'

'It wouldn't interest you, Irene. You're too law-abiding.'

Her face puckered with concern. 'Have you committed a crime?'

'I done my country a service,' he boasted, 'and I had a good laugh while I was doing it. That's all I'm ready to admit.'

Slicing off a piece of fish, he thrust it into his mouth and munched away. Irene was disturbed. A meal that had been quite pleasant had turned into a cause for alarm. Ernie Gill was a diehard Liverpudlian who'd sworn time and again that he would never leave his native city. Yet here he was, strutting around London in his best suit and revelling in the idea of making mischief. What was his real reason for leaving Liverpool and what sort of trouble had he created since he'd arrived in the capital? On balance, Irene decided, she did not want an answer to either question. It was best not to know.

Harvey Marmion was collating all the information gathered by his team of detectives. He was so immersed in his work that he didn't hear the knock on the door and was only aware of his visitor when Joe Keedy's shadow fell across the desk.

'Good morning, Joe,' he said, looking up.

'I hear that we've found one of our mystery men.'

'That's right. His name is Howard Fine and he's the young tailor who worked briefly at Mr Stein's shop. He's definitely not our killer. When his former boss was being stabbed, Fine was in Brighton with his family.' He glanced at the sheet of paper in front of him. 'According to this, he has a perfect alibi.'

'He needs interviewing nevertheless.'

'Yes, I'm having him brought in today.'

'What about the other former employee?' asked Keedy. 'You know – the man who left after a big row?'

'We're still looking for him.'

'He was called Porridge or something like that.'

'Cyril Burridge,' corrected Marmion with a laugh. 'People who knew him say that he was a first-rate tailor with many productive years in the trade.'

'Then why did he suddenly disappear?'

'We'll ask him when we find him, Joe. We'll also ask him why he and Stein fell out after such a long time together. David Cohen, who managed the shop, said that Burridge seemed set to spend the rest of his life working in Jermyn Street.'

'So what went wrong, Inspector?'

'The only person who can tell us that is the man himself.'

'If he's that experienced,' said Keedy, 'he must have found a job elsewhere by now.'

'Oh, he has. Burridge was snapped up by one of Stein's bitter rivals in Savile Row. It was the first place our lads looked but it seems that Burridge is on leave at the moment.'

'Where has he gone?'

'Nobody seems to know,' replied Marmion. 'When they called at his house, there was nobody there.'

'Do you think he's gone into hiding?'

'It's beginning to look like that, Joe.'

He handed a report about the man to Keedy who flicked through it before putting it back on the desk. In his opinion, Burridge had to be considered as a suspect. He reasoned that someone who had been in the business for so many years would be familiar with Stein's routine and very much aware of what the safe in the upstairs room had contained. Another factor weighed with Keedy.

'Burridge is not a Jewish name, is it?'

'No,' replied Marmion. 'He's a chapel-going Yorkshireman from Barnsley. That's what Cohen told me anyway. I had the feeling that Burridge was not the manager's best friend. He could be blunt.'

'They speak their mind in Yorkshire.'

'I'm all in favour of plain speaking, Joe.' He rose to his feet. 'It means that you know where you stand with people.' He checked his watch. 'I'd like you to interview Mr Fine, if you will. He's on his way here right now. It's probably a waste of time but you might just get a nugget or two out of him. There's no harm in trying.'

'What will you be doing, Inspector?'

'I'll be grilling some other people who took part in the raid on the shop. While we were away, our lads tracked down three of them in all but not – alas – the man with the petrol can.'

Marmion went on to inform him that John Gatliffe had been released on bail but that Oliver Cochran had been refused bail and was remanded in custody. The inspector had no fears that Gatliffe would abscond. The soldier was ashamed of what he'd done and was ready to take his punishment. Instead of returning to his family as a courageous soldier, he'd had to slink home with his tail between his legs and explain the situation to his parents. Cochran, by contrast, still maintaining his innocence, *was* likely to make a run for it if set free. He was better off behind bars where he could not intimidate his friend.

'We may have done the pair of them a favour,' said Keedy. 'Prison might turn out to be a lighter option than being stuck in a trench while the Germans use them as target practice.'

'I fancy that Cochran and Gatliffe would disagree. Compared to the regime they'll face in prison, the army will seem like a relief. And think of the humiliation they're going to suffer.'

Keedy remembered the ordeal endured by Ruth Stein.

'I'd rather think about the humiliation the girl suffered.'

Marmion nodded. 'So would I, Joe – so would I.'

'I'd better go and see if Mr Fine has arrived.'

'Ask him if there were any tensions at the shop.'

'I don't think he was there long enough to find out.'

'You never know.'

When Keedy left the room, Marmion resumed his seat and began to sift through the paperwork. He was soon interrupted by a tap on the door. As it opened, a young detective constable stepped into the room. He cleared his throat before speaking.

'There's a gentleman outside who insists on speaking to you, Inspector,' he said.

'Then show the fellow in.'

The constable beckoned to someone in the corridor and a well-dressed man in his fifties strode purposefully into the office.

'Inspector Marmion?' he enquired.

'That's me, sir,' said Marmion.

'I'm Cyril Burridge. I understand you've been looking for me.'

Irene Bayard visited the shoe shop as a customer rather than as the sister of its manager. Dorothy, however, insisted on giving her preferential treatment and served Irene herself. While her sister was trying on a third pair of shoes, Dorothy tried to probe.

'When will you be seeing Ernest again?' she asked.

'We haven't set a date.'

'It's good for you to have a friend in London.'

'He's not that kind of friend, Dot.'

'He proposed to you, didn't he? So he must be keen.'

'Yes,' said Irene with a sigh. 'He's keen all right.'

'What happened yesterday? All you've told me is that you had a nice lunch together. There must have been more to it than that.'

'There wasn't.'

Having put on both shoes, Irene stood up and walked up and down to test them for comfort. Then she stood in front of the mirror to see how they looked. Dorothy waited while her sister had another stroll up and down the shop. Irene eventually sat down again.

'The left one is pinching my foot slightly,' she said. 'Perhaps I'll need a larger size after all.'

'I'll get a pair for you to try.'

Dorothy darted off into the storeroom. Irene removed the shoes and turned one over to see the price marked on the sole. Her sister came back with a pair in the same style. Dorothy put them on.

'How do they feel?' asked Dorothy.

'Much better, thanks.'

'You've always had wide feet.'

'It comes from spending so much time on them, Dot. When I worked for Cunard, I was always at someone's beck and call. It will be nice to have a job where I can work sitting down.'

'Did you tell Ernest about the toy factory?'

'Yes.'

'Does he have a job yet?'

'He was going for an interview yesterday.'

'Where?'

'I've no idea,' said Irene, slipping on both shoes then standing up and promenading again. She stopped in front of the mirror and examined the shoes from various angles. 'These are really comfy.'

'Does that mean you'll take them?'

'Yes . . . yes, I think I will.'

She sat down and took them off so that Dorothy could pop them back into the box. Irene put on her own shoes, picked up her handbag and crossed to the counter. Her sister had moved to the till. Dorothy felt slightly cheated that she'd been told so little about the lunch Irene had shared with her friend. Expecting a full account, she'd got no more than a couple of sentences out of Irene. She probed again.

'So you will be seeing him again in due course?'

Irene pursed her lips. 'I suppose so.'

'You don't sound very enthusiastic.'

'We've got so little in common.'

'How can you say that, Irene? You worked together for years and the pair of you survived the sinking of the *Lusitania*. I'd have thought that would give you a bond for life.'

'Well, it hasn't.'

'Listen,' said Dorothy, 'why don't you invite Ernest for tea one Sunday? I'd so like to meet him.'

'No,' said Irene, decisively. 'I'm not having him in the house. Let's be clear about that. If he calls when I'm not there, he must not be allowed in. Do you understand?'

Dorothy was taken aback by the sharpness in her voice.

'I'm sorry, Irene,' she said, 'but, frankly, I *don't* understand.'

Cyril Burridge was an unlikely tailor. He was a big burly man in his fifties with the broad shoulders of a manual worker and an ugly face decorated by a walrus moustache. His expensive suit had been cleverly cut to hide his paunch. Marmion sensed a dormant anger in his visitor. When he'd offered Burridge a seat, he got him to talk about his time at the shop in Jermyn Street. Burridge was laconic. Into less than two minutes, he condensed the story of well over twenty years.

'Why did you leave?' asked Marmion.

'It were time to go.'

'Mr Cohen said you had a disagreement with Mr Stein.'

'So?'

'What was the disagreement about?'

'It's a private matter.'

'Not if it's relevant to this investigation, Mr Burridge. I need hardly remind you of the seriousness of the crimes committed. Someone murdered your former employer. To find out who the killer was, I need every detail I can gather about what went on inside the business. In other words,' Marmion stressed, 'privacy does not exist.'

Burridge glowered at him for a few moments then he sniffed.

'It were about money,' he confessed.

'You wanted an increase in your pay?'

'We all want that, Inspector.'

'Why are you being so evasive?'

'Ask Mr Cohen about that.'

Marmion sat back to appraise him. Burridge was well defended. He was ready to cooperate with the investigation but only on his terms. He was like a batsman at the wicket, confident of being able to hit any ball that was bowled at him. Those he could not smash to the boundary, he would deflect with a flick of the wrist. The inspector changed his grip on the metaphorical ball and tossed it at him again.

'Why were you so difficult to find, Mr Burridge?'

'You didn't look hard enough.'

'Nobody seemed to know where you'd gone to.'

'I don't advertise my whereabouts.'

'It seemed odd that you should vanish around the time that Mr Stein's shop was attacked and when he himself was murdered.'

'You're a policeman. You have a suspicious mind.'

'You don't find it odd, then?'

'No,' said Burridge. 'I had leave owing to me. I took it.'

'Why did you choose that particular week?'

'Ask my wife – it were her idea.'

Marmion's latest ball was met with a straight bat. It was frustrating. Having come ostensibly to help the inquiry, Burridge was doing the opposite. All he was interested in was establishing his innocence. He showed no sadness over the death of his former employer and no regret over the fact that the premises where he had worked for so many years had been burnt down. Burridge seemed to have cut himself off comprehensively from the past.

'I gather that you and Mr Cohen did not get on,' said Marmion.

'Is that what he told you?'

'Not in so many words, sir. It was something I sensed.'

'David Cohen were a good manager.'

'But you'd never describe him as a bosom pal, would you?'

'We had different opinions sometimes.'

'Did that lead to arguments?'

Burridge smiled. 'What do you think?'

'Did you ever argue about money?'

'No.'

'Did you complain about the way that the business was run?'

'I did the job I were paid for, Inspector.'

'How did you get on with the rest of the staff?'

'Ask them.'

'I'm asking you, Mr Burridge.'

The Yorkshireman shrugged. 'We got on well enough.'

Marmion doubted that. Burridge was the sort of man who would enjoy throwing his weight around when dealing with junior colleagues. In certain circumstances, his physical presence and gruff manner could be rather menacing. Marmion could see why the suave and reserved David Cohen had hinted at difficulties with Burridge. In both character and attitude, the two men would never be natural bedfellows. Marmion stepped up his attack.

'Did you like Jacob Stein?' he asked.

'He were my employer.'

'That's not an answer.'

'I respected him.'

'But you didn't actually like him.'

'Do you like *your* boss, Inspector?'

'That's beside the point.'

'Mr Stein gave me work. I were grateful for that.'

'But not grateful enough, I suspect,' said Marmion. 'How much did you see of his brother, Herbert Stone?'

Burridge scowled. 'Too much.'

'Did he come to the shop often?'

'Too often.'

'Why was that? He had his own business to run.'

'Mr Stone liked to keep his finger in every pie.'

'Are you saying that he had a financial interest in the business?'

'Mr Cohen is the man to ask that.'

'As a matter of fact,' said Marmion, 'he isn't. He was surprisingly reticent on the subject. He wouldn't even tell me how harmonious or otherwise the relationship between Mr Stein and his brother had been.' Burridge stifled a grin. 'I was hoping that your famed honesty would allow you to enlighten me on the subject.'

'Happen.'

'My guess is that Mr Stone used to browbeat his brother and interfere in the running of the business.'

'I can see that you've met him.'

'He's an assertive gentleman.'

'That's a kind way of putting it, Inspector,' said Burridge. 'I'd have called him a bloody nuisance.'

'Did he have some involvement in the business?'

'Yes, he did.'

'And did that entitle him to make decisions relating to it?'

'Mr Stone thought so.'

'Was his brother afraid of him?'

'Everyone were afraid of him – except me.' Burridge took out his watch and glanced at it before returning it to his waistcoat pocket. 'How much longer do you need me here, Inspector?' he asked. 'I've got work to do. Instead of questioning me, you should be looking at people who might be glad that Mr Stein is dead.'

'Such as?'

'Start with his brother.'

Marmion was amazed. 'You surely can't be accusing Herbert Stone of being party to the murder.'

'You heard my advice. Take it or leave it.'

'You must have some reason for naming him.'

'I've got lots of reasons.'

'What are they?'

'Find out,' said Burridge, getting to his feet. 'Look into the way that the business was structured.' He fingered his moustache. 'Will that be all, Inspector?'

Marmion was on his feet. 'Not quite, sir,' he said. 'Why was Howard Fine sacked?'

'He should never have been taken on in the first place.'

'Was he such a poor tailor?'

'Howard never fitted in.'

On that enigmatic note, Burridge gave a nod and departed.

Unlike most of the people Keedy interviewed, Howard Fine was eager to cooperate. He was a tall, slim, dark-haired man in his twenties, wearing an immaculate suit that the sergeant coveted the moment he set eyes on it. They were in a small featureless room that had no natural light coming in. Seated directly under the lampshade, Fine was bathed in an unreal glow. His handsome clean-shaven face was split by a nervous grin and his hands gesticulated whenever he spoke.

'How long were you with Mr Stein?' asked Keedy.

'Five or six weeks in all, Sergeant.'

'Did you like it there?'

'Of course,' said Fine. 'It was the sort of job that every tailor dreams of. Jacob Stein has a big reputation in the trade. I couldn't believe my luck when I was taken on by him.'

'How did that come about, sir?'

'There was a vacancy and I applied for it. That's to say, I was tipped off about the vacancy by my uncle who was kind enough to put in a good word for me with Mr Stein. Not that it was as simple as that,' Fine went on, anxious to dispel any notion of nepotism. 'I had to show examples of my work and compete with two others on the shortlist. Eventually, I landed the job.'

'Did you enjoy it?'

'Yes and no. I enjoyed the work itself but I never felt that I was fully accepted. I don't know why, Sergeant. I'm affable by nature and do my best to get along with everyone. Somehow it never worked.'

'Could you be a little more specific, Mr Fine?'

'Well,' said the other, 'it came down to two people, I suppose. I hardly saw Mr Stein himself but I had to deal with Mr Cohen and Mr Burridge every day. Mr Cohen – he's the manager – resented me for some reason. He was always criticising my work.'

'What about Mr Burridge?'

'He was much more of a problem. I hate arguments, you see, and run a mile if someone confronts me. Mr Burridge was always doing that. He didn't just resent me – he hated me and I still don't know why. I mean, I tried my best. What more could they ask?'

'So,' said Keedy, wishing that the man would twitch less, 'there was obviously tension at work.'

'It wasn't *my* fault.'

'I'm sure it wasn't, sir.'

'I was bullied by Mr Burridge and sniped at by Mr Cohen. To tell you the truth, it began to get on my nerves. At least I don't have that problem in my new post.'

'And where might that be, Mr Fine?'

'I work for a bespoke tailor in Brighton,' said Fine, beaming. 'It's not as grand as being in the West End but I'm much happier and I'm able to live at home with my parents. All in all, it's worked out for the best. Let's face it,' he added, lowering his voice, 'if I'd stayed with Mr Stein, my job would no longer exist. What a tragedy that would have been. Not that it compares with what happened to Mr Stein, of course,' he said, hastily. 'I wouldn't want you to think I'm *that* self-centred. I was shaken rigid when I heard about the murder. It preyed on my mind for days. I do hope you catch the man who killed him.'

Fine launched himself into a paean of praise about Jacob Stein, saying what an honour it had been to work for him, albeit for only a short time. Keedy let him ramble on for minutes then halted him with a forthright question.

'Why did he give you the sack?'

Stopped dead in his tracks, Fine looked almost insulted.

'If Mr Stein liked your work enough to take you on,' said Keedy, 'why did he dismiss you?'

'He didn't dismiss me,' said the other, petulantly. 'If truth be told, he wanted me to stay.'

'Then who got rid of you – was it Mr Cohen?'

'No – he didn't have the authority.'

'Somebody must have sacked you. Who was it?'

Howard Fine winced, his nervous smile replaced by a grimace.

'It was Mr Stein's brother,' he said. 'Herbert Stone.'

CHAPTER THIRTEEN

Herbert Stone would never win any awards for patience. Once his brother's funeral was over, and once he felt that he'd convinced Ruth of the seriousness of her sin in attempting suicide, he turned his attention to the investigation once more. Instead of hounding Harvey Marmion directly, he went over the inspector's head and spoke to the commissioner. They met in the latter's office at Scotland Yard. Sir Edward Henry gave details of the progress made so far but was unable to announce the arrest either of the killer, or of the man believed to have used petrol to accelerate the blaze. Stone was peeved.

'Why is it taking so long, Sir Edward?'

'Evidence has to be pieced together bit by bit.'

'Put more detectives on the case,' suggested Stone.

'That's not possible,' explained the commissioner. 'The events in Jermyn Street are not the only crimes with which we have to deal. There are scores of other cases demanding urgent attention. I'm doing my best to deploy my men to the best advantage but – with a depleted force – I can't spare any more of them at the moment.'

'Perhaps I should hire some private detectives.'

'That's your right, of course, but I wouldn't advise it. No private detective has the resources that Scotland Yard can offer, nor the experience of someone like Inspector Marmion. You seem to have forgotten that he's already solved one serious crime,' said Sir Edward. 'Incidentally, how is your niece?'

Stone's face darkened. 'Ruth is still suffering badly.'

'Was she heartened by the news of the two arrests made?'

'She will be in due course – when she's pulled herself together.'

'I've dealt with victims of crime for many years,' said the commissioner, 'and what I've noticed is that their greatest need is for reassurance. They want to feel safe and that the outrage will not occur again. It's only after those two imperatives have been met that they begin to think about punishment for the offenders.'

'I've thought about nothing else,' said Stone, icily.

'In arresting the two men, we've given your niece some peace of mind. They no longer represent a threat to her. The healing process can finally begin.'

'It may not be as easy as that, Sir Edward.'

'Why not?'

'Ruth is an unusually sensitive girl.'

Stone did not tell him about the despair into which his niece had sunk, nor did he mention the abortive attempt at killing herself. They were private matters that had to be kept strictly within the family. What he did explain was that, hopefully, Ruth's brother was on his way home. Stationed with his regiment in Mesopotamia, Daniel Stein had missed his father's funeral and there was no certainty that word of it had actually reached him because the expedition was on the move. Writing to his nephew's commanding officer, Stone had asked for compassionate leave so that Daniel could return home to mourn with the rest of the family. He and his sister had always been close. Stone believed that seeing him again might help to bring Ruth out of her depression. Before that could happen, however, Daniel would have to make the long and perilous journey home.

'This war has played havoc with families,' observed Sir Edward. 'And as far as I can see, there's no end in sight.'

'Daniel is needed here. I expressed that need in the strongest terms, yet I still haven't had a response.'

'Correspondence does go astray, I fear.'

'Then I'll keep on sending word until it gets through.'

'You do that, Mr Stone. Perseverance is everything.'

They chatted for a few more minutes then Stone rose to leave. After a farewell handshake, he moved to the door, pausing when he remembered something.

'You might tell Inspector Marmion that I'm considering the hire of private detectives,' he said.

'Why should I do that?'

'It might act as a spur to him if he knows he has competition.'

'Nobody can compete with the inspector,' said Sir Edward.

'It won't be the first time I've had to take matters into my own hand,' explained Stone, pointedly. 'When one of my warehouses was razed to the ground, I realised that I couldn't rely on police protection. That's why I've brought in a private firm to guard my property.' He arched an eyebrow. 'You might mention *that* to the inspector as well.'

* * *

When both interviews were concluded, the detectives discussed them over a cup of coffee. Marmion felt that he'd had the more productive session, picking up a whole new line of inquiry from Cyril Burridge. Keedy was as astonished as the inspector had been that the name of Herbert Stone was put forward as a possible suspect.

'Mind you,' said Keedy, thoughtfully, 'it does chime in with something that Howard Fine told me.'

'What was that, Joe?'

'The person who booted him out of a job was Herbert Stone.'

'Who gave him the right to do that?'

'He just took it.'

'That decision should surely have lain with Jacob Stein.'

'I put that point to Fine.'

'What was his response?'

'He said that Stone was always poking his nose into the shop and asking to see the accounts. He obviously has some stake in the company but Fine didn't know what it was.'

'We need to dig a little deeper on that front.'

Keedy shook his head. 'No,' he said, 'I can't accept that Stone is behind it all. What possible motive would he have for killing his brother and seeing the premises go up in smoke? Unless the place was heavily insured, of course – can we find out if it was?'

'I've already sent someone off to do just that,' said Marmion. 'And I agree that Stone would not be my prime suspect either. On the other hand, we didn't see any sign of grief when he realised that his brother might be dead. I'd be devastated if anything like that had happened to Ray.'

'How is your brother?'

'He's still doing good work in the name of the Salvation Army.'

Keedy grinned. 'Brass bands and soup kitchens, eh?'

'Don't mock them, Joe. They relieve distress. How many people can you say that about?'

'Very few.'

'There you are, then.'

'No disrespect to your brother but I think that people in the Salvation Army are holy fools – full of good intentions, yes, but altogether too misguided.'

'I must remember to invite you over next time that Ray and Lily come to tea. By the end of the meal, I guarantee, they'll have you banging the tambourine and singing hymns as loud as anyone.'

'Don't bet on that.'

'You're ripe for conversion,' teased Marmion.

'Oh no I'm not,' said Keedy with a chuckle. 'But since we're on the subject of tea at the Marmion household, I haven't really thanked you for inviting me last Sunday. Please pass on my thanks to the family.'

'It was good to see you off duty, Joe.'

'I could say the same about you. And it was lovely to see Ellen and Alice again. They both looked wonderful. I had a long talk with your daughter,' he said, recalling their time alone in the kitchen. 'Alice is so intelligent. I can see why she frightens most men off.'

'I'm still not sure if that's good or bad.'

'She seems perfectly happy with things as they are.'

'That's true.'

'Alice told me that her mother wants grandchildren.'

'They can wait,' said Marmion, philosophically.

'Not indefinitely.'

'The right time will come.'

'The right time or the right man?'

Marmion smiled. 'Ideally, both of them will arrive together.'

It was a cloudy day and the promise of rain encouraged Alice Marmion to walk briskly along the pavement. She was on her way home from school and her bag was bulging with the books she had to mark. It was impossible to miss the signs of war all around her. At the outbreak of the conflict, there had been little visible difference in the streets beyond the fluttering of a few Union Jacks. Flags were much more in evidence now and so were people in uniform. Recruiting posters stared down from advertising hoardings. Walls were daubed with patriotic slogans. As a young man limped past on crutches, Alice knew that he'd lost his leg somewhere in combat, one of an untold number of amputees invalided out of the forces.

She arrived home to see her mother hunched over a newspaper.

'I thought you'd stopped reading the paper, Mummy.'

'I tried to,' said Ellen, 'but, whenever I go shopping, people are talking about the latest news. If I want to join in the discussion, I have to make an effort to keep up.' She looked up. 'Good day at school?'

'Yes,' said Alice, 'it was very good, as it happens.'

'The children are lucky to have a teacher like you.'

'That's what I keep telling them.'

Ellen's tone was meaningful. 'It's what you do best.'

'All right, Mummy, don't labour the point. You've said all there is to say on the subject of my future. Why not wait until I've actually made my decision?'

'I'm hoping your pupils will make it for you.'

Alice put down her bag and went into the kitchen to fill the kettle.

After she'd lit the gas and put the kettle on the hob, she came back into the living room. Ellen was still reading a report.

'Do they say anything about that Zeppelin raid we had in London last night?' asked Alice.

'Yes – it's the first of many according to this. It's terrifying when you think about it,' said Ellen. 'It's not enough for the Germans to fight on land and sea. Now they want to drop bombs on us from the sky. It's inhuman.'

'It's no more than we'll do to them in time.'

'Every day brings more bad news. First, it was all those setbacks in Gallipoli and now it's the fighting in Flanders. The battle of Ypres keeps going on and on.'

'Daddy and Joe Keedy were fortunate not to get too close to it.'

'They got close enough.'

'What does it say in the paper?'

'It just lists the casualty figures. It's not one big battle but a series of small ones in the northern sector of something called the Ypres Salient. It started last month when the German 4th Army attacked the Allied front line.' She peered at the article. 'I'm not sure if I'm pronouncing it right but it was the Battle of Gravenstafel Ridge. That's when they began to use gas attacks.' Ellen put the paper aside. 'I can't read any more. I keep thinking about Paul.'

'He's nowhere near Ypres, Mummy.'

'How do you know that? He may have been moved.'

'Worrying will get us nowhere.'

'I tell myself that every day, Alice, but I still fret over your brother. He has his whole life ahead of him. It would be cruel if—'

'I know,' interrupted Alice, 'but it's the same for every other family with sons in the army. All we can do is to watch and pray.'

Ellen gave a resigned nod and went off into the kitchen. Alice took the opportunity to pick up the paper and read the main stories. The news was dispiriting. Vast amounts of money and manpower were being dedicated to the task of winning small amounts of territory. It seemed pointless to her. Lives were being uselessly sacrificed for what appeared to be minimal gains. Her brother's letters talked of the severe deficiencies experienced by those in the trenches, yet he was not in a combat zone. Alice thought how much worse it must be for those compelled to lurk in a hole in the ground until someone blew a whistle and ordered them to race towards the enemy machine guns. Like her mother, she could not bear to read too much and set the paper aside. When Alice finally went into the kitchen, Ellen was pouring hot water into the pot. She slipped the tea cosy into position.

'Your father is so glad that Joe Keedy didn't join up,' she said.

'Lots of other policemen did.'

'I know, Alice.'

'You don't go into the police force unless you like some sort of physical action and the best place to get that is in a war.'

'Your father thinks very highly of Joe. He says that he's going to be an outstanding detective.'

'He's got a good teacher in Daddy.'

'The very best,' said Ellen with a proud smile.

She put milk into two cups then used the strainer as she poured tea into them. Ellen added sugar before stirring. They took their tea back into the living room and sat down.

'You have to feel sorry for Joe, I suppose,' said Ellen.

'Why?'

'Well, I didn't know this until your father mentioned it. I thought that what stopped Joe from joining the army was a desire to stay at Scotland Yard.'

'I thought that as well.'

'There was another reason, Alice. It seems that he's been seeing a young lady for some time – a nurse at St Thomas' Hospital.'

'Oh.' Alice was shocked. 'I didn't know that.'

'Joe didn't want to go abroad for months on end,' said Ellen. 'The irony is that his plan has backfired.'

'I don't follow.'

'*She's* the one who volunteered to go to the front. While Joe is left here, his young lady is on her way to work in a field hospital. That was why he was able to come to tea on Sunday, you see. Since she's no longer here, Joe was at a loose end.'

The news was like a punch in the stomach for Alice. She had fond memories of her time alone with Keedy and felt that he'd enjoyed her company as well. Now, it appeared, she was merely a distraction for him while his beloved was abroad. The faint hope she'd started to nurture was snuffed out like a candle. It was a painful moment.

Since she was at home all day for the rest of the week, Irene tried to make herself useful, helping to clean the house and offering to do some shopping. When she asked Miss James if there was anything she could get for her while she was out, the old lady surprised Irene by joining her on the outing. They left the house together and walked arm in arm. Miss James carried her white stick and used it to tap the pavement in front of her. Irene soon got used to the sound it made. She also grew accustomed to the regular greetings that Miss James attracted from passers-by. The old lady was clearly an established figure in the area. She recognised all the voices and was able to put names to faces. There was something oddly comforting about it. Irene wondered how long it would take her to acquire the same sort of popularity in the community. She tried to memorise the names of the various people who spoke to Miss James.

It was a long walk to the shops but the old lady made no complaint about that. She was much more robust than she looked and kept up a steady pace. It was when they turned into the main road that Miss James stopped.

'Is he still there, Mrs Bayard?' she asked.

'Who do you mean?'

'Someone has been following us since we left the house.'

Irene looked over her shoulder. 'I don't see anyone.'

'Oh, he's there somewhere.'

'How do you know that, Miss James?'

'There's nothing wrong with my ears, dear.'

They walked on until the shops came into view but it was no longer a pleasant stroll for Irene. She was on edge. Every few seconds she looked uneasily behind her. There was nobody in sight but she trusted the old lady's instinct. Someone *had* followed them. She was sure of that now and it was unsettling.

Marmion found time that afternoon to call on the commissioner in order to bring him up to date on the progress of the investigation. Sir Edward Henry was wearing one of Jacob Stein's suits over a white shirt with a wing collar. His black shoes were gleaming. Marmion wished that he could look as elegant but his build seemed to vitiate any attempt at being stylish. He told the commissioner about the interviews with the two former employees of the firm. Sir Edward was startled to hear that one of them had pointed the finger of suspicion at Herbert Stone.

'That's a preposterous suggestion,' he said.

'It may seem so on face value, Sir Edward, but I still think we should pay some heed to it. Mr Stone was clearly more involved with his brother's business than we imagined.'

'What could he possibly gain by his brother's death?'

'That's what we need to find out,' said Marmion.

'Then you're going on a wild goose chase, Inspector,' said the commissioner with clear disapproval. 'My advice would be to look elsewhere for suspects. I'd exonerate Mr Stone from any connection with the destruction of the shop in Jermyn Street.'

'Then why did Mr Burridge direct our attention at him?'

'It must have been done out of spite.'

'He didn't strike me as a spiteful man.'

'You said that he was singularly unhelpful.'

'Exactly, Sir Edward – that's why we should take seriously the one piece of information that he gave voluntarily.'

The older man snapped his fingers. 'I'd dismiss it like that.'

'Mr Stone's role in the business will bear investigation,' said Marmion, doggedly. 'The more we know about the politics inside that shop, the better we'll be able to understand what was going on.'

'This case is nothing to do with what was *inside* the shop,' said the other. 'It was provoked by the German name on the outside. Yes, I know that you think that the murder was orchestrated but I'm coming around to the view that it was a random act by an opportunist who went upstairs to rob the safe.'

'How would an opportunist know where the safe was kept?'

The commissioner pondered. 'I can't answer that, Inspector.'

'And why stab Mr Stein to death? From what we've learnt about him, he was not a strong man. Someone who wanted to grab the contents of the safe could easily have brushed him aside.'

'It took years to build up that business, remember. However unequal the odds, I don't think Mr Stein would have given up without a fight. That was probably his undoing,' said Sir Edward. 'If he'd let the man take what he wanted and concentrated on escaping a burning building, he'd still be alive today.'

'I very much doubt that,' insisted Marmion.

Rather than start an argument with him, the commissioner decided that they should agree to differ. He told Marmion about Stone's visit and his threat to hire private detectives to handle the case. The inspector found the news interesting but unsurprising.

'I told him that no private detective had our resources,' said Sir Edward, 'and would certainly not have your abilities.'

'Mr Stone is not entirely persuaded of my abilities, I fear.'

'Then he should be. You identified, chased and arrested the two villains implicated in the rape of his niece. There's not a private detective alive who could have got the authorisation that *we* obtained.' Sir Edward plucked at his moustache. 'I should have made that point to Mr Stone. It beats me why he should even entertain the notion of hiring private help. It would have no positive value to him.'

'Yes, it would, Sir Edward,' said Marmion. 'Mr Stone can *control* a private detective. He can't control us.'

'You're imputing a very dark motive to him.'

'We have to look at this case from every conceivable angle.'

'Are you saying that he'd deliberately muddy the waters?'

Marmion was firm. 'I'm ruling nothing out.'

'Well,' said the commissioner, 'it's not for me to interfere. You're in charge. All that I can do is to offer advice. With regard to Mr Stone, I believe that you're barking up the wrong tree but . . . only time will tell which of us is right.' He brushed a speck of dust from his sleeve. 'What does Sergeant Keedy feel?'

'He's sticking to his theory that there's an anti-Semitic element.'

'Is he following up that line of inquiry?'

'He is, Sir Edward,' said Marmion. 'His first port of call is a man I could not recommend more highly.'

'Why is that, Inspector?'

'He's my brother, sir – Major Marmion of the Salvation Army.'

Raymond Marmion had been a committed Salvationist for a long time and had been promoted to the rank of major after fifteen years as an officer in the organisation. The silver crest on his uniform denoted his status. Younger than his brother, he had the same solid frame and an open face with the sheen of religiosity. His receding hair threw the high-domed forehead into prominence. Though he had heard a great deal about Marmion's brother, Keedy had never met him before and he was struck both by the similarities between the two men and by their glaring differences. They met in Raymond's tiny office in a ramshackle building. Keedy immediately noticed the graze on the other man's temple.

'No,' said Raymond, touching the wound gingerly, 'my wife has not been attacking me with a beer bottle. Lily would never do that. I was hit by a stone while trying to help someone up from the pavement. It's not the first time that's happened, unfortunately.'

'You're a brave man to work here,' complimented Keedy. 'The East End is a jungle at times. If the kids are not hurling missiles at you, they're trying to knock helmets off policemen on the beat. They have no respect for authority.'

'And still less for the word of God, alas. But,' Raymond went on, 'you didn't come here to discuss our mission. I take it that my brother sent you here. How can I help?'

Keedy did not need to give full details of the case in hand. Since he always kept an eye on his brother's work, Raymond had been following its progress in the newspapers. He gave a sympathetic hearing to Keedy's theory then opened a drawer in the table to take out a sheaf of papers. He found the relevant page.

'This is what you need, Sergeant,' he said.

'What is it?'

'It's a list of organisations – tiny groups in some cases – that try to blame the woes of the world entirely on the Jews. We don't have pogroms here, thankfully, but we have people who conduct their own forms of persecution. If you've been in the police force for any length of time,' continued Raymond, 'then I don't need to tell you how much immigrants have suffered in the East End.'

'I remember the riots from years ago,' said Keedy.

'Russians seemed to get the worst of it because of their large numbers. Many of them had been hounded out of their own country for committing the crime of being Jews. Eastern Europe in general drove them west.' Raymond gritted his teeth. 'They came with nothing, Sergeant – except hope, that is. It was soon extinguished.' He handed the list over. 'I'll need to keep that but you're welcome to jot down those names.'

Keedy studied the paper. 'Very few seem to have addresses.'

'That's deliberate. They move around all the time, holding meetings in different places so that they can't be tracked.'

'How many of these groups are still active?'

'It's difficult to say,' replied Raymond. 'Some disappear for long periods then suddenly spring back to life. And, of course, the real militants may belong to a number of groups, shifting to the one that's planning some action at any particular time.'

'Beatings, destruction of property, poison pen letters?'

'All that and much more – they had a field day when the *Lusitania* went down. That was a signal to go really wild. German homes and businesses were the principal targets but Jewish immigrants from other countries were caught up in the wave of violence. I speak from personal experience,' said Raymond. 'We sheltered some of them in this very building.'

'Have things died down now?'

'There are still rumblings below the surface.'

Taking out his notepad, Keedy copied the list onto a blank page. When he'd finished, he handed the sheet of paper back to Raymond.

'Thank you, Major. You've been very helpful.'

'I'm always ready to assist the police.'

'The inspector has obviously got you well trained. I hope that we'll be in a position to help you in return one day.'

'Oddly enough, I was about to suggest that.'

'Oh?'

'Do you play a musical instrument, Sergeant?'

'No,' said the other, 'I'm tone deaf.'

'Then it sounds to me as if you're better off with a bass drum. You're strong enough to carry it and clever enough to beat it. Can we count on you joining our band on Sunday morning?'

Keedy was alarmed. 'Hey, now hold on a moment,' he said, backing away. 'I'm not volunteering for the Salvation Army.'

'Don't you want to save sinners with rousing music?' asked Raymond, grinning broadly. 'It's very rewarding work.'

'I'll take your word for it, Major.'

'Our door is always open.'

'The inspector warned me that you'd try to recruit me.'

'I've been trying to recruit Harvey for almost twenty years but he says that he has important work to do.' He indicated the crucifix on his collar. 'What's more important than serving Jesus Christ?'

The detective wisely chose not to reply. Although there was a humorous note in Raymond's voice, Keedy had no wish to be drawn into an argument with him. Even on their brief acquaintance, he could see how plausible and persuasive Major Marmion was. Keedy had been brought up in the Anglican Church but rarely attended services now. Religion was something that had gradually faded from his life. It was not the moment to rekindle it.

Raymond gave him a firm handshake and pumped his arm.

'It was a pleasure to meet you, Sergeant Keedy,' he said.

'The pleasure was mutual.'

'You have a devoted admirer in the family.'

'Oh,' said Keedy, misunderstanding, 'Inspector Marmion is not always full of admiration for me. If I make a mistake – and I do that from time to time – he comes down on me like a ton of bricks.'

'I wasn't talking about Harvey. I was referring to my niece.'

Keedy was jolted. 'Alice?'

'Who else? Your name often comes up when we all get together. Alice speaks very well of Joe Keedy.'

'Thank you for telling me.'

The news brought a smile to his face and ignited a memory of their time together washing the dishes the previous Sunday. Until he turned up at the house, Keedy had forgotten how attractive Alice Marmion was. It had been months since he'd last seen her and she'd matured in the interim. It made him look forward with anticipatory delight to their next meeting. Conscious that Raymond was watching him, Keedy became serious and waved his pad.

'This list will be extremely useful, Major,' he said.

'It's not comprehensive, I fear. Old groups emerge in new forms all the time and some may consist of no more than a handful of people. Of one thing, however, I can assure you,' said Raymond, seriously. 'Anti-Semitism is as virulent as ever.'

They moved with speed. When the lorry drew up outside the synagogue, they jumped out and unloaded cardboard boxes filled with firewood and newspapers. The boxes were piled against the double doors. Then the man in the dungarees doused them liberally in petrol from a large can. Lighting a cigarette, he took a couple of puffs before tossing it into the biggest of the cardboard boxes. There was an immediate explosion and flames began dancing against the doors. Seconds later, the lorry sped off down the street.

CHAPTER FOURTEEN

Ruth felt increasingly oppressed. Though the wider family was still mourning the death of Jacob Stein, they also kept a close eye on his only daughter in case she should be tempted to take her own life again. Suffocated by their love, Ruth was simultaneously worn down by their surveillance. Privacy was a thing of the past. There was always somebody there and she came to see her nearest and dearest as so many warders changing shifts outside her cell. It was her mother's turn to be on duty that morning.

'How are you feeling today?' she asked, solicitously.

'I'm fine, Mother.'

'Did you have a better night?'

'Not really,' said Ruth.

'What kept you awake?'

'It was the usual thing.'

'You must stop blaming yourself for what happened,' said Miriam, gently. 'Those two evil men were to blame – not you. They've both been arrested and will be convicted of the crime. Doesn't that give you a feeling of relief?'

'No, it doesn't.'

'Why not?'

'I can't explain it.'

'Are you still afraid of them?'

'Yes, Mother.'

'But they're safely locked up.'

'One of them is,' said Ruth. 'The other man is out on bail.'

'He can't touch you here.'

'That's not the point.'

'Then what is?'

'You wouldn't understand.'

Though Miriam continued to press her for details, her daughter had taken refuge in silence. It was impossible for Ruth to untangle the confused mixture of heightened emotions and irrational fears swirling around inside her. She was taxed by the apparent pointlessness of her existence yet racked by guilt because she had tried to bring it to an end. She felt irredeemably responsible for tarnishing the family's hitherto spotless reputation.

Miriam reached for what she hoped would be a possible solution to her daughter's distress, assuring her that everything would seem different when her brother, Daniel, returned. Because there was such a strong bond between them, he had always been able to cheer up his sister. His mere presence, Miriam felt, would act as a fillip to Ruth.

'He'll get your Uncle Herman's letter before long,' she said.

'You keep saying that.'

'Daniel is thousands of miles away. We're not sure where his regiment actually is at the moment but your uncle will find him somehow.'

Ruth was certain of it. Her uncle was very tenacious and usually got what he wanted in the end. But she had misgivings about the potential return of her brother. While she missed Daniel terribly and longed to have him back home, she feared that the trust between them would be shattered when he learnt what she had tried to do. Shocked by her suicide bid, he would condemn it along with everyone else. Instead of being a loving brother offering her succour, he might turn out to be one more person maintaining a vigil over her.

They heard a car sweep onto the drive and come to a halt. Its door was opened and slammed then footsteps approached. The sound of a key being inserted in the lock told them that it was Herbert Stone, who was allowed to let himself in at any time. He came striding into the living room where the two women were seated on the sofa. Hoping for news about her son, Miriam got to her feet.

'Is there any word of Daniel?' she asked, then she saw the mingled fury and sorrow in his face. 'What's wrong, Herman?'

'I've just heard appalling news,' he said. 'Someone tried to burn down the synagogue last night.'

In view of recent developments, Marmion felt that David Cohen had not been as forthcoming as he should have been with regard to details about the way that the business in Jermyn Street was run. As a result, he decided to call on the former manager at home to press him for more information. Cohen was surprised to find the inspector standing on his threshold when he opened the front door but he quickly recovered his poise and invited the visitor in. They adjourned to the living room.

Marmion turned down the offer of refreshment and plunged straight in.

'Why didn't you tell me that Mr Stein's brother had a stake in the firm?' he asked.

'It didn't seem pertinent.'

'Everything relating to the business is pertinent, Mr Cohen.'

'I wasn't deliberately withholding information from you,' said Cohen. 'You must make allowance for the circumstances, Inspector. When we talked the first time, I was looking at the shop in which I'd worked for many happy years burnt to the ground. I was overcome by emotion.'

'I took that into consideration, sir. I still think that you were unnecessarily taciturn when asked how the two brothers got on.'

'I happen to value the concept of loyalty.'

'You allowed it to cloud your thinking. I'm sure that you're as anxious as we are to catch the perpetrators of the crimes but we can't do that if you conceal vital facts from us. Mr Stein is dead,' Marmion emphasised. 'You're not being disloyal if you tell me that his brother exerted undue influence over him.'

'Perhaps not,' conceded the other.

'So what *was* the relationship between them?'

David Cohen took time to assemble his answer. Even though he was spending leisure time at home, he was neatly attired in a suit. Marmion wondered if the man ever wore casual clothing. It seemed wholly out of character for him. Cohen began with a warning.

'What I'm about to tell you, I do so in strictest confidence.'

'I respect that, sir.'

'Nobody outside the family is aware of the true situation.'

'And what situation would that be, Mr Cohen?'

Cohen inflated his chest. 'The business was not always as successful as it became,' he admitted as he breathed out. 'There was a time early on when it ran into difficulties.'

'Did Mr Stein have a loan from his bank?'

'He felt it easier to borrow from his brother,' said Cohen. 'That way, the bank was kept unaware of the fact that there'd been a wobble in his fortunes. Thanks to the injection of new capital, the business quickly righted itself.'

'But it remained in debt to Mr Stone.'

'He was Herman Stein in those days, Inspector, and he was very acquisitive by nature. He believed that his loan had bought him a strong position in the firm. Even after it was repaid, he continued to put in an appearance and keep abreast of the accounts.'

'That must have been disconcerting for his brother.'

'It was.'

'How did the other employees view his interference?'

'They resented it.'

'Did they complain?'

'They left it to Mr Burridge to do that,' said Cohen. 'He was the unofficial spokesman and not simply because he was the oldest. Cyril Burridge was a born complainer.'

'Yes,' said Marmion with a wry smile, 'I've met the gentleman. I can imagine him speaking out.' He waited for a response that never came. Cohen was not to be drawn. 'What do you know about the insurance arrangements for the shop?'

'Nothing at all, Inspector – I left that to Mr Stein.'

'Was he punctilious about such things?'

'Very punctilious,' replied Cohen.

'Then I'm bound to ask why he put the arrangements in his brother's hands.' Cohen was taken aback. 'It seems that the whole policy was reviewed a couple of months ago. Thanks to Mr Stone, the shop was carrying much heavier insurance than before.'

Once again, Cohen held back any comment. Marmion could see that the man was startled, yet he refused to express it in words. Nor did he ask how the inspector had come by the information. Insulated by consecutive layers of caution, the manager simply bided his time. Marmion tried to pierce his defences.

'You didn't like Mr Burridge, did you?' he challenged.

'Is that what he told you?'

'I deduced it from the way you talked about him.'

'His work was above reproach, Inspector.'

'What about his manner?'

'One learns to accept people's idiosyncrasies.'

'Are you claiming that there was no conflict between you?'

'I was there to make sure that everyone did his job,' said Cohen, smoothly, 'and that's what I did. Mr Burridge is an expert tailor.'

'Then why didn't you fight to retain his services?'

'The decision was not left in my hands.'

'What if it had been?'

Cohen gave a cold smile. 'That's idle speculation and, as such, of no earthly use to us. Mr Burridge left because of a dispute over his wages. I did not hold the purse strings, Inspector.'

'I'm beginning to wonder what you actually *did* do,' said Marmion, irritated by his companion's habit of dodging questions. 'You seem to have managed the business with your eyes closed.'

'I find that remark offensive,' said Cohen, huffily.

'Then that makes us quits, sir, because I find your evasiveness equally offensive. I'm trying to find out who killed your employer and all that you can do is to fend me off. Since you can't give me a straight answer with regard to Mr Burridge, let's turn to Howard Fine. Were you pleased that he was dismissed?'

'I felt that it was best for the firm.'

'Why was that, sir?'

'He was not our sort of tailor.'

'He was personable, had excellent credentials and came from a good Jewish family. I would have thought he was ideally qualified to work for Jacob Stein.'

'That was how it seemed at first.'

'What went wrong, Mr Cohen?'

'Mr Stone is best placed to answer that, Inspector. He made the decision to terminate his contract.'

'Did his brother endorse the decision?'

There was a long pause. 'He came to do so after a while.'

'So there was some dissension at first – is that correct?'

'It did cause a ripple or two,' confessed Cohen. 'The fact is that both Mr Fine and Mr Burridge were soon replaced with people who did their respective jobs just as well. Until the tragic events of last week, the business was thriving.'

Marmion detected the slightest hint of a smirk around the man's lips as if Cohen was congratulating himself on the way that he was refraining from committing himself in any way. It prompted the detective to ask a question off the top of his head.

'Did you see anything of Mr Stone socially, sir?'

'No, I didn't.'

'What about his brother?'

'Mr Stein and I did have an occasional drink together, Inspector, and my wife and I were privileged to dine with him and Mrs Stein now and again. Also, of course, I worshipped at the same synagogue.'

'Indeed? Then I have some sad news for you.'

'Really?'

'An attempt was made last night to burn it down,' said Marmion. 'Luckily, the alarm was quickly raised and the fire brigade got there in time to put out the blaze before it did any significant damage.'

Cohen was distraught. 'That's an appalling thing to do!'

'We've mounted a police presence outside the building and warned other synagogues to take precautions against attack.'

'Do you think attacks are likely elsewhere?'

'No, Mr Cohen,' said Marmion, calmly, 'I don't believe that they are. I think it's more than possible that your synagogue was picked out because it was the one that Jacob Stein attended. He's being persecuted even though he's now in his grave.'

When she woke up that morning, the problem that she had taken to bed with her was still there to vex her. Who had been following them the previous day? It was a question that tormented Irene. Though she had seen nobody with her own eyes, she put her trust in the instincts of Miss James. Someone had tailed them to the shops. Irene kept asking herself who it was and what his motive could have been. The obvious candidate was Ernie Gill but he lived on the other side of London and had promised not to get into contact with her until she felt ready. The onus was on Irene to arrange their next meeting.

Over her mid-morning cup of coffee at the house, she came round to another explanation and it was not reassuring. The person following them must have been a thief. Seeing someone as vulnerable as Miss James, he had been waiting for an opportunity to snatch her handbag and run off. Irene's presence stopped him doing that. She agonised over whether or not to confide her fears in the old lady herself, then decided against it. Miss James rarely ventured out alone. She almost invariably had company that would act as protection. The best thing was to forget the whole episode.

As she was deciding how to spend the rest of the day, Irene heard the click of the letter box and the thud of mail hitting the carpet. She went out and picked up three letters, checking the names on them as she walked back to the kitchen. Two were addressed to her sister but one was for her and she recognised the handwriting of her landlady in Liverpool. Using a knife to slit open the envelope, she took out a cutting from the local newspaper. Beneath a photograph of a small house whose windows had been smashed in was an article that made her gasp. When she noted the date given in the article, her blood ran cold. It was too great a coincidence. Her mind was racing. She had something much more sinister to worry about now than being followed by a mysterious stranger.

Thanks to the quick response, the damage to the synagogue had been swiftly curtailed. The fire had gained a purchase on the double doors but had been unable to spread before the fire brigade arrived. That did not minimise the shock felt by those who routinely attended the synagogue. Several of them had come to view the smoke-blackened doors and to weigh up the implications of the attack. Joe Keedy was shown the full extent of the damage by Rabbi Hirsch. When he broke away, the sergeant was confronted by Herbert Stone.

'What are you going to do about this?' demanded Stone.

'As you can see, sir, we've assigned two uniformed policemen to stand guard here. That will continue around the clock.'

'It's too little, too late. We needed protection *beforehand*.'

'We had no indication that the place was in danger.'

'When the situation is highly volatile, as it is at present, then it's always in danger. You should have foreseen that, Sergeant.'

'We're not fortune-tellers, Mr Stone,' said Keedy, determined not to be browbeaten. 'We can't predict the future. The question you should be asking is not why this synagogue was attacked, but why none of the others in London was singled out.'

Stone blenched. 'Is that true? Ours is the only one?'

'Yes, sir.'

Keedy was not pleased to see him. He had simply come to take stock of the damage and to see if there were any clues that pointed to the culprits. Unhappily, there were none so far. A man walking his dog reported seeing a lorry driving away at high speed but it could not definitely be connected with the blaze. Detectives were still going from house to house in the vicinity in search of potential witnesses.

Stone clearly took an almost proprietorial interest in the synagogue and, judging by the way the two men talked together earlier, he seemed to be an intimate friend of Rabbi Hirsch. Since he could not avoid speaking to Stone, Keedy took advantage of the opportunity to question him.

'I understand that you had more than a passing interest in your brother's business affairs,' he said. 'Is that true, sir?'

Stone's jaw tightened. 'What if it is?'

'You even had some say in who was employed there.'

'Jacob always turned to me for advice.'

'It was rather more than advice, Mr Stone. When I interviewed Howard Fine, he told me that you'd dismissed him in person.'

'He should have gone much sooner,' said Stone with disdain.

'Why was that?'

'He did not *belong*, Sergeant.'

'Your brother apparently thought he did.'

'He was the only one who did. Fine was a disruptive influence.'

'In what way?' asked Keedy, surprised. 'He struck me as a rather harmless and inoffensive fellow.'

'You didn't have to work alongside him.'

'Neither did you, sir.'

'I picked up the vibrations from the other members of staff,' said Stone, bristling. 'Burridge loathed him and – though he was far too well bred to voice his concerns – so did Mr Cohen, the manager. Howard Fine was a mistake. That's why I sent him on his way.'

'Do you think that he could be vindictive?'

Stone glared. 'His type often can be.'

'What exactly do you mean by "his type"?' asked Keedy.

'I leave you to guess. But if you're asking if he should be treated as a possible suspect, the answer is no. Howard Fine wouldn't have the guts to seek revenge,' said Stone, contemptuously. 'As far as I was concerned, his departure was a case of good riddance to bad rubbish.'

'Yet he was able to find employment almost immediately.'

'Then he's someone else's problem now.'

Keedy was puzzled. When he'd spoken to Fine, there'd been no hint of vengefulness in the man. He'd accepted his dismissal and found more amenable work elsewhere. Evidently, there had been a deeper rift in the Jermyn Street shop than the tailor had indicated. What had actually happened during his time there, and why was Stone showing such animosity towards a man with whom he hardly ever came into contact? What had Howard Fine done to upset him?

Stone shifted the conversation to another former employee.

'You're going to ask me about Burridge next, aren't you?' he said.

'I might as well tell you that I wasn't sorry to see him go. That was no reflection on his work, mind you – it was exceptional. But his manner could be abrasive,' said Stone. 'He was respectful towards me and my brother, of course, but Mr Cohen had difficulties with him.'

'Did he complain about them?'

'No, Sergeant – David Cohen wouldn't do that. He never told tales. He believed in settling differences by means of tact and diplomacy.'

'According to the inspector,' said Keedy, 'Cyril Burridge was far from being either tactful or diplomatic. In fact, the wonder is that he lasted so long in your brother's shop.'

'He had his virtues,' conceded Stone, 'and he knew how to keep his head down whenever Jacob and I were about. When he was given his notice, however, he told me precisely what he thought of me and he didn't mince his words.' He smiled, darkly. 'My back is broad,' he boasted. 'Insults like that just bounce off me.'

Keedy wanted to pursue the topic but the rabbi was beckoning Stone over to him. The sergeant managed to get in one more question.

'How is your niece bearing up, sir?'

'Not too well,' admitted Stone. 'Ruth is still reeling from what happened to her and to her father. She's still very fearful.'

'There's no need to be,' said Keedy. 'Gatliffe would never dare to go anywhere near her and Cochran is safely locked up in prison. She has nothing to fear from either of them.'

When the telephone call came, Sir Edward Henry was as annoyed as he was disturbed. After ridding himself of some biting criticism, he left the room and headed down the corridor to Harvey Marmion's office. He knocked on the door then let himself in. Seated behind his desk, Marmion looked up from the report he was studying. He could see from the commissioner's expression that something dramatic had occurred.

'What's the trouble, Sir Edward?' he asked.

'I've just had a phone call from the Home Office.'

'And?'

'The staff at Wandsworth can't do their job properly.'

Marmion understood. 'Oliver Cochran?'

'Yes,' said Sir Edward. 'Somehow – God knows how – he's managed to escape and is on the run.'

Major Raymond Marmion was such an irregular visitor to the house that Ellen always made a fuss of him when he did turn up. He had called in that afternoon to borrow his brother's lawnmower and was immediately pressed to have tea, sandwiches and a slice of home-made chocolate cake. To someone who deliberately led a fairly spartan existence, it was a rare moment of indulgence for him.

'Since I joined the Army,' he said, relishing the cake, 'I've had to *make* far more tea than I ever have chance to drink. I just get so much more pleasure out of satisfying the needs of others.'

'You're a saint, Ray.'

'We don't believe in canonisation.'

'Well, you should do.' Ellen cut herself a slice of cake. 'I hear that Alice came to see you to discuss this mad idea she has of joining the Women's Emergency Corps.'

He was more tolerant. 'Is it such a mad idea, Ellen?'

'We think so. Alice has a profession to follow.'

'She feels that she wishes to help the war effort.'

'Is that what you advised?'

'Good Lord, no,' he said, smiling. 'I'd never try to tell Alice what to do. I merely provided a pair of ears so that she could go through the pros and cons. She's well aware of the disadvantages of the scheme, so it's not an easy decision. It partly depends on this friend who teaches at the same school.'

'Her name is Vera Dowling. She's a rather timid creature.'

'Miss Dowling is ready to follow Alice's lead, it seems, but she's getting impatient. Alice thinks that her friend may get fed up with waiting and will volunteer even if she has to do it on her own.'

Ellen did not like the sound of that. Vera Dowling was a young woman who needed someone else to tell her what to do. If she was suddenly deciding to take independent action, it would act as a spur to Alice and that was worrying. Ellen tried to explain why she and her husband opposed the notion. Raymond listened with his customary patience and attention, making sure that he didn't take sides. It was important for his sister-in-law to air her grievances so he let her talk uninterrupted.

Barely a minute after Ellen had finally reached the end of her peroration, they heard the front door being opened. Alice had come home from school. At the sight of her uncle, she grinned broadly and rushed to embrace him. Then she looked at her mother and back again at Raymond.

'Something's been going on,' she said, suspiciously. 'I sense a conspiratorial air in this kitchen.'

Raymond held up both hands. 'Don't look at me,' he said. 'I only came to borrow your father's lawnmower.'

'You'd better wear ear plugs when you use it, Uncle Ray. It makes the most terrible clanking noise.'

'I can put up with that.'

Alice saw the cake. 'I wouldn't mind a slice of that, Mummy.'

'I'll make a fresh pot of tea,' said Ellen.

'Thank you. Then you can tell me what you were saying about me before I came in.'

'You weren't even mentioned, Alice.'

'Then why is there such an atmosphere?'

Ellen clicked her tongue. 'You're imagining things.'

While her mother went to the sink to fill the kettle, Alice turned to her uncle. Honest by nature, her uncle would never dissemble. He anticipated her question and sought to divert it.

'You *were* the subject of discussion, Alice,' he told her, 'when I had an unexpected visitor yesterday.'

'Oh – who was that?'

'Sergeant Joe Keedy.'

'Why did he come to see you, Uncle Ray?'

'He knows how long I've worked in the East End and how closely I've watched the activities of dissident elements in the area. We often have to pick up the pieces afterwards, you see. I was able to help him with a list of names.'

'And you talked to him about me?'

'Let's say that your name came into the conversation.'

Alice was curious. 'What did Joe have to say?'

'It's not what he had to say but the way that he said it.'

'I don't follow.'

'You've made something of a conquest, Alice.'

'Oh, I don't think so,' she said with a touch of sadness. 'Joe is only interested in his girlfriend. She's a nurse, apparently, and she's gone to Flanders to work in a dressing station.'

'I can only tell you what I heard,' said Raymond.

'And what was that?' asked Ellen, lighting the gas.

'I heard a man who is extremely fond of my lovely niece.'

Alice was pleased. 'Did he say that in so many words?'

'He didn't need to,' explained Raymond. 'It was the way that Joe said your name. That's what gave him away.'

It was encouraging news but Alice was not quite sure how to take it. While she was delighted to have made a good impression on Keedy, she was critical of him for taking an interest in her when his affections were already engaged elsewhere. Her own feelings about him had not changed – Alice still thought him a handsome, engaging and thoroughly mature man. That put him streets ahead of any of her other admirers. Yet he was unavailable. She had to keep reminding herself of that. Keedy was already spoken for and she had to respect that fact. When she came out of her reverie, she saw that her mother was offering her a slice of cake on a plate.

'Oh,' said Alice, taking it from her, 'thank you, Mummy.' She had a first bite of the cake before announcing her decision. 'By the way, Vera and I have made up our minds at last.'

Ellen braced herself. 'Have you?'

'Yes – we're going to join the WEC.'

As soon as Keedy entered Scotland Yard, he saw Marmion coming towards him with a sense of urgency. Instead of being able to report on his visit to the synagogue, the sergeant was turned round and bundled into a waiting car. Marmion settled in beside him and the vehicle set off.

'Oliver Cochran has escaped,' he said.

Keedy gaped. 'How the hell did he do that?'

'Let's worry about that when we have him under lock and key. We have to catch him as soon as possible, Joe. If this gets into the press, they'll start asking about the offence with which he's charged and Ruth Stein's name may be leaked.'

'We must stop that happening, Inspector. I've just spoken to her uncle. The girl is still struggling badly. The last thing she needs is to see her name all over the newspapers. What's the situation?'

'We've launched a manhunt. Cochran won't get far.'

'He's young and strong. If he's clever enough to escape from Wandsworth, he could be very difficult to find.'

'I don't think so,' said Marmion, confidently. 'He realises that he can't stay at liberty indefinitely. In my view, that isn't why he broke out of prison. Cochran has only one purpose in mind.'

'What's that, Inspector?'

'He wants to get his revenge on John Gatliffe.'

CHAPTER FIFTEEN

He sat on the riverbank with his rod beside him, unable to summon up the energy or the interest to do any fishing. At least he was alone and free from the sustained disgust of his parents. Gatliffe had no rest at home. His mother and father had been horrified to hear that he'd been charged by the police, even though he insisted that he did not molest Ruth Stein in any way. His father had wanted to disown him and throw him out of the house. Only the intercession of his mother stopped it happening but she punished him in another way. While her husband ranted and threatened, she subjected her son to silent hostility, treating him to long withering stares and refusing to do anything for him beyond making meals that he was forced to eat by himself. Staying at home brought him unrelenting pain and guilt. Gatliffe had therefore fled to the river. Even though it was a dull and chilly day, he was content. They could not hurt him there.

He'd been wrong. He could see that now. He should never have confessed to the crime. It had not only ruined his life but broken his closest friendship. He and Oliver Cochran had grown up together, making light of the deprivation they suffered in a poverty-stricken area and supporting each other to the hilt at all times. They were no strangers to petty theft but had always got away with it because they were such convincing liars. Their respective parents had no idea how often they had gone astray. Mr and Mrs Gatliffe thought that their son was a decent and law-abiding young man. The revelation that he had been involved in the rape of a girl in the West End had come as a thunderbolt.

He'd let his friend down. That's what hurt Gatliffe most. In being unable to defend himself against police interrogation, he'd betrayed Cochran and would never be forgiven. In hindsight, the situation was clear. He should have maintained his innocence. There was no certainty that the girl would be able to identify them in court and she might well lose her nerve before the trial took place. According to Cochran, that often happened. The girl in the alley had not been his first victim. While Gatliffe had kept watch, Cochran had once raped a drunken girl after a dance. Though she'd vowed revenge, there'd been no repercussions – no report to the police, no hostile questioning, no charges. Even if there had been, Gatliffe would have been prepared to lie outrageously on his friend's behalf. Why hadn't he done so this time?

He sought for ways to make amends, to win back a friendship that had been the mainstay of his life. He had to convince Cochran that he was still on his side and would go to any lengths to get him off the charge they were both facing even if it meant committing perjury. Brooding on his folly, he glanced into the dark water and saw a face appear in it behind his own. Gatliffe sat up in alarm and turned round to find Oliver Cochran hovering over him.

'What're *you* doing here, Ol?' he croaked.

Cochran gave a crooked grin. 'Guess.'

She had to know the truth. After hours of thinking it over, Irene Bayard decided that she could stand it no longer. The cutting from the *Liverpool Echo* had raised a frightening possibility. At first, she tried to dismiss the notion as a wild fantasy but the strategy failed. It was the date that was critical. She'd checked it in her diary. When Irene was staying with her sister in London, her landlady in Liverpool often sent her cuttings from the local newspapers that she deemed might be of interest. None had had such a stunning effect as this one, nor held such potential significance for her. Yes, it *could* be an unfortunate coincidence – she prayed that it was – but the signs indicated otherwise. Irene had to find out.

Reaching for her handbag, she took out the slip of paper on which she'd scribbled an address then she tried to work out the best way to reach that part of the city. Minutes later, she left the house and went striding off along the pavement.

Gatliffe scrambled quickly to his feet and took a precautionary step backwards. One glance at Cochran's face told him that he was in dire trouble.

'Have they let you out, Ol?' he asked.

'I let myself out.'

Gatliffe was astounded. 'You mean that you *escaped*?'

'Remand prisoners have more leeway. They gave me too much.'

'So the police will be out looking for you.'

'Bugger the police!' snarled Cochran.

'I'll help you to hide,' said Gatliffe, anxious to placate him. 'You obviously can't go home and we can't take you in. But there must be somewhere you can lie low.'

'Forget it, Gatty.'

'What about that derelict house by the canal?'

'I told you to forget it. I'm not looking for a hiding place.'

'Then what are you looking for?'

He saw the glint in his friend's eye and stepped even further away. Cochran wanted retribution. He knew where to find Gatliffe. That was the whole purpose of his escape from prison. He was there to inflict punishment. Gatliffe's mouth was dry. He glanced around but there was nobody to whom he could call. Nor could he hope to outrun Cochran. His friend was much faster than him. His only hope lay in appeasing Cochran.

'I've changed my plea,' he said with a hollow laugh. 'I told the police we were nowhere near Jermyn Street that night. They can't *prove* it, Ol. I mean, that girl wouldn't dare to come forward. Think of the one you shagged after that dance. She knew it was a waste of time going to the police. It's the same here. They got nothing on us. If we stick together, we're in the clear.' His mouth was drier than ever. 'Well, aren't we?'

'You should've kept your trap shut, Gatty.'

'I know.'

'Because of you, we're up to our necks in shit.'

'I've told you – I'm pleading not guilty now.'

'It's too late.'

'The case might not even come to court.'

'I don't care about that now,' said Cochran, advancing on him. 'Killing you is all I care about.'

'But we're friends, Ol. I'll stick by you.'

When he backed away again, Gatliffe came up against the trunk of a tree. He was cornered. Cochran was on him in a flash, grabbing him by the shoulders and banging him hard against the tree. Then he landed a series of stinging punches. Gatliffe tried to fight back at first but he soon buckled under the onslaught and resorted to covering his head with his arms. The blows were unremitting. When he could not beat him to the ground, Cochran used his feet instead, kicking him repeatedly until he doubled up in pain. Shoving him down on the bank, he dived on top of Gatliffe and got both hands to his throat, slowly applying pressure.

Gatliffe became desperate. Realising that he might be throttled, he took hold of Cochran's wrists and wrenched them away so that he could speak again.

'There's no need for this, Ol,' he bleated. 'We're friends.'

'You betrayed me, you bastard.'

'Get off. You're hurting me.'

But Cochran was in no mood for mercy. Pulsing with anger and prompted by the need for revenge, he went for the throat again and squeezed hard. Gatliffe began to panic and found a surge of strength that allowed him to grasp his friend by the arms and force him sideways. Locked together, the two of them rolled over and over on the grass until they fell into the water. It was very shallow but the shock of the cold water made Cochran release his hold at last. Gatliffe struggled to his feet, spitting out water. When Cochran surfaced, he, too, was spluttering but was the first to recover. As Gatliffe tried to wade to the bank, he was gripped from behind and hurled back into the river, disappearing from sight for a few seconds.

Cochran was not going to let him go a second time. As soon as Gatliffe's head rose above the water, Cochran grabbed his hair and pushed him down again, determined to keep him there until he drowned. Gatliffe flailed wildly but he could not shake off his attacker. It was only a question of time before his resistance was broken. Cochran was exultant, laughing at his triumph, thinking of nothing else but of meting out the ultimate punishment to his friend.

He was so obsessed with getting his revenge that he didn't see the two detectives running along the bank towards him. Keedy was in the lead but Marmion was only a yard behind him. Sizing up the situation, they didn't hesitate for a second. They flung off their hats, tore off their coats, then plunged straight into the water. While Keedy knocked Cochran over with a crash tackle, Marmion helped the victim, taking Gatliffe by the scruff of the neck and hauling him up to the surface. Gasping for air, he was so weak that Marmion had to carry him to the bank.

Keedy, meanwhile, was involved in a frenzied contest with Oliver Cochran. Waist-deep in the water, they traded punches, then grappled. Cochran did everything he could to get free, struggling, spitting and even trying to bite his assailant. Keedy did not stand on ceremony. Pulling one hand away, he bunched his fist and pounded Cochran's face until the man yelled in agony, ending with a vicious right hook that caught him on the ear and momentarily dazed him. Keedy was quick to overpower him, twisting one arm behind his back and forcing him to the bank. Marmion was waiting to snap handcuffs onto the escaped prisoner. Cochran was not finished yet. Even though both detectives had hold of him, he managed to swing a foot and kick Gatliffe who was still sprawled on the grass.

Keedy pulled the prisoner out of reach of his former friend.

'It's all over, Cochran,' he said. 'You're going back to prison.'

Uniformed policemen were now hurrying along the bank. When they arrived, Keedy handed over Cochran. As they dragged him away, he was howling with rage. Marmion assisted Gatliffe to his feet.

'How do you feel now?' he asked.

'He tried to kill me,' said Gatliffe in horror. 'Olly tried to drown me.' He gave a shudder. 'Thank God you came, Inspector!'

'The person to thank is your mother, sir. When we called at your house, she told us you'd gone fishing and where we'd be likely to find you. We had a feeling that Cochran might have got here first.'

'It's where we always used to come. It was our special place. Me and Ol spent hours fishing here.'

'Well, you won't ever do it again,' said Keedy. 'Cochran's fishing days are over.' He glanced down at his sodden clothing. 'Look at the state of me,' he moaned. 'I'm soaked to the skin.'

'We *all* are, Joe,' said Marmion, examining his own dripping trousers. 'Let's find somewhere to dry off – come on.'

The address she'd been given was in one of the less salubrious areas of the city. An air of unspecified danger hung in its grimy streets. Had she not been so determined, Irene would have turned back and sought the safety of her own home but she had not come this far to be thwarted. Ignoring the lustful stares and the coarse comments she attracted from ragged men loitering in doorways, she walked quickly on and averted her gaze from the scrawny women who looked at her smart clothing with an amalgam of envy and hatred. Disappointment awaited her. When she reached the house where Ernie Gill was lodging, she was told that he was not there. The most likely place to find him, she was informed, was in the pub two streets away.

It was bad news for Irene. If Gill had been drinking, he might become unpredictable but that could not be helped. She simply had to see him. Though it meant braving the denizens of the Three Tuns, she was not afraid. Irene pushed open the door of the lounge bar and stepped into the fug. Through the curling smoke from cigarettes and pipes, she tried to pick out Gill from the dozen or more people there, conscious that all eyes were on her. An old man spoke up.

'Eh, 'ow much d'you charge, darlin'?' he asked.

There was a roar of laughter at Irene's expense. She rose above it and took a few steps forward so that she could peer around. Three men were sitting at a table in a corner. One of them leapt to his feet and came scurrying across to her.

'Is that *you*, Irene?' asked Gill in amazement. 'What on earth are you doing here?'

'I need to speak to you, Ernie.'

'That's wonderful. Let me buy you a drink.'

'No, no,' she said, touching his arm as he turned towards the bar counter. 'I only came for a talk.' She looked around. 'Is there somewhere more private than this?'

'Let's go into the snug.'

As he took her through a swing door into a tiny room, there were jeers from the other patrons and a barrage of crude remarks. They sat down either side of a small, round, beer-stained table. Gill grinned expectantly.

'This is a lovely surprise, Irene,' he said.

'It's not a social call.'

'How did you find me?'

'A lady at your house suggested I might try here.'

'That would be Maggie – Maggie Thompson. She's Brad's wife. He's the friend who took me in.'

'She told me that you spent a lot of time here,' said Irene with disapproval. 'Whereas you reckoned you were looking for a job.'

'I found one,' he said, proudly. 'I start tomorrow at a barber's not far from here. It's not the same as working on a liner but it's a job. What about you? I thought you'd have started in that toy factory by now.'

'Not until next Monday.'

He leered at her. 'So what did you want to speak to me about?'

'I want to ask you about this, Ernie.'

She opened her bag and fished out the article from the *Liverpool Echo*. She slapped it on the table in front of him and watched his reaction. He was nonplussed at first. Puzzlement gave way to wariness then turned into positive alarm. He read the article twice.

'Well?' she pressed. 'What have you got to say?'

'I'm . . . very sorry that it happened.'

'You were involved, weren't you?'

'No!' he cried.

'You were part of the gang that smashed up that house.'

'Of course I wasn't, Irene.'

'Look at the date. It was the day we landed back in Liverpool.'

'So?'

'You told me that you went out drinking then decided to go in search of a German family you knew about. It was them, wasn't it?' she challenged, pointing at the press cutting.

'I never went anywhere near this place.'

'The wife managed to escape but the man was beaten to a pulp. He hung on in hospital for days but eventually died. That means the people who attacked him committed murder.' She grasped his wrist. 'Were you one of them, Ernie? Are you a killer?'

'No – I swear it on my mother's grave!'

'But you boasted about killing Germans.'

'That was just talk.'

'It didn't sound like it to me.'

'Irene,' he said, putting a hand to her cheek, 'you've got it all wrong. I've got faults and lots of them but you surely can't think me guilty of *this*. What sort of a man do you think I am?'

'That's what I started to wonder.'

'Listen, I *did* go out boozing that night, I admit it. And I did go off with a few others to a house where a German family used to live. But they weren't there any longer. They'd moved away.'

'So why did you say you taught them a lesson?'

'I was just showing off.'

'"We did what needed to be done," you said.'

'I wanted to impress you.'

'Impress me!' she repeated, indignantly. 'Do you think I'd be impressed to hear about an innocent family being assaulted?'

'It never happened, Irene.'

'Yes, it did, and this article gives all the details. The police are still looking for the men involved. Is that why you came to London all of a sudden, Ernie? Are you on the run?'

'Don't be stupid!' he said, angrily.

'There's no need to shout at me.'

His tone softened immediately. 'I'm sorry. I didn't mean to do that. It's just that I hate being accused of something I didn't do. Since we're old friends, you deserve to know the truth.' As he chose his words with care, he chewed his lip. 'I *did* go out looking for trouble that night. I admit it. But we never found it. We ended up getting drunk and singing rude songs about the Germans.' He gave her a dazzling smile. 'Are you satisfied now?'

'What about that group you know here in London? The one you said I'd be too law-abiding to join. You told me that you hit and run.'

'Oh, that only lasted for days. Brad took me along. They were all talk, really. I soon got bored with them. I am who I am, Irene – the same Ernie Gill you've known all these years.'

Irene looked at him, then down at the article, then back at him again. She was not sure what to believe. Hoping with all her heart that he had nothing to do with the crime, she still had vestigial doubts.

'How do I know that you're telling the truth?'

His voice became earnest. 'Fetch me a Bible,' he told her, 'and I'll swear on that. You know me, Irene. I'm a good Catholic boy. I wouldn't lie with my hand on the Holy Book.'

'There's no need to do that.'

'How else can I convince you?'

There was a pleading note in his voice. Irene looked deep into his eyes but saw no hint of guilt or dissembling. She looked down at the article once more then she picked it up and scrunched it in her hand. Her smile was edged with slight embarrassment.

'I think I owe you an apology, Ernie.'

'Not at all,' he said, effusively. 'I'm glad you came. You did the right thing, Irene. I can see exactly what you must have thought and I'm glad I was able to set the record straight.'

'So am I.'

'I take my hat off to you for walking in here the way you did. Ladies like you don't come in here by themselves. They know the kind of greeting they'll get. It was very brave of you.'

'I *had* to know the truth,' she explained.

'And now you've heard it. Come on,' he said, getting up. 'This is no place for you, Irene. I'll walk you to a place where you can get some transport home. Ernie Gill, a murderer,' he went on, laughing. 'You should know me better than that. I wouldn't hurt a fly.'

* * *

Ellen Marmion had been torn between concern and amusement when the two of them turned up soaking wet. Since his house was closer, Marmion had asked to be driven there so that he and Keedy could change into dry clothing. Shoes, socks, trousers, shirts, ties and underclothes were discarded and hung on the clothes line. While the inspector was able to put on a different suit, Keedy had to make do with borrowed items of clothing that neither fitted properly nor suited his taste. He was embarrassed when Alice came in from the garden in time to catch him in a pair of trousers that were noticeably too baggy.

'What happened?' asked Alice.

'Joe is a hero,' replied her father. 'He saved a man from being killed and arrested an escaped prisoner. Unfortunately, it all took place in a river.'

As he supplied more details of the incident, Alice's interest and admiration grew. She tried not to notice that Keedy's shoes were sizes too large for him or that his coat and trousers did not match. Keedy stressed that it was Marmion who'd rescued and resuscitated John Gatliffe. As a precaution, he'd been taken to hospital and examined before being released. Cochran had been returned to Wandsworth.

'Does this mean you'll get some good publicity for a change, Daddy?' said Alice. 'You and Joe should be in all the newspapers.'

Marmion shook his head. 'We're more likely to be blamed for letting him escape than for actually catching him.'

'But it was the prison officers who should be blamed for that.'

'The press don't make distinctions, Alice. They lump us all together as the forces of law and order. If they have an excuse to take a potshot at us, they will.'

'Yes,' said Keedy. 'They're already criticising us because we haven't caught the man who killed Jacob Stein yet.'

'They can't expect instant results,' said Ellen.

'They can and they do.'

Alice wanted to hear Keedy's version of the arrest of Oliver Cochran but he was too modest to give it. Instead he told her about the fire at the synagogue and what he found when he went there. It was the first time that Marmion had been with his daughter since she made her decision. Ellen cued her in.

'Alice has something to tell you, Harvey,' she said.

Marmion turned to his daughter. 'Do you?'

'Yes,' said Alice. 'I'm going to join the WEC.'

'Talk her out of it,' urged Ellen. 'You help him, Joe.'

'This is nothing to do with me,' said Keedy, holding up a hand.

'It's nothing to do with me either,' said Marmion, calmly. 'Alice is old enough to make up her own mind and we must respect that.'

'Thank you, Daddy,' said Alice.

Ellen was simmering. 'How can you say that, Harvey?' she asked. 'You were as strongly against the idea as I was.'

'I was,' conceded Marmion, 'and I left Alice in no doubt about my opinion on the subject. But we can't let this drag on forever, Ellen. If the decision has been made, we should have the grace to accept it.'

'You can't just let it go like that.'

'What would you have me do?'

'Let's discuss this in the kitchen.'

'There's nothing to discuss.'

'I think there is,' said Ellen, eyes flashing. Forcing a smile, she looked at Keedy. 'You'll have to excuse us a minute. We won't be long.'

She led the way into the kitchen and Marmion followed her. When the door was shut behind them, Alice was uncertain whether to smile or to apologise.

'Oh dear!' she said. 'You've caught us at a rare moment, Joe. My parents almost never have an argument. It's my fault that they're about to have one now.'

'You're entitled to run your own life, Alice.'

'Tell that to Mummy and Daddy.'

'I wouldn't dare.'

'Did you ever have arguments with your parents?'

'All the time,' he said. 'When I told my father that I didn't want to stay in the family business, he almost exploded. My mother was just as bad. She kept going on about the importance of tradition.'

'I can't see you as an undertaker somehow,' she said, then put a hand to her mouth to smother her laughter. 'Especially in a pair of trousers like the ones you've got on.'

'They were all that your father could find.'

'You always take such a pride in your appearance.'

'I like to look smart, Alice. It's important.'

They looked at each other with mutual affection and there was a long silence that neither of them had any inclination to break. They were simply savouring each other's company. Alice felt drawn to him once more but controlled her feelings when she recalled that he was not available. She picked up an envelope from the mantelpiece.

'We had a letter from Paul this morning,' she said.

'Yes – so your father said.'

'I don't know how he can be so cheery. Living in a trench sounds like being in purgatory. I'd hate it.'

'So would I, Alice. But your brother is an optimist. Paul always tries to see the good side of things.'

'There *is* no good side of things at the front, Joe.' She put the envelope back on the mantelpiece. 'But I daresay you'll get your own reports to that effect.'

He frowned. 'Why should I do that?'

'According to Daddy, you have a friend who's just gone to Flanders to work as a nurse there.'

'Oh – you mean Pam,' he said, noting the wistfulness in her voice. 'I don't think Pamela will bother to write to me. When she told me her decision, we agreed to go our separate ways. She's going to be fully occupied from now on.'

'Yes,' said Alice, barely able to keep a smile off her face. 'I suppose that she will be. Once you commit yourself to the war effort, you don't have much time for anything else. I know that when I join the WEC, I can expect to work much longer hours than I do now.'

'When do you start?'

'Oh, we're going to wait until the end of the term. We can't just hand in our resignations and walk out. Vera – that's my friend – has promised her parents that she'll wait until July. I'll do the same.'

'So until then,' he said, looking her up and down, 'you'll have some free time on your hands.'

She nodded happily. 'What about you?'

'I'm going to be working flat-out until this case is solved. That will probably mean giving up my Sundays as well. But it will be worth it when we nail the killer and the arsonist.'

'And what happens then, Joe?'

He grinned. 'It will be fun finding out.'

Herbert Stone seemed to be spending more time at his brother's house than at his own. It was not just a question of consoling Miriam and helping to monitor Ruth's behaviour. He had to see to his brother's business affairs. That meant that he spent hours in the office, going through the relevant books and documents. It took a huge load off his sister-in-law's shoulders and she was duly grateful. As he was about to depart after another session at the house, Miriam took his hand.

'Thank you, Herman,' she said with a tired smile. 'You've been a tower of strength.'

'I've only done what any brother would have done.'

'We'd have been lost without you.'

'It's nothing,' he said, kissing her lightly on the forehead. 'Has Ruth gone to bed yet?'

'She went up a few minutes ago.'

'Then I won't disturb her. I thought she seemed much better today. Our words are finally getting through to her.'

'She was very upset to hear about the fire at the synagogue,' said Miriam. 'But she rallied this afternoon. It was possible to have a proper conversation at last.'

'Do you think she's out of danger?'

'I do hope so, Herman.'

'If only her brother would come home,' he said, irritably. 'It would make all the difference.'

'Why is it taking so long for news to get through?'

'I don't know, Mimi. All that we can do is to wait.' He jumped in surprise when the grandfather clock immediately behind him started to chime. 'Goodness – is *that* how late it is?'

'You'd better go home.'

She escorted him to the door and opened it for him. After giving her a farewell kiss, he put on his hat and walked across to his car. It was mid-evening and the vehicle was in shadow. He was about to get into it when he noticed that his front wheels were missing and had been replaced by piles of bricks. Someone had smashed his windscreen as well. Stone stood there, quivering with fury.

Miriam was still at the door. 'Is something wrong, Herman?'

CHAPTER SIXTEEN

Irene was halfway back to the house before she realised that she'd forgotten to ask Ernie Gill if he'd followed her when she went to the shops with Miss James. It no longer mattered. Her prime objective had been to find out if he was involved in a murder in Liverpool. Now that he'd convinced her that he was completely innocent of the charge, she chided herself for having suspicions about him. Relieved that he'd not committed a heinous crime, she also absolved him of lying in wait to trail her. Why should he do that? What did he stand to gain? When he could go drinking with friends, he'd have no motive for making such a long journey in the hope of a glimpse of her. Irene had been wrong to suspect him of stalking her and even more wrong to imagine his being capable of murder. When they worked together on the *Lusitania*, Gill had sometimes played unwelcome pranks but that was the extent of his misdemeanours. She felt thoroughly ashamed at the way that she'd confronted him. It was a poor reward for a man who'd come to her rescue at sea.

When Irene let herself into the house, Dorothy was waiting.

'Where have you been?' she asked. 'I expected you here when I got back. It's getting dark outside.'

'I had to go out, Dot.'

'Have you been shopping again?'

'No,' said Irene. 'I went to see Ernie.'

'I thought he lived miles away.'

'He does.'

Dorothy laughed. 'I think that you're closer to him than you like to admit, Irene. When will I get to meet this admirer of yours?'

'How many times must I tell you? Ernie is just a friend.'

'I wouldn't go all that way if someone was . . . just a friend.'

'It won't happen again, Dot.'

'We could have him here for tea one Sunday.'

'No,' said Irene. 'I told you before. He's not coming here.'

'But I'd like to meet him. Miss James said that he had a nice voice and was obviously fond of you. Why hide him away?'

'I wouldn't want him to get the wrong idea.'

'Chance would be a fine thing,' said Dorothy with a sigh. 'I'd settle for a man getting *any* sort of idea about me but I don't seem to interest them. I don't know why.'

Irene was sympathetic. 'It may happen one day.'

'Who'd look at a woman of my age?'

'They still look at me.'

'I'm going to die an old maid – just like Miss James.'

'You're not at all like Miss James,' said Irene, hugging her. 'You hold down a good job and you do just about everything for the church. Don't keep putting yourself down, Dot. In your own way, you've been really successful.'

'It doesn't feel like it.'

'People rely on you. You're important in their lives.'

'There is that, I suppose.'

'I know a way to cheer you up,' said Irene, heading for the cabinet. 'Let's have a glass of sherry, shall we?'

'The bottle's almost empty.'

'That's why I bought another one when I went shopping.'

Irene took two sherry glasses from the cabinet, then filled one of them from a bottle. There was just enough left in it for the other glass. She handed one to Dorothy and picked up the other.

'Good health!' she said.

'Health, wealth and happiness,' said Dorothy, taking a sip. 'I needed that. I feel better already.'

'Let's go and sit down.'

'What about the cooking?'

'That can wait.'

Irene went into the living room and sat on the sofa. Dorothy chose the armchair opposite her. She saw her sister glancing round.

'I know what you're thinking,' she said. 'This place is dowdy. It badly needs decorating. I just never got round to it. By the time I've got home from work, I've run out of steam.'

'I'm here now, Dot. We'll do it together.'

'Unless you get a better offer, that is.'

'What do you mean?'

'Well, I'm not persuaded that you're here for good, Irene. You're too good a catch. Ernie Gill may not be your choice but I don't think you'll be short of offers.' After another sip of sherry, Dorothy was emboldened. 'Pass one of them on to me, will you?'

* * *

Before he returned to Scotland Yard, Joe Keedy went back to his flat and changed into a different suit and a pair of shoes that fitted. He now felt confident enough to face his colleagues again. Since they teased him about the care he took with his appearance, they would have ribbed him unmercifully if they'd seen him in the clothing borrowed from Harvey Marmion. That had all been given back to the inspector. Keedy was himself again, able to look in a mirror without wincing. Detectives had gathered more information about the raid on Jacob Stein's shop and Keedy had been given the task of going through all the statements and picking out the most salient. He was poring over his desk when the commissioner came in.

'I thought you'd have gone home by now, Sergeant,' said Sir Edward. 'After your heroic endeavours, you deserve a rest.'

'I've almost finished.'

'Is there any fresh evidence about the fire at the synagogue?'

'I'm afraid not, Sir Edward.'

'There's another outrage to add to the list, I fear.'

'Oh – what's that?'

'It's not on the same scale as the others but it's annoying enough. When he telephoned me, Mr Stone was extremely annoyed.'

'I would have thought he spent most of his time in a state of annoyance,' said Keedy, dryly. 'What's his complaint this time?'

'Somebody attacked his car.'

'When was this?'

'Earlier this evening,' said the commissioner. 'In the time that it was parked outside his brother's house, two wheels were stolen and the windscreen was smashed. The drive is screened by a thick hedge, apparently, so somebody could slip in there unseen.'

'Does he have any idea who was behind it?'

'None at all – he wants *you* to solve that little mystery.'

Keedy laughed mirthlessly. 'With respect to Mr Stone,' he said, 'we do have other crimes to address. I don't think you can compare two missing tyres with murder and arson.'

'He believes the latest incident may be connected to the others.'

Keedy pondered. 'It's possible, I daresay, but it was his brother who was the designated victim, not Mr Stone. This could just as easily be the random act of someone who just doesn't like him. From what I've seen of him, I'd say that he has a gift for making enemies.'

'He does, alas. I fancy that he lists us among them.'

'Did you tell him about Cochran's escape from prison, Sir Edward?'

'I told him how promptly you and Inspector Marmion retrieved the situation. He had the grace to offer a word of praise for you.'

'Is he going to pass on the news to his niece?'

'No, Sergeant,' said the commissioner. 'He was adamant about that. Miss Stein will not be told. She'd be unnecessarily alarmed. It's better that she's kept in ignorance.'

'I'll wager she's been told about her uncle's motor car.'

'That's different. Well,' said the other, stifling a yawn, 'I must be on my way and I'd advise you to do the same. I see that the inspector has already gone home.'

'But he hasn't, Sir Edward.'

'Then where is he?'

'He's still very much at work.'

'His office was empty when I walked past.'

'Inspector Marmion has gone back to Jermyn Street.'

He knew that it was him. Though the man was standing in shadow on the opposite pavement, Marmion was certain that it was none other than Cyril Burridge. He strolled across to him.

'Good evening, Mr Burridge,' he said.

'What are you doing here, Inspector?'

'I was about to ask the same of you, sir. As for me, I came to take a look inside the shop, now that it's safe to do so. When the light started to fade, I gave up.' He nodded towards the shop. 'It's much bigger than it seems from the outside.'

'We needed plenty of storage space.'

'Is this a nostalgic visit, Mr Burridge?'

The tailor was brusque. 'I don't believe in nostalgia.'

'You must have *some* happy memories of working here.'

'I choose to forget them, Inspector.'

As he looked at him, Marmion wondered how he'd managed to work alongside David Cohen for so many years without any major disagreements. The big, gruff, barely civil Yorkshireman would have been a difficult colleague for anyone, especially so for someone as refined as the manager. With customers, Marmion assumed, Burridge was able to shed his curt manner. The inspector recalled what he'd learnt about the financial affairs of the firm.

'I can see why you resented Mr Stone.'

'We all did.'

'Does that include Mr Cohen?'

'Ask him.'

'In effect, I did. He was non-committal.'

Burridge snorted. 'That's David Cohen for you!'

'He praised your work as a tailor.'

'I've never had complaints.'

'But you were prone to make them, I gather.'

'Happen.'

Marmion waited for a longer response but he got none. Burridge was prickly and unhelpful. Something must have drawn him back to the site of the tragedy and Marmion refused to believe that the man was entirely without sympathy. Burridge had to be mourning the employer whom he'd claimed to respect when first interviewed. Most of his working life had been spent in Jermyn Street. In spite of what Burridge said, it was bound to weigh with him. He might be free from any hint of sentimentality but he was not heartless. Beneath the bluff exterior, Marmion guessed, the tailor was deeply moved by what had happened to Jacob Stein.

'How did the two brothers get on?' asked Marmion.

'That were their business.'

'Not if it had an impact on you, and you've already admitted that it did. You told me that Mr Stone interfered too much.'

'I were being polite.'

'Who made his suits?'

'His brother had that job.'

'You were never asked to take over?'

'I'd have refused, Inspector.'

'Why is that?'

'Would *you* like to be his tailor?'

'I can't say it would be an appealing prospect.'

'It weren't.'

'Do you think he'd be too finicky?'

'I need to like my clients.'

'That lets Mr Stone out, then.'

'Oh, you're wrong,' said Burridge, sarcastically. 'He were my favourite of the two brothers. It's just that I'd have preferred to measure him for a coffin rather than for a suit. Question answered?'

'Answered with beguiling honesty,' said Marmion. 'While you're being so candid, sir, perhaps you'd answer this. Why didn't Jacob Stein stand up to his brother?'

'I wish I knew.'

'You must have a theory.'

Burridge smiled. 'I try to avoid foul language.'

'Did you know that there's been another incident related to the family? An attempt was made to burn down the synagogue they attended. What's your reaction to that?'

'First I've heard of it,' said Burridge, looking surprised.

'Are you sorry to hear the news?'

'What happened?'

'The fire brigade got there in time to prevent any real damage.'

'I'm glad to hear that.'

'Do you have no other comment?'

Burridge hunched his shoulders. 'No – should I?'

'Well, it does rather undermine your suggestion that we should take a closer look at Herbert Stone with regard to the events that occurred here. There may be some financial gain once the insurance claim is settled,' said Marmion, 'but that's not proof positive that he was in any way connected with the crimes. And a devout Jew like Mr Stone would hardly set fire to his own synagogue.'

'True.'

'So you can cross him off your list of suspects.'

'I don't have one, Inspector. You're the detective.' He adjusted his hat. 'My wife will be wondering where I am. I must go.'

'Answer this before you do, sir. It's a question that I put to Mr Cohen and he was unable to help me.'

'Nothing unusual there.'

'Howard Fine was appointed by Mr Stein then dismissed by his brother. Why?'

'Ask Mr Stone.'

'My colleague, Sergeant Keedy, did just that, sir. Mr Stone said that he simply didn't belong and was causing unease among the rest of the staff.'

'There's your answer.'

'He didn't explain *why* Mr Fine didn't fit in.'

Burridge gave him a shrewd look. Marmion had the feeling that he would not get a reply but he was mistaken. After thinking it over, the tailor eventually spoke, lowering his voice as he did so.

'Have you *met* Howard Fine, Inspector?'

'No,' said Marmion, 'he was interviewed by Sergeant Keedy.'

'And is the sergeant a man of the world?'

'I'd say that was a fair description of him, sir.'

'Then I'm surprised he didn't notice something about Howard. On the other hand,' Burridge continued, 'it got past Mr Stein as well. Howard were very good at concealing it.'

'What are you talking about, Mr Burridge?'

'Howard Fine talked endlessly about his wife.'

'Is there any law against that, sir?'

'No, Inspector. It just seems an odd thing to do when you're not actually married.'

'Do you mean that he was just living with a woman?'

'Howard were not interested in women,' said Burridge, sourly. 'Only in men like him.'

Careful not to advertise his destination, Howard Fine asked the taxi driver to drop him off outside a bank. He paid his fare and waited until the taxi had driven away before walking around the corner. Impeccably dressed and carrying a cane, he strolled gently along the pavement until he came to a large house with steps leading up to the front door. He paused to make sure that nobody was watching him then he went up the steps. The door opened before he even reached it. The steward was a dapper individual in his forties.

'Good evening, Mr Fine,' he said, standing aside to let his visitor step into the hall. 'We haven't seen you for a while, sir.'

'I had to spend a week or so in London,' said Fine.

After closing the door, the steward took his hat and cane.

'We're glad to have you back in Brighton, sir.'

'I'm very glad to be back.'

Keedy was startled. 'Are you telling me what I think you're telling me?'

'I'm only reporting what Mr Burridge said to me.'

'How reliable are *his* instincts?'

'I don't think he'd make a mistake about a thing like that.'

'Then I shouldn't have done so either.'

'You weren't looking for it, Joe,' said Marmion.

'There were signs, Harv. I should have spotted them.'

The detectives had met in a pub at the end of an eventful day to share a drink and compare notes. Glad to be back in his own clothing again, Keedy was in a good mood until he was jolted out of it by the news that Marmion had just passed on. He ran a hand through his hair and pursed his lips.

'That explains why Mr Stone dismissed him,' he said.

'Yes, I don't think he'd have any sympathy for gentlemen of that persuasion,' said Marmion. 'I fancy that the actual dismissal would have been nasty, brutish and short.'

'Then why did Fine have no recriminations about it?'

'That's a good question, Joe.'

'He gave me the impression that he was glad he left and that he'd found a better situation. I got the feeling that he might have enjoyed working in Jermyn Street much more if Cyril Burridge hadn't constantly bullied him.'

'Now we know why Burridge acted like that.'

'Yes, Harv, he doesn't sound as if he believes in tolerance.'

'Burridge wouldn't know the meaning of the word.'

Keedy took a long swig of his beer and smacked his lips.

'After the day *we've* had,' he said with feeling, 'that tastes better than ever. I don't know how you can drink whisky when there's beer of this quality to be had.'

Marmion raised his glass. 'I prefer it, Joe.'

They sipped their drinks and fell into a companionable silence. The pub was frequented by detectives from Scotland Yard and they could see several of their colleagues. Keedy was already close to finishing his first pint but Marmion was nursing his whisky and soda and taking only an occasional taste. It was Keedy who resumed the conversation.

'So where do we go from here?' he asked.

'I would have thought that was obvious.'

'You want me to interview Mr Fine again?'

'He needs looking at more closely, Joe. He certainly has cause to bear a grudge against Mr Stone.'

'Perhaps it was him who removed the wheels on that car.'

'I doubt that,' said Marmion. 'Everything I've heard about Howard Fine suggests that he's not a man to get his hands dirty.'

'He could have paid someone else to do it.'

'It seems like a paltry form of revenge.'

'Not if you're the owner of the car,' said Keedy. 'Mr Stone was livid, apparently. His car is a symbol of his success, Harv. It must have hurt his pride when he saw the damage.'

Marmion seemed to go off into a trance for a while. When he eventually came out of it, he saw that Keedy had finished his drink.

'My round, I think,' he said.

'Tell me what you were thinking first. You were miles away.'

'Oh, it was nothing.'

'It was something to do with the case, if I know you.'

'It was, Joe,' admitted Marmion. 'I was just thinking how much easier it would be if it was the *other* brother who was murdered.'

'Herbert Stone?'

'Yes – at least we'd have plenty of suspects. Everyone seems to have a motive for killing him. Jacob Stein, however, had no real enemies – or, at least, none that we've so far found.'

'Howard Fine might be a candidate. Then there's Burridge.'

'Both will bear closer investigation.'

'You know what I think, Harv,' said Keedy. 'If I was a betting man, I'd put money on one of those anti-Semitic groups.'

'Have you been sifting through them?'

'Yes – thanks to your brother. He was very helpful.'

'Ray gets to see the seamy side of life in his job. And people trust him in a way that they wouldn't do with the police. If Ray gives you information,' said Marmion, 'it's reliable.'

'With your permission, I'd like to send some men off to do some sniffing around. It may be possible to infiltrate some of these groups.'

'Choose them with care, Joe. We don't have the manpower to cover them all.' After a long sip of his drink, he rose to his feet and picked up Keedy's empty tankard. 'Let me get you another.'

'Thanks, Harv. Oh, by the way, who won the argument?'

'What argument?'

'You remember – the one that you and Ellen had earlier today when we called in at the house. When Alice announced her decision, you took it in your stride. Ellen wasn't happy about that.'

Marmion chuckled. 'She certainly wasn't.'

'So who won the argument?'

'I suppose that I did, Joe.'

'You mean that your wife has accepted the decision now?'

'No,' said Marmion, 'I mean that Ellen came to see that my strategy is best. Now that Alice has made her decision, it's the worst possible time to tackle her. She's full of enthusiasm for the idea. Any opposition would only encourage her. Give her a few weeks, however,' he went on, 'and she may be more vulnerable to persuasion. There's a long time to go before the end of term. We must bide our time.'

'You're a cunning old fox.'

'My strategy may not work, of course.'

'I'm sure it won't.'

'What makes you think that?'

'I had a long talk with Alice earlier on,' said Keedy. 'She takes after you, Harv. When she's set on a course of action, she'll stick to it, come hell or high water.'

Alice was a voracious reader. She liked nothing better of an evening than to bury her head in a book. Ellen did not interrupt her. Though she was sorely tempted to raise the subject of the Women's Emergency Corps, she held back on her husband's advice. While Alice was reading, her mother sat beside her sewing basket and repaired items of clothing.

She'd just finished putting a button on Marmion's trousers when her daughter looked up.

'Why don't you say it, Mummy?'

'Say what?'

'Come on – I know it's on the tip of your tongue. I'm surprised you haven't gone round to Vera's house and tried to get her parents on your side. If you want to discuss it, speak up.'

'I'd rather not say anything, Alice,' her mother told her. 'We've had enough rows about it. It's time for an armistice.'

'I couldn't agree more,' said Alice with relief. 'Thank you.' She saw the trousers. 'Don't you think it's time you taught Daddy to sew on his own buttons?'

'He's all fingers and thumbs.'

'I bet that Joe does all his own sewing.'

'Is that what he told you?'

'No – but it stands to reason.'

'Why?'

'He lives on his own. Who else would do his running repairs?'

'What about that lady friend of his?'

'I don't think any man would keep a lady friend very long if he expected her to do his sewing. It's not very romantic. Well,' said Alice, developing her argument, 'think back to the time when Daddy was courting you. How would *you* have felt if he'd turned up and asked you to darn his socks?'

Ellen laughed. 'I take your point.'

'In any case, Joe doesn't have a lady friend at the moment.'

'What happened to the nurse?'

'They came to the parting of the ways.'

'When did you discover that?'

'It was while you and Daddy were in the kitchen.'

'Did Joe simply come out with it?'

'No,' said Alice, 'I sort of drew it out of him.'

Ellen laughed again. Since she'd been a young woman, Alice had brought home a succession of boyfriends but they never seemed to last long. Ironically, it was the ones Ellen liked most who disappeared first. They found Alice too intelligent and assertive. Her mother had long felt that she needed an older man and the name of Joe Keedy had crossed her mind more than once. It was a friendship she'd be ready to condone but she knew that her husband would have objections.

'You like Joe, don't you?' she said.

'I always have, Mummy.'

'He obviously likes you.'

'Oh, I don't really think I'm his type,' said Alice. 'If I had been, something might have happened long before now.'

'I rather hoped that it would.'

'You can't force these things.'

'Well, at least you have a clear field now.'

'Mummy!'

'There's no need to sound so scandalised, Alice. I'm only being practical. If a man is involved with someone else, then it's wrong to set your cap at him. When he's on the loose, however . . .'

'I'm not going to chase *any* man,' said Alice, firmly. 'I never have and I never will. That's not the sort of person I am. Let's not discuss it any further. I've got my book to read.'

Ellen was repentant. 'I didn't mean to upset you.'

Hiding behind her book, Alice wondered why she felt so jangled.

* * *

When she said her prayers that night, Irene asked to be forgiven for entertaining such terrible thoughts about Ernie Gill. He'd always been given to boasting and she should have known not to take his words too literally. She'd placed far too much weight on the fact that the incident in Liverpool had occurred on the very day that he returned there. The whole city was full of people with a rabid dislike and distrust of German immigrants. Many of them had already been on the rampage. It would probably happen again. Why should she assume that Gill was guilty of murder on such slender evidence? It was grossly unfair on him. As she got into bed, she writhed in embarrassment at the memory of her visit to the Three Tuns. It would take a long time for her to live it down.

There was nothing sinister about Gill's arrival in London. Like many other people, he'd come to the capital in search of work. It was what she'd done herself, after all. While she had a sister to go to, Gill had a friend. Admittedly, Brad Thompson lived in a disreputable area but it was only a temporary arrangement. Once Gill found his feet, he would no doubt move to a better lodging. The question that gnawed away at her was whether or not she wanted to see him again. Irene would certainly avoid him in the short term. She needed time to get over the awkwardness of their latest encounter. Gill had his job as a barber to go to and she'd soon be starting at the toy factory. They'd both be far too preoccupied to enjoy much of a social life.

Meanwhile, she could settle into her new existence. She would soon make new friends at work and enjoy Christian fellowship at church on Sundays. It would be a full and satisfying life, free from the dangers of being torpedoed by enemy submarines. She still had nightmares about the sinking. In her waking hours, however, she kept reminding herself that she'd survived, a blessing bestowed on her for a purpose. That purpose – she felt humiliated to recall it – was most definitely not to make unwarranted accusations against an innocent man. Ernie Gill was her friend. It was time she learnt to trust him.

The car was parked in a yard at the side of the garage. It took them less than a minute to gain entry. Closing the double doors behind them, they loaded the vehicle with combustible materials. The man in the dungarees lit a cigarette, then took several puffs before holding it out to one of his companions.

'Here you are, Ernie,' he said. 'I think it's your turn.'

CHAPTER SEVENTEEN

Harvey Marmion had acquired a well-deserved reputation for being conscientious and few people arrived earlier at Scotland Yard than he did. When he got there next morning, however, he discovered that the commissioner was already at his desk and in urgent need of help. Summoned by a secretary, Marmion hurried along the corridor and found that Sir Edward was besieged by Herbert Stone. The visitor wasted no time on pleasantries. With an accusatory glare, he turned his fire on the newcomer.

'You're as much to blame as anyone, Inspector,' he said, puce with rage. 'You should have arranged protection for me.'

'Against what, Mr Stone?' asked Marmion.

'There's been an incident,' explained Sir Edward.

'Yes, I heard about the car wheels being removed.'

'This is more serious, Inspector. Some time in the night, Mr Stone's car was set on fire.'

'It was utterly destroyed,' said Stone. 'I left it at the garage to have new wheels put on and the windscreen repaired. Somebody broke in for the sole purpose of setting it alight.'

'I'm sorry to hear that, sir,' said Marmion.

'You are indirectly responsible.'

'I don't accept that.'

'Neither do I,' said the commissioner.

'The fire at the synagogue was a signal,' argued Stone. 'Whoever killed my brother is directing his aim at me.'

'That's a rather exaggerated claim,' Marmion pointed out. 'I know that you're closely associated with the synagogue but so are lots of other people. Each of them might feel there was something personal in the attack. My own view is that it's your brother's link with it that may have provoked the outrage. When I released the body to Rabbi Hirsch,' he remembered, 'he told me that Jacob Stein had been his most generous benefactor.'

Stone shifted his feet. 'My brother was a generous man.'

'He was identified with that particular synagogue.'

'So am I, Inspector – so am I!'

Stone was determined to portray himself as the victim of all the crimes so far committed. Marmion and the commissioner held their peace while their visitor insisted that his brother had been killed as a punishment for him, Herbert Stone, and that the attack on the synagogue and on his motor car were additional acts of persecution. When the man finally paused for breath, Marmion asked a question.

'Can you name any discontented former employees?'

'You already know them – Cyril Burridge and Howard Fine.'

'I was thinking about people who worked for you in one of your warehouses, sir. As well as being a successful importer, I believe that you have widespread business interests. Can you think of anyone you sacked who might have taken umbrage?'

'People often make wild threats when they're dismissed,' said Stone, flapping a hand, 'but they rarely act on them.'

'All the same, I think you should compile a list of names, sir.'

'That's sound advice,' added the commissioner.

'If you *have* become the target of someone with a grievance against you, then the culprit must lie in your past.'

Stone's brow crinkled as he went slowly through a mental list. Marmion took the opportunity to exchange a glance with Sir Edward, who was clearly grateful for his arrival. The shop, the synagogue and the car were connected by one thing – fire. The pattern was clear. What Marmion could not fit so easily into it was the murder of Jacob Stein. Was that a parallel crime or one obscurely tied to the others? Herbert Stone came back to life again.

'I can give you a few names,' he conceded.

'That would be very useful, sir,' said Marmion. 'And while we're talking about employees with a potential grudge, why didn't you tell me the real reason you sent Howard Fine packing?'

'I don't know what you mean.'

'You suspected that he was a homosexual.'

'Really?' exclaimed the commissioner. 'That is a surprise.'

'It was no surprise to me,' said Stone, scowling. 'I saw through his little charade the moment I laid eyes on him. For my brother's sake, I gave Howard Fine the benefit of the doubt. When the truth became unequivocal, I sent him on his way.'

'How did he react?'

'It was with a barefaced denial, Inspector. But it was no use. I had evidence, you see. I'd hired a private detective to find out if his phantom wife really did exist.'

'I'm not sure I'm following all this,' said the commissioner.

'He tried to pass himself off as a married man,' said Marmion. 'It was all a ruse behind which to hide his true sexuality. Not that I blame him for that. People take an unduly harsh view of men with those proclivities.'

'They should be hanged, drawn and quartered,' snarled Stone.

'I don't think that medieval barbarity is the answer, sir.'

'I was not having that fop polluting my brother's shop.'

'I understood that he was a very skilful tailor.'

'He was living a lie, Inspector. I exposed it.'

Stone made the announcement so grandiloquently that Marmion could imagine how much he must have enjoyed sacking Fine. He wondered how the tailor would have reacted. Instant dismissal would surely have had a profound effect on Fine and given him a strong motive to strike back. If that were the case, his target should have been Stone and not his brother. Marmion was confused.

'When he was interviewed by Sergeant Keedy,' he recalled, 'Mr Fine claimed that he lived with his parents in Brighton.'

'That was another lie,' said Stone. 'It's true that he lives in the family house but his father is dead and his mother is in a nursing home.' He smirked. 'My private detective was very thorough.'

'Perhaps you should have hired him to guard your car, sir.'

Stone glowered. 'I find that remark flippant, Inspector.'

'Then I withdraw it at once,' said Marmion, pleased to see the smile on the commissioner's face. 'It was only a passing comment.'

'What are you going to do about last night's outrage?'

'If you tell me the name of the garage, I'll send detectives there to investigate. Meanwhile, I'd advise you to exercise caution. There does appear to be someone stalking you.'

'I need a police bodyguard.'

'I don't believe that it's justified, sir,' said the commissioner.

'But I'm under threat, Sir Edward,' wailed Stone. 'You've seen what they did to my car.'

'That's tantamount to an attack on your property, Mr Stone, but not on your person. If someone had designs on your life, they'd surely have struck by now.'

'I agree with Sir Edward,' said Marmion. 'I don't believe your life is in any way in danger. When I urge caution, I'm really asking you to keep your wits about you. The best way to avoid further incidents is to anticipate them. I believe you already have private security at your warehouses. Extend it to your other businesses.'

'And even to your home,' suggested the commissioner.

'It's *your* job to do that, Sir Edward,' protested Stone.

'Our job is to catch the person or persons responsible for all the crimes linked to your family. Once that is done, you'll be liberated from any perceived threat.'

Stone got up in a huff. 'I knew I was wasting my time asking for help. Your attitude is disgraceful.'

'Before you go, sir,' said Marmion, pencil and pad in hand, 'I'd like the name and address of the garage. Then there's the list of people who may feel offended at the way you dispensed with their services.'

Snatching pencil and pad from him, Stone scribbled several lines then paused while he checked the list. He added another name and address then thrust the pad back at Marmion. Slapping the pencil down on the desk, he muttered a farewell and stormed out. The others sighed with relief.

'I'm so glad you came to my rescue,' said the commissioner, gratefully. 'Mr Stone was already here when I arrived. He seems to think that Scotland Yard exists solely to deal with problems relating to him and his family.'

'He needs someone to blame, Sir Edward. It never occurs to him that he somehow provoked the two incidents with his car. In his codex, *we* are at fault for not mounting a twenty-four-hour guard around him and his property.' Marmion glanced at the pad. 'I'll send someone over to the garage then have these names checked out.'

'Where did you secure that information about Howard Fine?'

'Cyril Burridge provided it.'

'I didn't know you'd spoken to him again?'

'We had a chance meeting in Jermyn Street.'

'It's made me look at Fine in a new light.'

'Sergeant Keedy had to revise his opinion of the man as well, Sir Edward. He noticed nothing untoward when he interviewed him. I've suggested that he talks to Howard Fine again. In fact,' said Marmion, glancing at the clock on the wall, 'even as we speak, the sergeant is on the train to Brighton.'

Dorothy Holdstock walked along with a spring in her step. Having her sister back home again had invigorated her. It was so refreshing to have someone with whom she could discuss things at the end of the day. She knew that Irene was, to some extent, convalescing after her ordeal. Such a distressing experience was bound to leave her nervous and apprehensive. Though her sister kept her spirits up remarkably well, Dorothy suspected that she was still suffering inside. She was glad that Irene had now found a job. Once she started that, it would give her life some stability.

Meanwhile, Dorothy had her own job to worry about. Since she had the keys to the shop, she had to get there ahead of the others. When she reached the front door, there was something she always did before she fumbled in her handbag. She looked in every direction to make sure that nobody was approaching. It was a precaution she took every time she opened or closed the premises. One could never be too careful. There was nobody about this time and yet the hairs on the back of her neck stood up. A warning bell rang somewhere inside her skull. She felt menaced. Someone was watching her.

Howard Fine was not pleased when he was intercepted as he left the house to go to work. Keedy got a very different reaction from him this time. Instead of being ready and willing to give any assistance he could, Fine was tetchy and uncooperative. Keedy observed that the man was wearing what looked like a Jacob Stein suit. It seemed a curious choice for someone who had left Stein's employ. At first, Fine tried to have the interview postponed but Keedy was insistent. In the end, they walked together to the men's outfitters where Fine now worked, so that he could invent an excuse to explain why he would be late that morning. He and Keedy then adjourned to a small café. Over a cup of coffee, the sergeant began to probe.

'Do you know where Mr Stein lived, sir?' he asked.

'What an odd question!'

'Could you answer it, please?'

'Yes, I do know his address,' said Fine. 'It's in Golders Green.'

'Are you aware that Mr Stone spends a lot of time there?'

'That's only natural, Sergeant. It's a house of mourning. He's there to offer moral support to his sister-in-law and her family.'

'Did you ever meet Mr Stein's children?'

'I met his daughter,' replied Fine. 'By the time I joined the firm, her brother, Daniel, was in the army and posted overseas. Ruth is a pleasant young woman.'

'You must have known that she was being groomed to take over the bookkeeping in due course,' said Keedy. 'She used to visit the office above the shop. Did you ever go to the office, sir?'

'No, I didn't. It was the holy of holies. Mr Cohen was the only employee who was allowed up there.'

'What about Mr Burridge?'

'He was kept downstairs with me. Where are these questions heading, Sergeant?' asked Fine, irritably. 'I do have work to do, you know.'

'So do I, sir. Your work only involves making a suit; mine has rather more significance. It concerns a foul murder and a case of arson, not to mention some ancillary crimes.'

He went on to tell Fine about the fire at the synagogue and the mischievous attack on Stone's car that left it with tyres missing and a broken windscreen. The tailor appeared to be shocked by the information about the synagogue but expressed no sympathy for the fate of Stone's vehicle. Instead, he was almost amused by what had happened. Keedy saw the smile flit across his features.

'You don't have much respect for Mr Stone, do you?'

'May I be frank?'

'It would be appreciated.'

'I loathe the man,' said Fine, crisply.

'Is that because he dismissed you?'

'It's because he invaded my privacy, Sergeant.'

Keedy could see the simmering fury in his eyes, something that had not been there at their first meeting. For his part, Fine realised that the sergeant knew his secret. There was no point in trying to deceive him on that score. Absent parents and a fake wife could not be invoked as a smokescreen. When the sergeant studied him, the tailor remained impassive.

'We had some trouble finding you,' said Keedy. 'Why didn't you leave a forwarding address with your former colleagues?'

'I had no wish for them to get in touch with me.'

'Were they so hostile towards you?'

'Cyril Burridge certainly was. The others displayed a more muted hostility – except Mr Stein, of course. He respected me.'

'How much time do you spend in London?'

'None at all, really,' replied Fine. 'The last occasion was when I came to see you at Scotland Yard. I must say,' he added, 'that it was more comfortable being questioned there than in surroundings like these. You didn't make me feel under suspicion last time.'

'Is that what I'm doing now, sir?'

'I don't think you came to Brighton just to see the pier.'

A new side to Howard Fine was emerging. He was petulant and waspish. His hatred of Herbert Stone was no longer concealed. Keedy was mildly unsettled by him. Since he had such a natural passion for the opposite sex, he could not understand a man who spurned it in favour of his own. Fine was calm, watchful and secretive. As he looked into the tailor's inscrutable face, Keedy had no idea what he was thinking. He fell back on a direct question.

'Are you sorry that Jacob Stein is dead?'

'No,' answered Fine, 'I don't believe that I am.'

'Why is that, sir?'

'It's because his brother will suffer as a result.'

'Are you sure about that?' asked Keedy. 'It's been suggested that Mr Stone might somehow be implicated in the murder.'

Fine was astonished. 'Who gave you that idea?'

'I can see that you don't agree with it.'

'I do and I don't, Sergeant.'

'You can't have it both ways, sir.'

'Then let me clarify my comment,' said Fine, leaning forward. 'I don't agree that Mr Stone was responsible for his brother's death. There's no reward for him in it and that petty tyrant is driven by the lure of reward. At the same time, however, there's something else you ought to consider. The man is certainly capable of murder.'

'What makes you think that, Mr Fine?'

'He made death threats to me.'

Keedy blinked. 'Did he do so to your face?'

'Oh, yes, and he didn't let it rest there. To prove that he was in earnest,' confided Fine, 'he had me beaten up one night by a hired thug. I was in hospital for two days.'

'Did you report this to the police?'

The tailor shot him a look. 'They're not anxious to help people like me, Sergeant. You should know that. Besides, I had no proof that Mr Stone was behind the assault. I heeded the warning,' said Fine, 'and got out of London altogether. He can't touch me down here.'

It was Alice Marmion's turn to do yard duty during the mid-morning break. Ordinarily, she would have spent her time preventing any arguments between the children from escalating into fights or picking up those who fell down in the playground. In fact, there were very few incidents calling for her attention, so she was given time to brood about what had happened the previous evening. The discussion with her mother about Joe Keedy had left her feeling resentful and she tried to understand why. She could not blame Ellen. Every mother wanted her daughter to marry a suitable man and raise a family. It was natural and expected. When she was younger, Alice had shared the same ambitions.

But the right man had failed to appear and children remained only a distant possibility. What upset Alice was the way that her mother subtly reminded her that time was against her. Most of her contemporaries were either married or engaged. Several were pushing perambulators. As she thought about it now, she realised that her age was the problem. She was too old to stay at home and have her life shaped by her parents. Loving and supportive as they were, they were also a handicap. Keedy's brief visit had given her great pleasure. She should have been allowed to wallow in her memory of it. Instead, Alice was forced into a spat with her mother. No relationship with a man could blossom with someone looking over her shoulder like that.

She had to move. That was the realisation that dawned on her. Alice had outgrown her family, yet stayed within its bosom. She needed a place of her own, even if it was only a bedsitter. It was something she could readily afford. Though she gave her mother a token rent each week, most of her salary was saved. Her expenditure was relatively small. Buying herself some freedom would be a wise investment. The longer she thought about it, the more convinced she became. There had been a time when Vera Dowling, who also lived with her parents, had suggested that they might find accommodation together. That arrangement had no appeal for Alice. Much as she liked her friend, she did not want her social life to be hampered by her. If she and Vera lived together, Alice could never invite a man to tea. Her friend would be in the way, another form of obstruction.

It was the moment to strike out on her own. On top of one important decision, Alice now made another. She would tell her parents that she was looking for somewhere else to live. It would give her freedom to grow. Her mother would protest but her father would be more sympathetic to the notion. He would also do something that made her tingle all over. He would pass on the news to Joe Keedy.

'Are you back already?' asked Harvey Marmion.

'It's almost noon, Inspector,' said Keedy.

'Is it? Where the hell has the morning gone?'

'Most of mine was spent on the train.'

'That was preferable to starting the day by going three rounds with Herbert Stone. He was camped in the commissioner's office when I got here.'

'What's his complaint this time?'

'It's a genuine one – someone set fire to his car.'

Marmion gave him an edited version of the conversation with Stone. He explained that detectives had been unable to find any telling clues at the garage but were still searching. Keedy was interested to hear that new names had come into play as potential suspects. The people concerned were being tracked down and interviewed so that they could be eliminated from the investigation.

They were in Marmion's office. He was behind his desk and Keedy flopped into the chair opposite him. It was the sergeant's turn to describe his morning. Referring to notes he'd made on his way back to London, he talked about his meeting with Howard Fine. When he mentioned the beating taken by the tailor, Marmion was roused.

'Why didn't he mention that to you before?'

'I think I've worked that out, Inspector,' said Keedy. 'He didn't want to tell me the reason he'd been threatened because it would have been too embarrassing for him. Now that I've had an insight into his private life, Fine was ready to talk about the incident.'

'Do you believe he was telling the truth?'

'I'm certain of it.'

'Well,' said Marmion, thinking it over, 'it certainly gives him a strong motive for wanting to hit back at Mr Stone.'

'He almost burst out laughing when I told him about the car.'

'Wait until he hears that it was set on fire.'

'I knew nothing about that when I spoke to him,' said Keedy. He looked at the sheet of cartridge paper in front of the inspector. 'What have you got there?'

'It's a plan of the shop in Jermyn Street,' explained Marmion. 'I did a rough sketch based on my visit there yesterday. Come and have a look, Joe.'

Keedy got to his feet and walked behind the desk. Standing behind the inspector, he peered over his shoulder at a ground floor plan. The names of the rooms had been marked. Keedy was surprised there were so many of them. Moving the sheet aside, Marmion pulled out the one underneath it. The second sketch was of the first floor of the building. Once again, rooms were named and the position of the safe marked in the office. When the two sheets were side by side, Keedy scrutinised them.

'What do you notice?' asked Marmion.

Keedy grinned. 'I notice that you'd never make a living as an architect,' he said with a grin. 'None of the lines are straight and it's obviously not drawn to scale. One of Alice's pupils could do better than that.'

'Accuracy doesn't matter. Study it with care.'

'What am I supposed to be looking for?' said Keedy.

'You should have spotted it by now, Joe.'

'There's no roof space – a building that size must have an attic.'

'That's irrelevant,' said Marmion. 'Besides, I couldn't get up there. I had to use a ladder to inspect the first floor.' He beamed. 'Come on, Joe. You're missing something very obvious.'

'Then put me out of my misery.'

'Count the doors.'

'Why should I do that?'

'Because they could give us the breakthrough we need,' argued Marmion. He used his fingers to indicate. 'There are one, two, three locked doors between the shop and the upstairs office.'

'So?'

'The man who killed Jacob Stein was not part of the mob that stormed into the shop. He wouldn't have been able to reach him.'

'He might have done so when the fire destroyed the doors.'

'That would have been far too risky.'

'Then that leaves us with only one possibility, Inspector,' said Keedy as he worked it out. 'The killer didn't *need* to get past three locked doors.'

'Your brain is clicking into action at last.'

'Why didn't we think of it before?'

'We didn't have my drawings at our disposal,' said Marmion, tapping the plans. 'Tell me why someone was able to wait until the safe was opened before he stabbed Jacob Stein in the chest.'

'I think that he watched and waited for the right moment,' Keedy deduced with growing excitement. 'The fire was lit as a diversion. Nobody went from the shop to the office because it was unnecessary. The killer was already upstairs in the building before the mob even arrived.'

'That *has* to be the answer.'

'It's bloody brilliant, Inspector.'

'I'll choose another way of saying that to the commissioner.'

'It sharpens the focus of the whole investigation.'

'It does, Joe. We come back to my original assumption that someone with a detailed knowledge of the layout of the premises has to be involved. Keys would have been needed to get the killer in there.'

'I thought Mr Stein had the only set.'

'Duplicates must somehow have been made, Joe. I doubt if he kept the keys on his person throughout the day. There must have been times when he went to the toilet or left the keys in his office.'

'David Cohen was the only employee allowed up there.'

'Then we must have him watched,' said Marmion. 'If I haul him in for questioning, it will put him on his guard. Put a man on him and we'll see just how loyal the manager really was to Mr Stein.'

'I still think there's an anti-Semitic element here.'

'Not if the culprit is David Cohen.'

'Then I'm inclined to think that he's innocent.'

'Reserve your judgement until we have more evidence,' said Marmion, sitting back and rubbing his hands. 'I think that we're on the right track at last.'

'Who the devil *was* the killer?'

'I don't know, Joe, but I feel that we have one hand on his shoulder now. It's only a matter of time.'

Irene Bayard could not be idle. After doing some chores around the house, she made Miss James a cup of tea, asked her if she could do any shopping on her behalf, then went out to catch the tram. It was well past noon when she headed for the shoe shop where Dorothy worked, hoping to tempt her out for a light lunch somewhere. Thrilled to see her, her sister was quick to accept the invitation. She took the two shopping bags from Irene.

'I'll put these in my office for the time being,' she said.

'Thank you, Dot.'

'I rather like the idea of being taken out for lunch.'

Irene laughed. 'I didn't say that I was paying.'

Having put the bags safely in the back room, and having given orders to one of her underlings, Dorothy led the way to the front door. As she stepped out into the street, she came to a dead halt and looked carefully in both directions before moving on.

'What's the matter?' asked Irene.

'Oh, it's probably just my imagination.'

'What were you looking for, Dot?'

'I'm not even sure that he was even there.'

'Who are you talking about?'

'That's the trouble, Irene – I don't know.'

'You're not making much sense.'

'I'm sorry,' said Dorothy with a gesture of apology. 'Something happened when I got here first thing today and it's been on my mind all morning. I don't often get feelings like this but they were too strong to ignore.'

Irene stopped and took her by the shoulders. 'Why don't you tell me what happened?'

Dorothy bit her lip before blurting out a question.

'Have you ever had the feeling that someone was watching you?'

'Yes,' said Irene after a pause. 'As a matter of fact, I have.'

CHAPTER EIGHTEEN

'Thank you, Ray,' she said, putting the lawnmower in the garden shed, 'but there was no need to bring it back so soon.'

'I always return things I borrow. Besides, Harvey has a lawn to mow as well. I don't want him wondering where his machine is.'

'He doesn't have much time for the garden these days, I'm afraid. Alice has taken over from him. She loves pottering about out here. Unlike me, she's got green fingers.'

'You have your own talents, Ellen.'

She pulled a face. 'I sometimes wonder what they are.'

Raymond Marmion had called in to hand over the lawnmower. Resplendent in his Salvation Army uniform, he looked as buoyant as ever. He was sad to hear the note of self-deprecation in her voice and sought to bolster her morale.

'You're a wonderful cook,' he told her, 'a supportive wife and a caring mother. That's three things in your favour and there are lots more.'

'I don't feel much like a caring mother at the moment,' admitted Ellen. 'All that I've managed to do is to upset Alice.'

'That's only because you care for her too much.'

'Do you think that I crowd her?'

'Not in the least.'

'It's what Alice feels, I'm sure, and she resents it.'

'Most children resent their parents at some stage,' he argued. 'I know that Lily and I irritate ours like mad from time to time. But they get over it.'

Raymond described some of the arguments he'd had with his children. He soon had Ellen laughing. It made her take a more relaxed view of her differences with her daughter. If Alice did join the WEC, it was not such a disastrous step. In some ways, she could see, it was an admirable thing to do. It's just that she would have preferred her to remain in the teaching profession. What irked her was the way she'd provoked such a sharp reaction when she'd offered advice about Joe Keedy. It had been a foolish thing to do, Ellen saw that now. She recalled how angry she'd been as a young woman when her own mother had tried to manoeuvre her into a romance.

Since her brother-in-law was there, she sought his opinion.

'What did you make of Joe Keedy?'

'I thought he was an interesting chap,' said Raymond. 'He's alert, committed to his job and obviously very efficient at it.'

'Did you know that he's captured an escaped prisoner?'

'Yes, I saw a brief mention of that in the newspaper.'

'Joe tried to play it down but Harvey was there at the time. He knows how brave and resourceful Joe was. The arrest took place in a river, so they got soaked to the skin in the process.'

Raymond smiled. 'And I thought that *my* job was hazardous.'

'It doesn't stop you doing it.'

'Nothing would ever stop me, Ellen – it's a mission.'

'I know.' She closed the door of the shed and took him back into the house. 'So Joe Keedy made a good impression on you, did he?'

'He'd make a good impression on anybody, especially the ladies.'

'Yes, he is rather dashing.'

'Yet I suspect that he puts work before all else.'

'Just like Harvey,' she said.

'It's probably just as well. If he was on the loose, Joe Keedy would break a lot of hearts.'

It was a timely reminder to Ellen that she and Alice were not the only women to be aware of his charms. Keedy was a roving bachelor. There had doubtless been many others who'd got close enough to him to entertain hopes of a deeper and more permanent relationship with the detective. He had always let them down. Ultimately, he valued his freedom. Ellen needed to remember that. In urging her daughter to go in pursuit of Keedy, she had been setting Alice up for an inevitable disappointment. It was another reason to reproach herself for raising the subject.

'I hope that I was able to help,' said Raymond. 'Joe seemed to think that I had. I don't envy him his task. He's courting danger.'

'You do that all the time, Ray.'

'Rude names and the odd missile are what I have to put up with for the most part, Ellen. That's not the case with Joe. Some of these groups he wants to investigate are full of violent men. They pledge allegiance to a doctrine that actually encourages them to use force.'

'Joe Keedy can defend himself.'

'It's just as well,' said Raymond. 'If he starts to probe too hard in the wrong places, he'll be in jeopardy.'

* * *

There were so many of them. That's what distressed Keedy. In their search for organisations with an anti-Semitic agenda, the detectives he'd assigned to the task had discovered several names to be added to the list given him by Raymond Marmion. Even more distressing than the number of groups was the propaganda that they put out. Keedy leafed through a pile of it and recoiled at its crudity and naked prejudice. Jews were reviled for things they could not possibly have done. There were absurd allegations of Jewish plots to seize power in Britain and impose punitive taxation. One pamphlet even accused them of being behind the sinking of the *Lusitania*. Every line of the posters incited hatred and the cartoons were grotesque. Anyone reading the literature churned out by the so-called guardians of British purity would think that the country was already overrun by Jewish immigrants and their network of spies. Keedy was appalled that such mindless bigotry still existed.

The reports on his desk suggested that most of the groups were more inclined to make vile threats than to implement them but there were those dedicated to direct action against what they saw as the relentless encroachment of Judaism. Of the names before him, Keedy took a special interest in the True British League. The headline on its leaflet was unambiguous: JEWS ARE A POISON INJECTED INTO THE NATIONAL VEINS. The leaflet went on to claim that every foreign office in Europe was controlled by Jewish moneylenders who had fomented the war in order to exploit it for profit. The charges were patently ludicrous but Keedy knew that there would always be those who believed them. It was time to get acquainted with the organisation. He had already dispatched detectives to infiltrate some of the groups that had aroused his suspicion. Keedy had saved the True British League for himself.

* * *

Sir Edward Henry was tied up in a series of meetings for most of the day. It was not until late afternoon that Marmion was able to see him. When he showed the commissioner the drawings of the shop, and told him of the deduction he'd made on the basis of them, he was given a verbal pat on the back.

'Well done, Inspector! You've explained the inexplicable.'

'It's only a theory, Sir Edward.'

'It has the ring of truth to me.'

'We shall see.'

'Let me get this right,' said the commissioner, recapitulating. 'You believe that someone was concealed in the building before that mob got anywhere near it. Where could he hide?'

'The attic is the obvious place. From that vantage point, he'd have been able to see that gang coming along Jermyn Street. Once the attack started and the diversion was created, he came down into the office, killed Jacob Stein and emptied the safe.'

'How could he know that the safe would be open?'

'He couldn't,' replied Marmion. 'That was pure luck. I think that he was only there to commit murder. When he saw that the safe had been left obligingly open, he helped himself to its contents.'

'The murder seems to have been planned so carefully.'

'Mr Stein paid for being a creature of habit.'

'I'm just grateful that his daughter was not there when the killer struck or she, too, might have been murdered.'

'She had a problem of her own to contend with, Sir Edward.'

'Yes – those two men lurking in the alley. It must have been a terrifying experience for her.' He touched Marmion's shoulder. 'I'm so pleased that you and Sergeant Keedy managed to apprehend Cochran so quickly. We can't have a rapist on the loose.'

'Cochran has another charge to face now,' said Marmion, 'and it's one of attempted murder. The sergeant and I will act as witnesses.'

'You caught him red-handed, so to speak.'

'I'm hoping that it will encourage Ruth Stein to face the man in court. If she knows he's certain to be convicted on the other charge, she has no worries that he'll be released to torment her again. That will reassure her.'

'We need to put Cochran and Gatliffe away for a long time.'

'I'm certain that that will happen, Sir Edward.'

'Good.'

Marmion updated him on the progress of the investigation. A detective had been deployed to watch David Cohen's movements. Other men had been told to gather more information about Howard Fine and Cyril Burridge. The people whose names were on Herbert Stone's list of potential enemies were also being contacted. Marmion had cast his net wide.

'What about Sergeant Keedy?' asked the commissioner.

'He's testing his own theory.'

'An anti-Semitic element is clearly present, Inspector.'

'He'll bring it out into the open. Since we were landed with this case,' observed Marmion, 'we've gathered a lot of significant evidence. What we lack is the connecting thread that runs through it and brings it all together. I'm looking to the sergeant to find it.'

He was there again. She sensed it. As soon as Dorothy came out of the shop, she knew that she was being watched. Though she looked in every direction, she saw no sign of her stalker. Taking out her keys, she locked up the shop then walked briskly away.

There was only one way to solve the mystery. Discounting the possibility that it could be a woman, she resolved to confront the man. It was a difficult thing for someone like Dorothy to do and she had to summon up all her courage. Eventually, she felt strong enough to take action. When she turned a corner, therefore, she didn't continue her walk along the pavement. She stepped into the porch of a house and waited. Twenty seconds ticked past. As she heard footsteps approach, her heart began to pound. Someone eventually came around the corner and stopped as if wondering where she had disappeared. Making an effort to control her nerves, she stepped out to face him.

'Are you following me?' she asked in a querulous voice.

'Good evening,' he said, raising his hat in greeting. 'There's no need to be alarmed. It's just that you remind me of a good friend of mine – Irene Bayard.'

'I'm her sister.'

'There – that explains it. I'm Ernie Gill, by the way.'

Dorothy relaxed. 'Irene has spoken about you.'

'I saw you yesterday and decided that I must be mistaken. So I came back for a second look today. You must be Dorothy Holdstock.' She nodded. 'There was just something about you that was so like Irene. I had to find out the truth. Did I upset you?'

'It was rather troubling, Mr Gill.'

'I'm sorry about that. Well,' he said, looking her up and down, 'it's good to meet you at last. Irene's told me a lot about you. What she didn't mention was that her sister was such a handsome woman.'

She was flattered. 'Oh, I'd never claim that.'

'Don't be so modest. I only speak as I find.'

'Thank you.'

'Irene and I worked together for many years.'

'So I gather, Mr Gill.'

'Call me Ernie – everyone else does.

'Except my lodger, Miss James, that is – she prefers Ernest.'

'She seemed a sweet old girl when I met her.'

'She is, Mr Gill . . . oh, sorry – Ernie.'

'How is Irene settling in?'

'Very well,' said Dorothy. 'She told me that she wished she'd moved in with me years ago. She only took the job with Cunard to get over the loss of her husband.'

'Yes,' he sighed. 'That really hurt her. I mean, he was so young.'

'She still hasn't fully recovered.'

Ernie Gill wasn't at all as she'd imagined. He was taller, thinner and older than the portrait in her mind. He had a pleasant voice and an easy manner, though there was a faint hint in his eyes of the intensity that Irene had warned her about. Dorothy's main emotion was relief that he had not been some anonymous stalker with designs on her handbag or, even worse, on her body. Gill was wearing a smart suit and was well groomed. He looked perfectly presentable and she could not understand why Irene had kept them apart.

'Does your sister ever talk about me?' he asked.

'Oh, yes. She's told me all about the rescue.'

'I wasn't going to let my favourite person drown. When I saw her flailing around in the water, I just had to go to her.'

'Irene is eternally grateful.'

'I simply acted on impulse, Miss Holdstock.'

'You can call me Dorothy – or Dot, if you prefer.'

'I'll stick to Dorothy. It was my mother's name.'

'I inherited it from an aunt.'

Gill was slowly getting her measure. It was not difficult to see why she'd remained a spinster. She had none of Irene's physical charms and was uneasy in the company of a man. Dorothy didn't know how to cope with flattery because she was so unused to receiving it. Gill found her dull and fatally old-fashioned.

'What else has Irene told you about me?' he probed.

'She said what a good friend you'd been to her.'

'You need friends on board a ship. Otherwise, voyages can get very boring, even on a liner like the *Lusitania*.'

'It seems such a coincidence that both of you decided to leave Liverpool and move to London together.'

He chuckled. 'Unfortunately, we moved here separately,' he said. 'If it was left to me, we *would* have moved here together.'

'Yes, she mentioned that you were . . . an admirer of hers.'

'I'm much more than that, Dorothy. You tell her. Oh, no,' he corrected himself. 'It might be safer if you didn't mention that we bumped into each other like this. For some reason, Irene didn't want me to meet you. Do you happen to know why?'

'To be honest, I don't.'

'Then let's keep this meeting as our little secret, shall we?'

Dorothy was uncertain. 'I suppose that we could.'

'At least you know who I am now.'

'Yes, that's true.'

'So you won't have to worry about your sister if she says that she's meeting Ernie Gill.' He flashed a smile. 'As you can see, I'm quite harmless. I'm just a nice, respectable, hard-working barber.'

'Irene said that you've already found a job.'

'Yes, I work strange hours but I really like it. I've made some new friends as well. In fact,' he went on, 'the move to London has been a success in every possible way – especially now that I've met you.'

Dorothy emitted an almost girlish giggle.

Joe Keedy could not go in one of the suits he usually wore. The address on the leaflet was in a rough area of the city and he didn't wish to look out of place. Returning to his flat, he changed into the tatty old clothing he kept by way of a disguise. With his flat cap on, he looked at himself in the mirror and decided that he could easily pass as a manual worker of some kind. When he set off, he had the leaflet from the True British League stuffed in his coat pocket.

It took him over half an hour to reach the Lord Nelson, a shabby pub with a fading image of the great naval hero on the sign that dangled outside. Keedy went in and showed the leaflet to the barman. After sizing him up, the man directed him to a door at the rear. Keedy knocked, opened the door and went into a rectangular room with beer crates stacked against one wall. Seated behind a bare table was a big brawny man in his forties with a gleaming bald head and a broken nose. Another man – younger, slimmer and whose wavy brown hair was parted in the centre – was reading a newspaper in the corner. He glanced up at Keedy then went back to his paper.

'What d'you want?' demanded the first man.

Keedy held up the leaflet. 'I came about this.'

'What about it?'

'I liked what it said.'

The man was cautious. 'Oh, yeah – why was that?'

'I hate Yids,' said Keedy with a snarl. 'I used to work in a factory that was taken over by one. First thing the long-nosed bastard did was to lower our wages. When I tried to organise a protest, he booted me out.'

'Where was this?'

'It was in Ashford, down in Kent.'

'What sort of factory?'

'We made furniture. I was a storeman.'

'What's your name?'

'What's yours?' asked Keedy, meeting his unfriendly gaze.

The man stopped to appraise him. His tone was hostile.

'We get lots of people who say they support our aims,' he said, 'but they turn out to be shit-scared of doing anything about it. You look as if *you* might be one of those.'

'Then you'd better ask Mr Liebermann.'

'Who's he when he's at home?'

'The rotten Jew who kicked me out of the factory,' said Keedy. 'He won't forget me in a hurry. His wife used to have this little dog she was mad about. She was always cosseting it. Well, she won't be doing that anymore,' he added with a cackle, 'because I killed the bleeding thing. It's the reason I had to get out of Ashford and come to London.'

Keedy heard the newspaper rustle slightly and realised that the man he was talking to was not in charge. It was the other one who was assessing him, listening carefully for any signs that he might be an impostor. Keedy walked over to him and pushed the paper aside.

'Since you don't want me,' he said, 'I'll find someone who does. I heard you were people who meant business but I can see I was wrong about that.' He turned on his heel and walked away. 'Thanks for wasting my time.'

'Wait!' said the man with the newspaper. Keedy halted. 'Why didn't you give a name?'

'It's because I'm as careful as you two are. The police are after me.

How do I know you won't pass my name on to them?' The big man guffawed. 'What's he laughing at?'

'Brad hates coppers,' said the other. 'He'd never help them.'

'Neither would I – unless they did what they ought to do and arrested every Jew in the country and deported them.'

'What do we call you, then?'

Keedy shrugged. 'Call me what the hell you like.'

'How long have you been in London?'

'I came here three weeks ago.'

'And is this the first time you've got interested in a group like ours and given serious thought to the Jewish conspiracy bent on taking over Britain?'

Unlike the first man, he had an educated voice and a shrewd gaze. If Keedy was to get accepted, he had to impress him somehow. He therefore claimed to have been part of a mob that stormed through the East End after news of the *Lusitania* tragedy broke. Having seen the police reports of the incidents, he was able to give accurate details of a particular attack. Drawing on information gathered by detectives, he talked about two other groups with similar objectives, saying that he tried to join them but found their activities were largely confined to holding public meetings and pamphleteering.

'If you believe in something,' he asserted, 'you should be ready to stand up for it. I've got no time for theories that never get put into practice. So unless you're the type of people who're ready to defy the law and use force, I'm off.'

'He sounds angry,' said Brad with approval.

'We've had angry people in here before,' recalled his companion. 'When we put them to the test, however, they turn out to be useless.'

'I'm not useless,' insisted Keedy. 'Just try me out.'

'There's more to it than poisoning a dog,' warned Brad.

'I didn't poison it. I strangled it to death with its lead. And if Mrs Liebermann had been there, I'd have strangled the old bitch as well.'

The younger man studied Keedy then turned to his friend.

'What do you think, Brad?'

'No harm in trying him out,' said the other.

'I fancy that he sounds too good to be true.'

'Then I'll be off,' snapped Keedy, looking round. 'If this dump is your headquarters, you're obviously short of cash. I want to join an organisation with the money to do something serious.'

'Oh, we've got money,' said the younger man. 'Thanks to an anonymous donation, we were able to buy a lorry. That makes it a lot easier to get around. And we've built up a healthy fighting fund.' He subjected Keedy to a long stare. 'Very well,' he said at length, 'let's put you on trial. Be here this time on Friday.'

'Where am I going?' asked Keedy.

'You'll find out.'

'Right – I'll be here.'

'We'll be waiting,' said Brad.

Keedy walked to the door and opened it. He turned back and addressed the younger man who was reading his newspaper again.

'You didn't tell me your name,' said Keedy.

'That's right,' replied the other, 'I didn't, did I?'

After a full day, Herbert Stone finally found time to call on his sister-in-law. He moaned about the destruction of his car and complained bitterly about the uselessness of the police. It was only after he'd ventilated his many grievances that he remembered his niece.

'How is Ruth?'

'She's still in a world of her own,' said Miriam.

'It's not healthy to be like that.'

'We've tried everything to bring her out of it, Herman.'

'Let me have another talk with her,' said Stone. 'I can usually get through to her. Where is she, Mimi?'

'Up in her bedroom – I'll go and fetch her.'

Leaving him in the living room, she tripped up the stairs. Her brother-in-law, meanwhile, took out a box of small cigars. Selecting one of them, he bit off the end and spat it into the fireplace. Then he lit the cigar and inhaled until it began to glow. A distant cry made him hurry into the hall. Miriam came running down the stairs.

'Ruth is not here,' she said in alarm. 'I've looked everywhere. She's just disappeared.'

Having started work early, Harvey Marmion habitually finished late, so it was a pleasant surprise to his family that he managed to get home by mid-evening. He had a welcoming kiss from his wife, then waved a greeting to Alice who was perusing a seed catalogue in the living room. Marmion followed his wife into the kitchen, which had a pervading aroma of cooked vegetables.

'What's happened?' he asked.

'Nothing much,' she replied.

'I can smell tension in the air.'

'It must be the cabbage or the onions.'

He lowered his voice. 'Have you and Alice had a row?'

'No, we haven't. In fact, I apologised to her for stepping on her toes a little yesterday. We're friends again.'

'So domestic harmony has been restored?'

'It is now that you're back home.'

He gave her a warm hug. Ellen had spoken too soon. Now that both her parents were there, Alice joined them to pass on her news. She'd refrained from telling her mother when she first got back from school because she knew that it would provoke an argument. Alice was relying on her father to respond more calmly and reasonably to her decision. When they saw Alice's expression, they sensed that an announcement was coming.

'Why don't we step into the living room?' suggested Marmion. 'There's less of a pong in there.'

'Cooked veg has a lovely wholesome smell,' insisted Ellen.

'Then I'll be glad to eat it when it's fresh out of a saucepan instead of having it the usual way – after it's been kept warm in the oven for hours.'

They adjourned to the living room and sat on the sofa.

'You're not at school now,' he said as his daughter remained on her feet. 'Take a pew – there's no charge.'

Alice perched on the arm of a chair and took a deep breath.

'I've been doing some thinking,' she said, 'and I reached a decision. I know it will come as a shock but I think we'll all benefit in the end.'

'That sounds ominous,' said Ellen, worried.

'What is this decision, Alice?' prompted her father.

'I'm going to find a place of my own.'

Ellen was aghast. 'You mean that . . . you're leaving home?'

'I feel that I need a little more space, Mummy.'

'But there's plenty of space here – especially since your father is at work most of the time. You've even got a free hand in the garden. What more space do you need?'

'Don't get so het up about it, love,' said Marmion with a hand on his wife's arm. 'Alice is not only talking about physical space.'

'That's right, Daddy,' said his daughter.

'Do you have anywhere in mind?'

'You're surely not going to encourage her, are you?' protested Ellen. 'I love having Alice here. Don't drive her away, Harvey.'

'I'm just respecting her right to do as she wishes.'

'Thank you, Daddy,' said Alice.

'So what's the answer?'

'I don't have anywhere particular in mind. Wherever it is, it won't be far away. It's not as if I'm emigrating.'

'This is Vera's doing, isn't it?' said Ellen. 'Mrs Dowling told me that she keeps going on about sharing accommodation with you.'

'That would be a big mistake,' observed Marmion. 'Not that it's up to me, of course, but Alice would get none of the space she wants if she moves in with Vera.'

'You're quite right, Daddy,' said Alice. 'I want to live alone.'

'Fair enough – I have no objection to that.'

'How can you say that, Harvey?' demanded his wife. 'Alice is our daughter. She belongs here. Well,' she continued, 'until she meets Mr Right and gets married, that is.'

Marmion smiled. 'Has it never occurred to you that she might stand more of a chance of meeting the elusive Mr Right if she didn't live under her parents' roof? Think how awful it was when I courted you and had to be grilled by your parents every time I took you out.' He put an arm around Ellen. 'Life would have been a lot easier for both of us if you'd been in digs somewhere.'

Ellen was dismissive. 'That's water under the bridge.'

'Your mother was so reluctant to let you go. You hated it at the time, yet you're behaving just like her now.'

'That's not true, Harvey.'

'We must be more understanding.'

'All I understand is that I'm losing a daughter.'

'Alice will probably be within walking distance.'

'It's not the same.'

'I may still be able to look after the garden, Mummy,' said Alice. 'Why not think of the benefits? You won't have to cook for me or do my washing or change my bed. I'm going to lighten your load.'

'That's not how I see it. You're running away from us. First, you defy us over joining the WEC, and now this.' Ellen was close to tears. 'Whatever next – that's what I ask?'

Alice continued to reassure her mother and Marmion added his own emollient comments but Ellen was in no mood to be pacified. For his part, the news had not come as such a shock. If anything, Marmion was surprised that Alice had stayed with them so long. He was glad that she felt ready to strike out on her own and could see the advantages for her. Ellen, however, could only see the disadvantages. Marmion steeled himself for a long discussion once they went to bed. His wife was not going to let the matter rest.

Irene had volunteered to cook the meal and had timed it so that it was ready only minutes after her sister returned home. They ate in the kitchen and compared their respective days. Dorothy said nothing about her encounter with Ernie Gill, though it was very much on her mind. After they'd eaten and done the washing up, they spent an hour or so playing cards. Irene noticed the difference in her sister. There was a muffled excitability about Dorothy that was untypical. When the game reached a natural break, Irene became inquisitive.

'There's something you're not telling me, Dot,' she said.

'What a funny thing to say!'

'Am I right?'

'No,' said Dorothy. 'You know me. I don't keep secrets from you.'

'Then why do you keep smiling?'

'We had a good day at the shop, that's all. It was the busiest afternoon for weeks.'

'I'm glad to hear that.'

'Let's play another game. It's your deal.'

'I thought you'd had enough.'

'I'm not stopping when I'm on a winning streak,' said Dorothy.

The cards were dealt and they picked them up. Irene could still see the smile hovering around her sister's lips but she accepted the explanation given. She was soon absorbed in the game, especially as her luck improved markedly. The odd thing was that Dorothy didn't seem to mind losing. That was unusual. She invariably bemoaned her fate if she was dealt a poor hand.

While Irene was concentrating hard on the game, her sister was preoccupied. The meeting with Ernie Gill had left her in a state of quiet elation, and not simply because he'd paid her a compliment. He'd interested her. Dorothy felt that she'd been given a wrong impression about him. She surmised that something had happened between him and Irene to make her sister wish to keep him as no more than a friend. Her curiosity finally got the better of her.

'When did you first meet Ernie Gill?' she asked.

'Oh, it was years ago, Dot. We met on deck. And no,' said Irene, quickly, 'it wasn't the start of a shipboard romance. I was pushing a grumpy old lady in her bath chair at the time.'

Dorothy shuffled the cards. 'When did he propose to you?'

'I've told you before. I try to forget that incident.'

'But he was paying you a compliment, Irene.'

'I suppose he was, looking back, and I must admit that I was amused by the coincidence.'

'What coincidence?' asked Dorothy starting to deal the cards.

'Well, it turns out that his mother was called Irene as well.'

Her sister gulped and her hands froze in mid-air. Gill had made a point of telling her that his mother's name had been Dorothy. Her good opinion of the man began to crumble.

'*What* did you just say, Irene?'

CHAPTER NINETEEN

Given the problems they'd had with Ruth, her disappearance was bound to cause panic. Herbert Stone joined Miriam in a frantic search of the whole house. They even scoured the garden. Ruth was not there and neither was her handbag. More telling was the fact that the window of her bedroom had been left wide open. It looked as if she'd climbed onto the roof of the shed below and lowered herself to the ground. Miriam was overwhelmed with guilt. In treating her daughter as a prisoner, she feared she'd forced her into a daring escape bid. As ever, Stone was quick to apportion blame.

'This is your fault, Mimi,' he said.

'I can't watch her all the time, Herman.'

'You should have been more vigilant.'

'I thought that's what I was being.'

'Why didn't you pick up the warning signs?'

'There haven't been any,' said Miriam. 'Ruth has been so dull and listless. It never crossed my mind that she could do anything as dangerous as climbing out of her room. What if she'd fallen?'

'That would have served her right,' he said under his breath.

In the hope that his niece had not long left, he ran out of the house and looked up and down the road. He even went to the road at the back of the property in case she'd left by means of the garden gate. It was all to no avail. By the time he got back to the front of the house, Miriam was standing in the drive. Stone was panting.

'I can't see her anywhere,' he said.

'Where on earth can she be?'

'If I had my car, I could go and look for her. But it's a complete wreck. And Jacob's car is still in that garage near the shop.' He scratched his head. 'Could she be with a friend, perhaps?'

'I don't think so,' said Miriam. 'Since that awful night, she's been afraid of meeting anybody. It's suited her to be shut away in the house. At least, it did until today.'

'When did you last see her?'

'It was no more than half an hour ago.'

'Then she can't have got far,' he said, looking up and down the road. 'The trouble is we don't know in which direction she went.'

Miriam was tense. 'You don't think she's going to . . . ?'

'No, I don't. If she was going to make another attempt, she'd hardly take her handbag with her. By the same token,' he reasoned, 'Ruth would take much more than a handbag if she was simply running away.'

'Why would she do that, Herman?' asked Miriam in disbelief. 'We're her family.'

'People behave strangely under stress.'

'Do you think she's done this deliberately to hurt us?'

'I don't believe she knows what she's doing, Mimi.'

She held back tears. 'We must tell the police.'

'I've lost all faith in them,' he said with a sneer.

'We can't let her roam about on her own. They need to start a search for her right away.'

He gritted his teeth. 'Leave it to me. I'll speak to them.'

They went back into the house. The telephone was in the hall. Stone was about to pick it up when a thought hit him. Miriam was now wringing her hands in anguish.

'This is dreadful!' she cried. 'Haven't we had enough pain to bear already? Why is Ruth *doing* this to us?'

'I'm not sure that she is,' said Stone, pensively.

'Ring the police and raise the alarm.'

'Yes, but what am I to tell them, Mimi?'

'Tell them that Ruth has run away, of course.'

'But *did* she?' he asked, worriedly. 'Did she go or was she taken? On a warm night like this, she'd have left her window ajar. It's not inconceivable that someone climbed up onto that roof, got into her room and seized her unawares.'

Miriam was distraught. 'Are you saying she's been *abducted*?'

'It's a consideration. When the synagogue can be attacked and my car can be vandalised on your drive, we have to accept that almost anything can happen.' His eyes darted and the veins stood out on his temples. 'Ruth may have gone,' he said, anxiously, 'but we mustn't jump to the conclusion that she did so voluntarily. She may have been kidnapped.'

Neither of them worked office hours. When they were engaged in an investigation, Harvey Marmion and Joe Keedy let it take over what was rightly their leisure time. If Keedy had important information to pass on, he knew that he could call at the inspector's house at almost any time without getting a frosty welcome. After making contact with the True British League, he felt that he needed to discuss his findings with the inspector. When he got to the house, the family had just finished their meal and were grateful to see him, if only because he relieved the taut atmosphere around the dinner table. Marmion was glad to talk about something other than his daughter's decision to move out. Ellen immediately offered to make their visitor a cup of tea and Alice was amused by his appearance.

'The last time I saw you,' she recalled, 'you were wearing some of Daddy's clothes and now you're dressed like a workman.'

'It was a necessary disguise, Alice,' he said, 'and at least this old suit fits me. When I put on your father's shoes, I realised that I could never step into them properly because they were far too big.'

'You'll replace me one day, Joe,' said Marmion. 'Who knows? You might even be promoted above me.'

'That will never happen, Harv.'

'You're the coming man. I'm one of the resident has-beens.'

He took Keedy into the living room so that they could talk alone.

'What was going on when I arrived?' asked Keedy. 'I thought I detected some tension in the air.'

'You did, Joe. Alice has decided that it's time to find a place of her own and Ellen positively hates the idea. I'm caught somewhere in the middle.' He gave a wry grin. 'Such are the trials of family life.'

'I'm on Alice's side. She's entitled to spread her wings.'

'Don't you dare say that to Ellen. It's a sensitive topic.'

'You can rely on me, Harv.'

When they'd settled down, Keedy described his visit to the Lord Nelson and gave his assessment of the organisation. He felt that it had serious intentions and was untroubled by inhibitions of any kind.

Whether or not it had been involved in any of the incidents under scrutiny, he was not sure, but he got the impression that the two men he met were more than capable of violent action. The scruffy pub that was its unofficial headquarters had made him think that the group was short of money and poorly supported. In fact, as he came to realise, the Lord Nelson was at the heart of an area in the East End where it was most likely to find recruits. People like Brad who lived cheek by jowl with Jewish immigrants were seething with resentment at their growing numbers and influence. He wanted his country to be reserved solely for those who were, in his opinion, truly British.

'Then it's no coincidence that they chose a pub called the Lord Nelson,' noted Marmion. 'Horatio Nelson was a British hero who kept hated foreigners at bay.'

'I never thought of that,' admitted Keedy. 'It wouldn't be quite the same if they met at the Black Bear or the Railway Inn.'

'Where does their money come from?' asked Marmion.

'They get contributions from bigots who think like them, I daresay. The one chap spoke about an anonymous donation large enough to buy a lorry.' He showed the leaflet to Marmion. 'And they print this sort of inflammatory stuff in large quantities. I'm told they have a sizeable fighting fund at their disposal.'

'Did they give you their names?'

'One was called Brad and he was clearly just a foot soldier. The other man pulls the strings. Like me, he chose to conceal his name.'

'And you say that he had an educated voice?'

'Yes,' replied Keedy. 'He spoke well, whereas Brad sounded as if he had a brain the size of a pea. He's the sort of character who talks best with his fists. His boss was very different. In fact,' he said, as the idea dawned on him, 'if you took away his suit and put him in a pair of dungarees, he'd answer the description of the man seen with the petrol can at the fire in Jermyn Street.'

He broke off as Ellen arrived with the tea. She put the tray down and told her husband to take charge of pouring. Then she gazed at Keedy with a blend of curiosity and wistfulness. After she'd left, he remarked upon it.

'That was a funny look Ellen just gave me.'

'It's much better than the hostile ones I was getting earlier, Joe. Hell hath no fury like a wife who thinks her husband isn't supporting her in the way she expects.'

'Thanks for the warning. I'll stay single.'

'Oh, don't misunderstand me,' said Marmion. 'I'm all in favour of marriage. I love it. But it does have its moments of turbulence.' He started to pour the tea. 'How does this group differ from the others that our lads have been watching?'

'It's smaller, more extreme and wilder in its denunciation of the Jews. If it ever got into power – God forbid! – it would initiate a series of pogroms. As it is,' said Keedy, 'the League is restricted to more modest targets.'

'Do you think that Jacob Stein's shop could be one of them?'

'I couldn't say, Harv. They gave very little away.'

'Are you going back on Friday?'

'I can't wait.' He took a cup of tea from Marmion. 'Thanks.'

While he poured his own tea, Marmion told him about his conversation with Sir Edward Henry and how the commissioner believed that the inspector had finally worked out how the murder must have been committed. There was something else to tell Keedy.

'You know that I've put David Cohen under observation,' said Marmion. 'Well, it's produced an interesting result.'

'What was it?'

'He was seen boarding a train to Brighton.'

'That's where Howard Fine lives.'

'There's no guarantee that Cohen is going to meet him, of course. It seems unlikely. We won't know the details of his visit until the man shadowing him gets back. But, if the two of them *are* in cahoots, it would explain a lot.'

'What about Cyril Burridge?'

'Oh, he's not linked to either of them. He disliked Cohen and despised Fine. In fact, I think you'd be hard put to find someone whom Burridge actually admires. There's iron in that man's soul.'

'How did it get there, Harv?'

'Search me,' said Marmion. 'I'm just glad that I don't have to work alongside someone as dour and unfriendly as that. Yet, by all accounts, Burridge is a happy family man, so he must be a different person at home. He lives with his wife and son, who – you won't be surprised to hear – is also a tailor. There's a daughter as well but she married and moved to Lincoln. There may turn out to be a connection between Cohen and Fine but I can safely say that neither of them would ever have been invited to the Burridge abode.'

They drank their tea and reviewed the case in detail. Keedy was about to offer a suggestion when they were interrupted by the sound of loud voices in the kitchen. Marmion was on his feet at once.

'The debate is still going on,' he said with a tired smile. 'I'd better separate the combatants before they come to blows.'

'Why not send Alice in here? If she's looking for a flat, I may be able to give her one or two ideas.'

'I won't say that in front of Ellen or she'll explode. But, yes, I will send Alice in for a chat. She needs to calm down as well.'

Marmion went out and the argument quickly subsided. Keedy finished his tea and put the cup back in the saucer. A moment later, Alice came into the room, distinctly shamefaced.

'I'm sorry about that noise, Joe. It was my fault.'

'You want to move on, I gather.'

'Mummy's trying to keep me here,' said Alice, 'but I've reached the stage when I need to live on my own.'

'I know that feeling very well.'

'By rights, I should have gone years ago.'

'That's exactly what I said.'

She peered at him. 'By the way, why are you dressed up like that?'

'I'm a storeman at a factory in Kent. At least, I was until I got the sack for trying to stir up trouble.' Alice was perplexed. 'I'm not serious. It was a story I had to invent to win somebody's confidence.'

'Did it work?'

'I hope so,' he said, 'or I could be in extremely hot water on Friday. But let's put that aside and talk about you. Ideally, what sort of area would you like to live in?'

'I haven't got that far yet, Joe. The way I'm feeling at the moment, I want to get out of London altogether.'

'This row with your mother has really upset you, hasn't it?'

'We both flew off the handle,' she confessed. 'I suppose that I'm to blame. I was so angry that I even threatened to leave the country altogether. I said that I'd go to the front as a nurse or something.'

'Hey, hold on,' he said. 'Don't *you* desert me as well.'

When she realised what she'd just said, her cheeks coloured slightly. She'd forgotten that Keedy's girlfriend had been a nurse and had left him to go to Flanders. Alice felt awkward but Keedy was not offended. He was feasting his eyes on her. The glow in her cheeks only added to her appeal. A slow smile spread across his features.

'I won't let you go abroad, Alice,' he said, softly. 'I like having you here. To be frank, I like it very much indeed.'

Dorothy Holdstock was in a dilemma. If she admitted that she'd met Ernie Gill, her sister would demand to know why she'd kept the information a secret for so long. On the other hand, if she didn't tell Irene about what Gill had said, she would be misleading her about the man. He'd lied about his mother's name to one or both of them. It was obviously a trick he used to ingratiate himself with people. Dorothy reproached herself for being so easily taken in. What was the real reason he'd followed her? And how did he know where she worked? She knew that Irene had not told him the address of her shoe shop. How had he found it out? There was another concern. Gill had clearly not meant to be caught trailing her. If she had not sensed his presence, how long would he have continued to dog her footsteps?

Not for the first time, she wished that she'd not been so naive, so ready to believe a man for the simple reason that he paid her a compliment. Gill was a plausible rogue. In essence, that's what Irene had been telling her all along. She had the sense to keep him at a distance whereas Dorothy had succumbed to his easy charm at their very first encounter. Instead of upbraiding him for daring to follow her, she'd ended up admiring him. She was being used. That was the point of it all. Gill had conceived such a passion for Irene that he was using her sister as a means of getting closer to her. He'd pressed her for details of what Irene had said about him. She was the only reason that he'd moved to London. After failing to woo her at sea, he was pursuing her on dry land.

Irene deserved to be warned but that could only happen if her sister confessed that she'd been deceiving her. Dorothy could simply not do that somehow. It would break the trust between them. It would also expose Dorothy as the impressionable and inexperienced woman that she was. Gill was cunning. In telling her to keep a secret, he'd made her his accessory. He'd won her over. Now that he'd been exposed as a liar, she felt that she'd betrayed her sister. Did she tell Irene the truth or did she remain silent? It was an agonising decision.

Ruth Stein had read somewhere that criminals always returned to the scene of the crime. Yet she was a victim. It simply did not make sense. Because of the vile memories it held for her, she had every reason to avoid Jermyn Street. What had taken her back there? The remains of the shop were illumined by the street lamp nearby. The place looked forlorn and abandoned. It was impossible to believe that it had once been a vibrant business. Ruth's gaze flicked upwards to take in the office where she and her father had been when the attack started. It was there that he'd met his death, although the full details had been kept from her. There was no glass in the two windows and the frames had been burnt to extinction. Her stomach lurched at the thought of her father's body being consumed by flames.

She had no idea how she'd got to the West End and only a dim memory of how she'd escaped from the house. Now that she was there, however, she began to discern a purpose in the visit. It was an act of confrontation, a determination to stand up to a terrible event instead of letting it dominate her. All that Ruth had wanted to do at first was hide her shame. Unable to cope with what had happened to her, she'd even considered suicide. That had been unforgivable and she'd sought ways to redeem herself. Facing up to her ordeal was, she dimly perceived, part of the answer. But it was something that she had to do on her own.

If her mother or her uncle had taken her there, it would not have been the same.

The rape had diminished her as a person. Having the courage to return to the place where it happened, she felt, was the first stage in the process of growth. Ruth had to rediscover her confidence and redefine herself as a young woman. She refused to spend the rest of her life cowering before a gruesome event. She had to get beyond it. Without realising it, her brother had helped. Daniel would be told the details of what had occurred that night. She didn't want him to come home and find her whimpering in her room. He'd be devastated that she'd tried to end her life but she might win back his love and respect if she demonstrated some spirit. In joining the army, her brother had shown bravery. It was time for Ruth to show a different sort of bravery, to prove that she could face a hideous experience in her past without flinching.

She walked to the rear of the building and stood beside the entrance to the alley. It was in shadow now. Only yards away from where she'd been assaulted, she wanted to walk to the exact spot but she began to falter. Ugly memories filled her head and her eyes misted over for a second. When she could see clearly, the alley was still there and so was the challenge. Ruth had to walk up it in defiance, as a means of boldly facing her attackers. Hands bunched tightly and with her heart beating like a drum, she took a first tentative step then a second, longer one. Though she was shaking all over, she went on with quickening strides, past the site of the rape and on to the end of the alley. The sense of achievement was thrilling and she felt a surge of power coursing through her. Ruth had gained a sense of control.

When she turned round, however, her elation evaporated. A figure had appeared at the other end of the alley, blocking her way. He was only there for an instant. In fact, he vanished so swiftly that she wondered if she'd really seen him. No longer afraid, she went back down the alley and out into the street. She felt proud of what she'd done but the fleeting encounter stayed in her mind. It was strange. Though she'd only glimpsed the figure in silhouette, she felt that she somehow knew the man.

It was two years since the Criminal Record Office had come into being. Initiated in 1869 and modified in 1871, it had originally been called the Habitual Criminals Register and was a list of all offenders who'd been convicted and imprisoned. Details were kept of their appearance, their crimes, their sentences and the dates of their discharge from various prisons. Photographs were a vital component of the records and, since 1901, fingerprints were also retained, thanks to the man who was now the commissioner. It was during his time as Inspector General of the Bengal Police that Edward Henry, as he then was, realised the importance that fingerprinting could hold in the fight against crime. His book, *Classification and Uses of Finger Prints*, had been adopted as a guide by the Indian Government and had led to the setting up in Britain of the Fingerprint Bureau.

'Where would we be without Sir Edward?' asked Marmion, looking at a set of fingerprints. 'He made our job a lot easier when he reminded us that each of us has a unique set of fingerprints.'

'Yes,' said Keedy, 'a set of dabs can be a great help.'

'Not that they're any use to us now, Joe. What you need is a nice clear photograph of him – assuming that he *does* have a criminal record, of course.'

'I'm certain he does, Inspector. You get a feeling about some people and Brad was one of them. He's seen the inside of a prison.'

'And he may well do so again.'

The two men were seated behind Marmion's desk as they leafed through the records. It was painstaking work but Keedy insisted that it would pay dividends. He was keen to identify the bald man whom he'd met at the Lord Nelson. All that they had to go on was a first name and a hunch but Marmion had learnt to trust his colleague's hunches. As he turned over another page, he remembered Keedy's visit to the house the previous evening.

'What did you say to Alice?' he asked.

'We had a pleasant chat, that's all.'

'Well, she was in a lovely mood this morning. And she was much more tactful with Ellen. Every time her mother tried to start an argument, Alice managed to calm her down.'

'I don't think *I* can claim any credit,' said Keedy.

'You perked my daughter up, I know that.'

'I simply told her she was making the right decision.'

'She'd need more than that to lift her spirits.'

Keedy beamed. 'It's the effect I have on women.' As a new face came into view, he took a close look. 'That's like him. In fact, it's *very* much like him but . . .' He shook his head. 'No, it's not him. He's got the same broken nose but the eyes are different from Brad's.'

'So is his name,' observed Marmion. 'He's Eric Hubbleday and he can't possibly be your man. Look what it says here.'

Keedy read the note aloud. 'Deceased – March 10, 1914.'

'Let's move on.'

As they continued to sift through the records, Keedy let his mind wander to other aspects of the investigation.

'Did you have a report on David Cohen's movements?'

'It was on my desk when I arrived.'

'What did it say?'

'Cohen took the train to Brighton, had a drink in a pub, then went to call on someone with whom he'd once worked.'

'Was it Howard Fine, by any chance?'

'You've guessed it, Joe.'

'What do you conclude from that?'

'When he talked about Fine, the manager wasn't telling the truth. Either both of them were involved in a plot to kill Mr Stein, or they're on – how shall I put it – intimate terms.'

'I thought that Cohen was a married man.'

'It's often the case,' said Marmion. 'When I was in uniform, I helped to raid a club in Soho. We went looking for pornography but what we found was a club for effete gentlemen. Almost all of them turned out to have wives and children.'

'Are you keeping the manager under observation?'

'Oh, yes – and I've got a pair of eyes on Howard Fine as well.'

'What motive could they have for killing Mr Stein?'

'One may well emerge, Joe,' said Marmion. 'What they did have were means and opportunity. Cohen had the keys to the shop, after all. He could have let someone in surreptitiously at night.'

Keedy was dubious. 'I don't see Fine as a killer somehow.'

'Looks can deceive. Think how many respectable-looking men have turned out to be ruthless murderers – Dr Crippen, for instance.'

As they talked, they continued to flick through the pages so that Keedy could study the photographs. Eventually, he slapped his hand down on a particular page.

'That's him, Inspector,' he said.

'Are you sure?'

'If I had any, I'd bet my life savings on it.'

'You were right about him having a record and it's not a very pretty one – assault and battery, malicious wounding and armed robbery. He was only released from Pentonville last year.'

'Do we pay him a visit?'

'No,' said Marmion, studying the face in the photograph, 'we have to catch him in the act of breaking the law. You meet up with him and that other man on Friday. If this True British League is really bent on destruction,' he went on, looking up, 'we'll be standing by to arrest the whole damn lot of them.'

'Does that include *me*, Inspector?'

Marmion slapped him jocularly on the back. 'You'll be the first we put the cuffs on.'

Miriam Stein was tugged repeatedly between relief and apprehension. Delighted that her daughter was back home, she feared for Ruth's mental condition. It was not in her nature to be so headstrong. In the space of a week, however, the girl had contemplated suicide, then climbed out of her bedroom and fled. Miriam had been overjoyed when a uniformed policeman brought Ruth safely back to Golders Green the previous evening. She'd also been amazed at how excited Ruth had been, accepting the strictures of her mother and her uncle with a quiet smile on her face. It was only now, after a late breakfast together, that Miriam was able to probe deeper into the mystery of what had happened.

'Why didn't you tell us where you wanted to go?' she asked.

'I couldn't do that, Mummy,' said Ruth, 'because Uncle Herman would have stopped me.'

'He might have tried to talk you out of it.'

'That comes to the same thing. He'd have got his way. I'd have been kept here and might never have been able to screw up my courage again. Don't you see? I had to go.'

'To be candid, Ruth, I *don't* see.'

'I had to overcome my fear of those two men,' explained Ruth. 'I was terrified of seeing them again in court when I gave evidence. I wanted the whole case to be dismissed. Then I saw how weak and cowardly that was of me, so I did something about it.'

'Yes,' said Miriam, ruefully, 'you frightened the life out of me and your Uncle Herman. He thought you'd been kidnapped.'

'I'm sorry about that, Mummy. I rather hoped that you wouldn't even notice that I'd slipped out. I hoped to be home before either of you even realised that I was missing.'

'We were on tenterhooks for hours.'

'I didn't mean you to suffer.'

'Your uncle was so frustrated,' said her mother. 'He couldn't go looking for you because he didn't have his car, and he couldn't use your father's car because that's still in the West End garage where the police had it towed to examine it. It was maddening, Ruth. However,' she went on, taking her daughter by the hand, 'if going back there helped you in any way, then I'm glad you did. I just wish that we'd known about it in advance. Didn't you trust us to understand?'

'No, Mummy, I didn't.'

'Why not?'

'I didn't understand myself until I got there.'

Miriam leant across her and gave her a kiss. When she sat up again, she took out a handkerchief and mopped up the tears that were forming in her eyes. She'd always believed that she had a close and trusting relationship with her daughter but the last week had fractured that illusion. Ruth was a complex and conflicted young woman. Adversity had reduced her to a point where her whole life had seemed pointless. Somehow she'd rallied. With no assistance from anyone else, Ruth had found the nerve to risk climbing out of the house in order to visit a place that Miriam could never bring herself to go because of its associations. Her daughter had somehow shrugged off those grim associations. She seemed completely restored.

'It wasn't just for my own benefit,' said Ruth, happily. 'It was for all the family. I wanted to make you proud of me again. I wanted you to see that I've got the strength to live through this. I'll get better,' she went on. 'I know it. I'm not going to let this ruin my life. I owe it to Daddy. It's what he would have expected of me.'

Bursting into tears, Miriam stood up and put both arms around her. The worst was over. The daughter that she knew and loved had come back to her at last. It was a miracle.

Irene was baffled. Her sister was so odd and nervous over breakfast that she wondered if she was ailing in some way. Dorothy insisted that she felt fine and left the house much earlier than usual. It was almost as if she'd wanted to evade scrutiny. Irene washed up the breakfast things and wondered what had provoked the strange behaviour. She continued to worry about her sister until the mail finally arrived. All of a sudden, Dorothy vanished from her mind to be replaced by someone else. As she read the latest cutting sent by her landlady, Irene felt so dizzy that she had to sit down. To make sure she'd not been mistaken, she read the piece again. There was no error. His name was there in front of her. She needed a nip of brandy to help her recover.

She was in a quandary and needed advice. Yet the only person she could turn to was her sister. Miss James was in the house but she couldn't possibly be told what Irene had learnt. It would distress the old lady too much. Dorothy was the person to help. Forgetting the strain existing between them at breakfast, Irene put on her coat and hat before venturing out. The cutting from the *Liverpool Echo* was in her handbag and its contents had lost none of their power to shock and frighten. They haunted her all the way. When the shoe shop finally came in sight, Irene almost ran the last forty yards.

Dorothy was astonished when her sister opened the door and stepped breathlessly in. She could see at once that something was amiss. One of her assistants was serving a customer, so Dorothy took Irene into the storeroom and closed the door behind them.

'You look terrible, Irene. What on earth has happened?'

'*This* has happened,' replied Irene, taking the cutting from her bag and handing it over. 'It's *him*, Dot.'

Dorothy read the item with rising horror. She could hardly breathe and prickly heat broke out all over her body. A sense of profound guilt burnt inside her. The article disclosed that the police conducting a murder inquiry in Liverpool were searching for a man named Ernest Gill.

'What am I to do, Dot?' asked Irene. 'He's my friend.'

'I know.'

'It must be a mistake. He'd never do such a thing. He swore to me that he wasn't involved. Should I believe him?'

Dorothy bit her lip and wrestled with her conscience. This changed everything. Her sister deserved to know the truth.

'I've got something to tell you, Irene,' she said.

'Have you?'

'It's about Ernie.'

CHAPTER TWENTY

Cyril Burridge sat on a bench in Green Park and ate the sandwiches his wife had prepared for him. His new colleagues preferred to have their lunch in a nearby restaurant but he spurned their company. Whenever possible, he liked to be out in the fresh air, especially on such a warm day. In his immaculate suit and homburg hat, he looked rather incongruous eating out of a lunch box but he ignored the curious glances he attracted. There was no escaping the fact that there was a war on. Soldiers on leave strolled past him in uniform with wives or girlfriends on their arms. Recruiting posters were featured on a hoarding. As he'd passed the vendor at the gate, Burridge had noticed that the newspaper headline told of more bombs being dropped on London by Zeppelins. The Germans were spreading their attack and causing grave concern in the capital. It was not shared by Burridge. He was more interested in tearing off a piece of bread and breaking it up so that he could toss it to the birds dancing around his feet. They pecked thankfully at the crumbs.

When someone sat down beside him, the birds flew away. He turned to berate the newcomer, only to discover that he was next to Inspector Harvey Marmion.

'Good day to you, sir,' said the detective. 'Your employer told me I might find you here.'

'I like to feed the birds.'

'That's a laudable habit, Mr Burridge.'

'Then why did you frighten them away?'

'They'll be back when they realise I'm no threat,' said Marmion. 'Those crumbs are far too inviting to leave.'

Burridge glared. 'What are you after this time, Inspector?'

'I want the usual thing, sir – more information.'

'Get it somewhere else. I know nowt.'

'I think you'd be surprised what you know. You just don't happen to think it's relevant. Tell me about Mr Cohen and Mr Fine.'

'I disliked them both.'

'How well did they get on together?'

Burridge spluttered. 'How should I know? I were there to work, not to watch the others.'

'Do you think Mr Cohen was aware of Mr Fine's . . . inclinations?'

'No,' said the tailor, 'he were taken in along with Mr Stein. I've got a sharper eye for these things.'

'Would you describe yourself as a prejudiced man?'

'Aye – and I'm proud of the fact. I've got my standards and no time for them as don't meet them. Howard Fine fell well short of those standards. I were glad when he went.'

As he fired the next question, Marmion looked him in the eye. 'Did you dislike him because he was a homosexual or because he was a Jew?'

'I've nothing against Jews,' said Burridge, angrily. 'I've spent most of my life working with and for them. They've always treated me fairly. No, Inspector, I'm not prejudiced in that way. When it comes to sodomites, however, then I'm very prejudiced, as every decent man should be. People like Howard Fine are a disgrace.'

'I daresay you passed on your low opinion to him.'

'He knew where I stood.'

'And did Mr Cohen share your prejudice?'

'Ask him. He does have a tongue in his head, you know. What I will say is that the manager were troubled when Fine were kicked out. I loathed Mr Stone, as you know, but I agreed with what he did. It's the only time Herbert Stone and me were of one mind.'

Marmion glanced down at the birds now hopping around only feet away from them. Burridge tossed them some more bread. They pecked away, sometimes fighting over the same crumb. Marmion was amused by their antics.

'I told you they'd soon come back,' he commented.

Burridge sniffed. 'I just wish *you* hadn't done so as well.'

'Do you find my questions so intrusive?'

'I find them dishonest, Inspector,' said the other. 'You ask one thing but you're thinking another. You're trying to trick me into saying what you want to hear.'

'And what's that, sir?'

'I haven't a bloody clue!'

Burridge's rebuff brought the conversation to an end. He began to wrap up the remaining sandwich before putting it into the box on his lap. When the Yorkshireman got up abruptly, the birds scattered. Marmion rose to his feet and fell in beside him. They walked towards the gate at the Piccadilly end.

'I'll come back to the shop with you,' he said.

'Well, it's not by invitation.'

'Really? I thought you were revelling in my company.' His sarcasm produced a throaty laugh from Burridge. 'Did you know that Mr Fine lives in Brighton?'

'I didn't know and I don't care.'

'What reason could Mr Cohen have for visiting him there?'

'Ask him.'

'They were hardly friends when Mr Fine worked in London.'

'How do you know?'

'I'm going on evidence so far gathered.'

'Then it's obviously insufficient,' said Burridge. 'People in the same trade congregate together. I'm sure it's the same with detectives. David Cohen were a tailor and so were Howard Fine. That's reason enough for them to meet in Brighton or anywhere else. There's another thing for you to ponder,' he continued. 'Mr Cohen holds a position in the Jewish Tailors' Guild. He's on the national committee. Even if he hated everything about Mr Fine, he'd do his damnedest to get him to join.'

Marmion kept pace with his companion's purposeful stride.

'Why did you become a tailor, Mr Burridge?'

'I had no choice. It were in my blood. My father were a tailor and so were my granddad.'

'And I believe your son is carrying on the tradition.'

'Oh, you've found that out, have you? Yes, Arnold is in the trade and so is my son-in-law, as it happens. Why are you checking up on my family, Inspector?' he said, resentfully. 'Are you planning to write my biography?'

'Every detail is useful, sir.'

Burridge was sardonic. 'Happen I should tell you about my Uncle

Reuben, then,' he said. 'He lives in Doncaster with Auntie Doris. They've got five children and a dog called Alfred. Then there's my brother, Martin, up in Scarborough, of course. Would you like to hear about the time he broke his leg on the ice?'

'All right, all right,' said Marmion, holding up a hand, 'that's enough, thank you. I hear you loud and clear.'

'Does that mean you'll leave me alone at last?'

'It means that I'll let you walk back to the shop alone.'

'Good.'

'But I'm glad that we had this brief chat.'

Burridge smiled. 'Did you get what you came for, Inspector?'

'Oddly enough,' said Marmion, 'I believe that I did.'

It was not until evening that they could discuss the problem in depth. Until then Irene sat at home with her mind in turmoil. Had her old friend been party to a murder in Liverpool? The dates tallied. On the day he'd got back to the city, Gill boasted, he'd gone out to attack a German family so far unscathed by the backlash after the *Lusitania* sinking. He'd later retracted his claim, yet his name was now linked in a newspaper to the murder. Irene tried desperately to explain it away, to exonerate him somehow. The article only said that the police wished to speak to him. They didn't describe him as a suspect, still less as a man on the run. And Gill hadn't behaved like someone being hunted. He moved around as if he had no qualms whatsoever.

Anxious to believe him, she was bound to take her sister's confession into account. Dorothy had told her about the encounter with Gill and about the way he'd sworn her to secrecy. Irene was shocked at her sister's dishonesty and chastised her for being so gullible. Two things, however, had become clear. First, Dorothy's unusual behaviour the previous day had now been explained and, secondly, Irene realised that the person who'd followed her and Miss James must have been Ernie Gill. Since he didn't know where Dorothy worked, he must also have trailed her. It was disconcerting to feel that the sisters were both being watched. If Gill really did have a job as a barber, how could he find the time to stalk Irene and Dorothy?

It all came down to the name of his mother. In stating that she'd been called Dorothy, he'd told a blatant lie and, in all probability, had done the same to Irene when they first met. That showed how unscrupulous he could be. Gill never expected that the two women would become aware of the deception. Now that they had, they felt cheated. Irene was seething. A friend she'd known for years had been revealed as an arrant liar with an obsessive interest in her. To get closer to Irene, he was even prepared to manipulate her sister. Yet his scheming didn't prove him capable of murder. The police could, after all, simply be after him in the hope that he might have information that could lead to an arrest.

When she heard the key in the front door, Irene rushed to open it. Dorothy came in with an expression of utter dejection on her face. She was so eager to resume the discussion that she didn't even remove her hat and coat. She simply sat on the sofa in the living room and grasped Irene's hands.

'I don't know how I got through today,' she said. 'I just couldn't stop brooding on it.'

'I've been doing the same, Dot.'

'What have you decided?'

'Nothing – I can't make up my mind.'

'You must report him to the police,' said Dorothy, firmly.

'What if he's innocent?'

'Then he'll be released to go his own way.'

'And the first thing he'll do is to come looking for us,' said Irene. 'If we tell the police his whereabouts, Ernie will be very cross with us.'

'He took part in that *murder*, Irene.'

'That's not what it said in the *Liverpool Echo*.'

'He's a suspect.'

'Not necessarily – he could just be a witness.'

'Go to the police right now. I'll come with you.'

'It's not as simple as that, Dot.'

'Please don't tell me he's a friend,' said Dorothy, scornfully. 'After the way he's treated the pair of us, you owe him nothing.'

'Yes, I do – I owe him my life.'

'He may have saved your life but he's taken someone else's. You read the report. That poor man was beaten senseless, Irene. While he was in hospital, he never even recovered consciousness. He just faded away. That's what Ernie Gill helped to do to him.'

'We don't know that for certain.'

'*I* know,' asserted Dorothy. 'If *you're* too scared to report him, then I'll do it myself. What was that address he gave you?'

Irene broke away from her and paced the room. Her brain seemed on the point of bursting. Arms folded and lips pursed, she walked up and down as she went over the arguments yet again. Eventually, she came to stand in front of Dorothy.

'He's got to have the chance to defend himself, Dot.'

'Let him do that in front of the police.'

'He needs to be warned beforehand,' said Irene. 'I wonder if I should go to the house again and speak to him.'

'That's the last thing you should do,' argued Dorothy. 'If he's a killer, you'll be an accessory. In warning him, you'd be aiding his escape. I can't let you do that, Irene. It's too dangerous. And there's something else,' she added. 'What if he turned nasty?'

'Ernie would never hurt me.'

Dorothy was curt. 'He'd hurt *anybody*, if he was cornered.'

Irene was more confused than ever. She didn't want to return to the house where Gill was lodging but she had a vague feeling that he deserved a chance. Irene had a sense of obligation that her sister would never comprehend. It couldn't be ignored.

'Well?' demanded Dorothy, 'what are you going to do?'

'I'm going to sleep on it, Dot,' said Irene. 'Everything may seem a lot clearer in the morning.'

Joe Keedy hated the delay. With the chance of some action in the offing, he was eager to get involved but had to kick his heels until Friday. When it finally came, he was in a state of high excitement. He was due to join members of the True British League that evening in what he suspected would be some kind of attack on property. At worst, he might get to arrest the leader of an odious organisation committed to violence against Jews; at best, he might be helping to solve the case that had been taxing them so much. Either way, Keedy stood to gain.

Harvey Marmion was more circumspect.

'Don't expect too much, Joe,' he advised.

'I have a good feeling about this, Inspector.'

'You could be setting yourself up for disappointment. They might have called off today's little adventure altogether, or you might get to the Lord Nelson to discover that nobody's there. What if they rumbled you?'

'Then they'd have thrown me out there and then,' said Keedy.

'It's a mistake to have high hopes, that's all I'm saying.'

'Fair enough. I accept that.'

'Thankfully, the commissioner has sanctioned the exercise. It's always good to have support from the top.'

'What if he *didn't* authorise it?'

Marmion chuckled. 'If I thought there was any chance of that happening,' he said, 'I wouldn't have told him about it. We'd simply have gone ahead.'

'There's that devious streak of yours coming out again,' said Keedy, laughing.

'I'm just being practical. Good results are what matter.'

'We're supposed to obey orders.'

'So was Nelson,' said Marmion. 'Luckily, he didn't always do so and achieved great victories as a result.'

Keedy grinned cheekily. 'Are you telling me I can disobey you whenever I fancy?'

'I'm telling you to exercise discretion, Joe. By the way,' he went on, picking up a sheet of paper, 'I had another report from the man I put on David Cohen. He's discovered something interesting.'

'Let me guess – Howard Fine is Cohen's illegitimate son.'

'There *is* a blood relationship between them, as it happens.'

'Really? I was only joking.'

'It's not that close. It turns out that the firm that Fine joined in Brighton when he left London is run by David Cohen's cousin.'

'Does that mean Cohen recommended Fine for the job?'

'Something of the kind must have happened.'

'Wheels within wheels, eh?'

'Yes, Joe,' said Marmion. 'The problem is that they keep turning faster and faster.' There was a tap on his door. 'Come in.'

The door opened and an attractive young woman entered with a folder. She walked to the desk and offered it to Marmion.

'This has just been sent to us, Inspector,' she said.

'Thank you.'

Handing the file over, she gave a polite smile of farewell and went out again. Keedy had not taken his eyes off her. As the door shut behind her, he gave a whoop of approval.

'That's one bonus of the war,' he observed. 'When I came to Scotland Yard, we only had male clerks. Now that manpower is scarcer, we've got something much nicer to look at.'

Marmion opened the folder and read the brief report inside.

'Forget her,' he said, standing up. 'I've got something even nicer to look at here.'

'What is it?'

'During an attack on a house in Liverpool, a man of German origin was beaten to a pulp. He died some days later. The police are searching for a man by the name of Ernest Gill.'

'So?'

'Someone walked into her local police station this morning and gave Gill's address. It's one that we've already come across, Joe.'

'When was that, Inspector?'

'It was when we looked at the criminal record of bald-headed Bradley Thompson. This man must be a friend of his because they live at the same house. He might well be a member of the True British League as well.' He gave the sheet of paper to Keedy. 'There's a description of Gill here. Make a note of it. You may be able to do our colleagues in Liverpool a big favour.'

Ernie Gill walked jauntily along the street beside his friend. They were both wearing dark clothes and Thompson's bald head was hidden beneath an oil-stained cap. They turned a corner and saw the sign outside the Lord Nelson swinging creakily in the wind.

'I like the League,' said Gill. 'They get things done.'

'That's why I joined, Ernie. I tried one or two other groups but all they did was talk and shove leaflets through letter boxes. The day after I came here,' said Thompson, 'we were painting slogans on the windows of Jewish shops. A week later, we were throwing bricks through them.'

'I enjoyed setting that car alight.'

His friend sniggered. 'Pity the owner wasn't sitting in it.'

They reached the pub and went in through the swing door. There were several people drinking in the lounge bar but they ignored them and headed for the room at the rear. As they entered, Thompson looked around with a smile of satisfaction.

'He's not here,' he said with contempt. 'I knew he wouldn't be.'

'Give him time, Brad,' suggested the man in the dungarees. 'I don't think he'll be frightened off somehow. Ernie wasn't, was he?'

Gill cackled. 'You can say that again. This is just what I want. I feel really at home here.'

'That's good, because we'll have plenty of work for you to do.'

'Where are we going this evening?'

'It's another commission.'

'Somebody must hate Jews as much as we do if he keeps on doling out money like this. What's his name?'

'I don't ask,' said the man. 'He gets what he pays for and we get some more cash for our coffers. We'll spend some of it in the bar here tonight.'

There was a general laugh of approval. As well as the man in the dungarees, there were two other members of the True British League. One was a short, emaciated, sallow individual in his fifties with a fringe beard flecked with grey. The other was a strapping young man with thick eyebrows meeting each other above a bulbous nose. Like Brad Thompson, he had the wild-eyed look of someone who was keen to exercise his muscles. While both men acknowledged the newcomers with a nod, they left the talking to their leader.

'I'll drive,' said the man in the dungarees, 'and Brad can sit beside me. The rest of you can travel in the back of the lorry. That goes for the new man as well.'

'He won't come,' said Thompson.

'Oh yes he will – he believes in our cause.'

'Lots of people do but they're too afraid to show it.'

'I'm not afraid,' said Gill, stepping forward. 'We need a group like this in Liverpool. Some parts of it are crawling with Jews, and Manchester's even worse.'

'The True British League is here to clean up London and drive the Jews out,' said the leader. 'One day, we may be able to carry the message to other cities. I've got an idea, Ernie,' he added, snapping his fingers. 'Perhaps you could start a branch in Liverpool.'

Thompson smirked. 'He won't be going back there in a hurry.'

'No,' said Ernie, laughing, 'I sort of outstayed my welcome.'

'The coppers are still looking for him.'

Without warning, the door was flung open and Joe Keedy stepped in. He was wearing the same rough apparel as before. He identified the man in the dungarees as the one to whom he'd talked on his first visit. Keedy recognised Brad Thompson as well but the other three faces were new to him.

'Here I am,' said Keedy, rubbing his hands together.

'Brad thought you'd be scared off,' said the leader. 'I knew that you wouldn't let us down.'

'I wasn't going to miss out on the fun.'

'Right, let's get on our way. Brad's in the cab with me. You're in the back of the lorry with Ernie and the others.'

'Which one's Ernie?' asked Keedy.

'I am,' said Ernie, stepping forward. 'Who are you?'

'I'm someone who doesn't want the country polluted by Jews.'

'That's all we need to hear,' said the leader. 'Follow me. We'll go out the back way.'

He took them through a door in the far wall and out into the courtyard. The lorry was waiting. While the leader climbed into the cab, Thompson went to crank the engine. Keedy clambered into the rear of the lorry and sat down. The others got in after him. After a couple of turns, Thompson started the engine then hauled himself up into the cab. The lorry pulled away with four men, two cardboard boxes and some cans of petrol in the back. As it swung into the street and picked up speed, it shot past a car parked in the shadows. Keedy was the only one aboard who knew that it would follow them.

The car turned into the drive and came to an abrupt halt. As the engine was switched off, the front door opened and Miriam Stein came out. Her brother-in-law climbed out of the vehicle.

'It's nice to see it back here again,' said Miriam, running a hand over the bonnet. 'I remember the day that Jacob bought it. He was so proud of his car.'

'It's a lovely smooth drive, Mimi.'

'We should have thought of it before.'

'Yes,' said Stone, 'it's the obvious thing to do. Since my own car was destroyed, I should have reclaimed this one from the garage right away. It just never occurred to me.'

'You've had a lot on your mind, Herman.'

'There's been one crisis after another. Talking of which,' he said, glancing at the house, 'how is Ruth?'

'She's surprisingly well. I still don't understand why she sneaked out of the house like that but she's come back almost refreshed. She's even eaten a proper meal at last.'

'That's encouraging.'

'And she's promised not to run off like that again.'

'I'll want more than an apology from her,' warned Stone. 'She put us through hell yesterday. I'll never forget the shock of seeing her bedroom window wide open.'

'Leave her be for a while,' advised Miriam. 'She needs rest.'

'What Ruth needs is to be under restraint.'

'That's the worst thing we could do to her, Herman. It was being watched all the time that made her want to get away. We took away her freedom. Ruth wanted it back.'

'And what did she do with her freedom?' he asked, irritably. 'She went gallivanting off to the West End. Ruth was asking for trouble. What was she trying to do?' he said, waving an arm. 'Get herself assaulted all over again?'

Miriam flared up. 'That's a terrible suggestion.'

'We have to be realistic. The streets are full of drunks at that time of night. Anything could have happened to her.'

'Thanks to the police, she got back home safe and sound.'

'Yes, but only after she'd given us a fright. I don't think you should be so forgiving, Mimi. We need to remonstrate with her. If I hadn't been so busy all day, I'd have spoken very sternly to Ruth.'

'I'd rather you didn't do that just now,' she said. 'Ruth knows she did wrong. Let's leave it at that for the time being.'

Stone saw the determined look in her eye. Miriam was asserting herself. After consideration, he agreed to back off from his niece for a while. About to go into the house, he was reminded of the last time he'd left a car on the drive.

'If you don't mind,' he said, 'I'll put it away in the garage. For some unknown reason, I've obviously become a target for someone.'

Keedy didn't need to trawl for information. It was readily supplied by Ernie Gill, who couldn't stop bragging about the way he'd helped to set fire to a synagogue, then destroy an expensive motor car. What he couldn't confirm was that he and the others had been instrumental in the attack in Jermyn Street. Quite apart from the man's activities in Liverpool, Keedy had enough to arrest him. Gill had freely confessed. Seated in the back of the lorry, it was difficult to follow the route they were taking. The vehicle lurched round corners and rattled over uneven roads. Keedy kept one eye on the car following them while trying to divert his companions from doing so.

At length, the river appeared on their left. The lorry then went through a maze of streets before juddering to a halt. Late evening shadows turned the buildings into massive dark blocks of stone. The area felt deserted. Jumping out of the cab, the leader banged on the side of the lorry. Gill passed the cans of petrol to him. Keedy watched as the other two men lifted boxes of kindling onto the pavement. When he got out of the lorry, Keedy was standing beside Brad Thompson whose tone was condescending.

'Keep your eyes open,' he said. 'We'll show you how it's done.'

'He wants to join in, Brad,' said the leader. 'Right?'

'Right,' confirmed Keedy. 'Where are we?'

'We're very close to a warehouse that needs burning down.'

'Who owns it?'

'A man named Herbert Stone – except that his real name is Herman Stein and he's a Jewish immigrant who ought to be driven out of Britain altogether with the rest of his kind.'

'Why not use the lorry?' asked Keedy. 'Why not drive up, start the fire then disappear fast? According to Ernie, that's what you did at the synagogue.'

'Ernie should learn to button his lip,' said the leader, shooting a look of reproach at Gill. 'It didn't work at the synagogue. The fire brigade got there too soon. We'll take no chances this time. The place is guarded. Our information is that there are four nightwatchmen on duty. Brad and the others will take care of them while you and me,' he continued, jabbing Keedy, 'will get inside and start a blaze.'

'I'd rather light the fire,' complained Gill.

'You stay with me, Ernie,' said Thompson. 'We'll knock out those nightwatchmen. That's why I gave you that cosh.'

The leader beckoned them close. 'This is how we're going to get inside the warehouse . . .'

Marmion had driven the car himself with a detective beside him and three more crammed into the back seat. They kept the lorry in sight and, when it slowed down to a halt, they turned into a street nearby and parked at the kerb. One man ran to the corner so that he could keep a furtive watch on the occupants of the lorry. Marmion had already guessed where they'd be going because he knew who owned a warehouse nearby. Herbert Stone was under attack yet again. It made their job easier. Instead of having to follow, the detectives could get ahead and prepare an ambush.

'This way,' said Marmion, gesturing to his men. 'We can cut through there and beat them to it. Follow me.'

They trotted down a narrow lane strewn with rubbish.

Keedy decided to make his move before any of the nightwatchmen got hurt. Thompson and Gill were each carrying a cosh, the older man had an iron bar and the younger one brandished a hammer as if dying to use it. Under his arm was a box of kindling. Keedy was carrying a large petrol can and the other box of kindling. The leader had the other two cans of petrol. Spread out, they moved stealthily and stepped into a doorway when an occasional vehicle went past. The warehouse came into view. They all knew the plan. Gill was to approach the building and distract the nightwatchman on duty in the gatehouse so that the others could move into position. When Gill had persuaded the man to open the door, he would offer him a cigarette, then cosh him when he was off guard. Once inside the building, they'd dispose of the other nightwatchmen while the petrol was splashed about and the kindling set alight. When the fire took hold, Keedy knew, there'd be no hope of stopping it.

Timing was everything. If he made his move too early, the detective might find himself isolated and he was no match for four armed men and their leader. If he left his intervention too late, a nightwatchman could be knocked unconscious. Keedy had to hope that Marmion and the others were at hand to come to his aid but he saw no sign of them. He began to fear that they'd been shaken off by the lorry as it twisted and turned through the docks.

The leader gave the order and Gill set off, ambling along and puffing at a cigarette. When he saw the light in the gatehouse, he paused to wave to the man inside. After a few moments, the nightwatchman pushed the window ajar so that he could hear Gill. They got into conversation. The barber was relaxed and unthreatening. He was so plausible that the nightwatchman was eventually tempted to open the door. Gill reached in his pocket for the cigarettes. It was the moment that Keedy had been waiting for and he sprang into life.

'It's a trick!' he yelled, running towards the gatehouse. 'Get back inside and lock the door.'

The man was baffled at first. When he saw Gill pull out the cosh, however, he didn't hesitate. Leaping back into the safety of the gatehouse, he locked the door and pressed the bell to alert his colleagues in the warehouse. Keedy, meanwhile, had tackled Gill with such power that he bowled him over and forced him to drop his weapon. Thompson was enraged at the betrayal. He charged after Keedy with his cosh held high but he got nowhere near him. Two detectives suddenly came out of the shadows to overpower him, relieve him of his weapon and, in spite of his frantic struggles, put handcuffs on him. Thompson was soon lying face down on the pavement with Gill beside him, also securely handcuffed.

The remaining two detectives used surprise to advantage, coming out of nowhere to take on other members of the gang. The older man was easily arrested and deprived of his weapon but the younger one was much stronger and put up a fight. Keedy had to lend a hand to subdue him. The leader had been quick to gauge the situation. When he heard Keedy shout his warning and saw five men emerge from hiding to attack them, he realised that it was futile to resist. They'd soon have to contend with four nightwatchmen as well. The odds were impossible. The leader therefore discarded the cans of petrol and took to his heels.

Harvey Marmion was after him at once. Having seen the group

approaching in the gloom, he'd picked out the leader from the way that he was conveying his orders with gestures. When the man fled, Marmion ran in pursuit, their footsteps echoing along the empty streets. The leader was obviously heading for the lorry. Marmion had to reach him before he could start the vehicle. Pushing himself to the limit, he tried to ignore the burning sensation in his lungs and the jabbing pain in his legs. He was determined to get his man.

The leader heard the footsteps getting closer. When he reached the lorry, he swung round and saw Marmion haring towards him. There was no time to escape in the lorry. Instead he grabbed the starting handle and held it up menacingly. It made the detective slow to a walking pace.

'I'm Detective Inspector Marmion of Scotland Yard,' he said, panting, 'and I've come to place you under arrest. The new member who joined the True British League the other night was my colleague, Sergeant Keedy.'

'Stand back,' warned the man, waving the starting handle.

'Put that down, sir – there's no way out.'

'At least I can spill a little blood before I'm caught.'

As Marmion came to a halt, two of his men sprinted around the corner to help him. They slowed down when they saw what was happening. On a command from Marmion, the detectives fanned out so that they formed a semicircle around the leader. With his back to the lorry and three detectives in front of him, the man seemed to give up. The hand with the weapon dropped to his side and he sagged in defeat. Marmion wasn't fooled. As he stepped forward to arrest him, he knew that the man would resist. When the inspector got close, the leader suddenly lashed at him with the starting handle. Anticipating the move, Marmion ducked beneath the weapon, diving into his midriff and slamming him hard against the front of the lorry. The other detectives moved in quickly to overpower the man and hold him while Marmion snapped on the handcuffs. He took a close look at the leader of the organisation. The dungarees and flat cap suggested a workman but his face belonged to a different class altogether.

'Are you the leader of the True British League?' asked Marmion.

The man was defiant. 'I'm proud to hold that title.'

'Your loathsome organisation has just been dissolved.'

'Not before we had our triumphs.'

'Was one of them in Jermyn Street, by any chance?'

'Yes, Inspector – we burnt some Jews out of business.'

'Who put you up to it?'

'Somebody who hates them for what they've done to this country and who believes in our mission to drive out the scum.'

'It was the same man who sponsored tonight's attack,' said Keedy, joining them with one hand on the shoulder of a forlorn Gill. 'According to Ernie here, they were paid by someone to set fire to the synagogue and to destroy Mr Stone's car.'

Marmion rounded on the leader. 'Who was your paymaster?'

'I don't know, Inspector,' replied the man.

'He's as guilty as you are. Do you want to take the rap while he goes free? That seems very unfair on you. Who is he?'

'God knows.'

'He must have a name.'

'He never told me what it was.' Marmion looked sceptical. 'That's the truth, I swear it. He just handed over money and gave us orders. We enjoyed working for him because he thought like us.'

'Tell us something about him,' urged Keedy.

'Yes,' added Marmion. 'How old was he? What did he look like? How did he dress? Describe his voice. Was he a Londoner?'

'Oh no,' said the man. 'He came from somewhere up North.'

The telephone call transformed him. When he came back into the room, Herbert Stone was actually beaming. Ruth and her mother were astonished by the dramatic change in his demeanour.

'What's happened?' asked Miriam.

'One of my warehouses was going to be burnt down,' he said, 'but the police foiled the attack. They've caught the men responsible. Inspector Marmion has finally got something right.'

'That *is* good news, Herman.'

'I want all the details. You'll have to excuse me while I drive over there. Goodnight, Ruth.'

'Goodnight, Uncle Herman.'

Miriam went out to see her brother-in-law off and left Ruth alone. Something had been puzzling her ever since she'd got back from her visit to the West End. She'd spent hours racking her brain for an answer that would simply not materialise. As she tried to solve the mystery once again, she thought of the figure she'd seen in profile at the end of the alley. Though there was something familiar about his outline, she still couldn't place him. It wasn't a close acquaintance but someone she'd met only briefly. Ruth went through a list of names in her head but none of them fitted the man in the alley.

Her mother came back into the room, smiling for the first time since the murder of her husband. Miriam was buoyed up by the news that arrests had finally been made.

'It's taken such a load off my mind,' she said with relief.

Ruth was too preoccupied to hear her. As she concentrated hard on the problem that had been vexing her, a light gradually illumined the figure in the dark alley.

'I know who it was now, Mummy,' she cried in delight. 'The man who watched me last night was Mr Burridge!'

Cyril Burridge and his son had dined in style at the Café Royal. As it had been a special celebration, no expense had been spared. Because of the nature of the celebration, Burridge's wife had been excluded. She was quite unaware of what her husband and son had done. They, however, were savouring their success.

'We're making the bastard sweat,' said Burridge, gleefully. 'I'll enjoy reading newspaper reports of the destruction of his warehouse.'

'Aye,' agreed his son, 'so will I.'

Arnold Burridge was a younger version of his father with the same build, facial features and mannerisms. They wore suits that they'd actually made for each other and seemed quite at ease in the plush ambience of the restaurant.

'Best meal I've had in ages,' said Burridge, 'though I still prefer a sandwich in Green Park.' He patted his stomach. 'Less fattening.'

'What do we do next, Dad?'

'Nothing at all, son.'

'But you talked about going for his house.'

'That can wait, Arnold. He'll be on the alert now. Let a few weeks pass before we strike again. Stone will start to think he's safe. That's the time to hit him.'

'I still think we should get rid of him altogether,' said Arnold.

'Oh, no – that would be letting him off the hook. I'm going to keep the swine alive so that we can make him *suffer*.'

He called for the bill, paid it and left a generous tip. Then the two of them got up and headed for the door. As they came down the steps into Regent Street, they saw a car draw up at the kerb. Burridge took no notice of it until Marmion and Keedy got out and intercepted them on the pavement. Marmion raised his hat.

'Good evening, sir,' he said, glancing at the Café Royal. 'This is a step up from a park bench, isn't it?' He turned to Arnold. 'This is your son, I gather. When we called at the house, we were told that you'd be here.' Burridge was silent. 'Well, since your father won't introduce us, Arnold, we'll have to do it ourselves. I'm Inspector Marmion and this,' he went on, indicating his companion, 'is Sergeant Keedy.'

'We'd like you to accompany us to Scotland Yard,' said Keedy.

'Why?' demanded Burridge.

'There are lots of reasons, sir. We could start off by discussing a fire at Mr Stone's warehouse that never took place because we were able to arrest the people you paid to start it.'

Arnold was startled but Burridge remained cool.

'I've no idea what you're talking about, Sergeant,' he said.

'Then let's try something else,' suggested Marmion. 'We can talk about the murder of Jacob Stein by someone who remained concealed on the premises until the mob arrived.' His eyes flicked to Arnold. 'We've every reason to believe that *you* were the killer.'

Burridge turned white and Arnold immediately looked for an escape. Pushing Marmion away with both hands, he darted off along the pavement, dodging people as he did so. Keedy was quickly in pursuit. Arnold was young and relatively fit but he'd just eaten a large meal and drunk a lot of champagne. He soon felt the effects of his indulgence. Keedy was gaining on him with every stride. In desperation, the tailor dashed across the road and almost collided with a van. Keedy went after him. By the time Arnold turned into Piccadilly, the sergeant was close enough to hurl himself forward onto the tailor's back, causing him to stagger then fall forwards to the ground. His forehead hit the pavement with a thud and he was completely dazed. Before he knew what was happening, Arnold was handcuffed and lifted to his feet. Keedy marched him back to the car in which an ashen Burridge was already sitting. A night of celebration had turned into a day of reckoning.

Eating out was a rare treat for Ellen Marmion. The restaurant could not compete with the Café Royal but the meal was delicious and, more importantly, she didn't have to cook it. The wine was exceptional. Also at the table were her husband, her daughter and Joe Keedy. It was the evening after the investigation had finally been concluded and all the loose ends had at last been tied up.

'The commissioner was thrilled with our success,' said Marmion, 'and couldn't stop congratulating us.'

'Who actually committed the murder?' asked Alice.

'It was Arnold Burridge, whose father used to work at the shop. It turns out that Arnold was due to join him there but was turned down at the last moment. That really rankled with Cyril Burridge. It was the latest in a long line of broken promises.'

'Yes,' said Keedy, taking over. 'Burridge was without question the finest tailor there and Mr Stein knew it. He offered to take him into partnership and bring Arnold into the firm as well. Neither of those things happened.'

'Why not?' asked Ellen.

'They believed it was because Jacob Stein had betrayed them. Wanting their revenge, they tailored what they thought was a perfect murder. Aware of the riots caused by the *Lusitania* tragedy, Burridge hired some extremists called the True British League to loot and burn down the premises. His son, meanwhile, was hidden in the attic, waiting for his chance to come down and stab Mr Stein to death.

'If he'd used a gun,' explained Marmion, 'the shot would have been heard, so he chose a knife instead. He'd got into the premises at night with duplicate keys made from David Cohen's set. Cyril Burridge had "borrowed" them when the manager wasn't looking.'

'They planned ahead very carefully,' said Keedy. 'Arnold waited until Ruth Stein had run out of the office before he went into it and murdered her father. And he had a piece of extraordinary luck.'

'The safe was open,' continued Marmion, 'so he helped himself to the contents. He not only got away with a lot of money, he also took documents that proved Mr Stein was no longer the sole proprietor of the firm. He'd been bought out by his brother, who made all decisions affecting the business from the shadows.'

'I see,' said Alice. 'It was Mr Stone who prevented Mr Burridge from becoming a partner. He refused to promote him because he wasn't a Jew. '

'He also refused to give him a large pay rise that had been promised as a reward for long service.'

'What a dreadful man!'

'The Burridges didn't realise how dreadful he was until they read through the documents in the safe. Stone was the real villain, not his brother. From that point on,' said Marmion, 'they turned their attention to Herbert Stone. With the money from the safe, they were able to employ the True British League again. Its members would stop at nothing, as Joe can tell you.'

'I joined them myself for a few days,' recalled Keedy, 'and I can't say I liked it. They were vile people, led by a disgraced lawyer, Simon Higlett, who'd fallen foul of his Jewish colleagues and blamed them for all the things he did wrong. He and his cronies got their pleasure from attacking Jewish families indiscriminately. Some of the leaflets they put out were disgusting. They made me feel sick. Thank God we've stopped them in their tracks.'

'What will happen to them, Joe?' wondered Alice.

'Four of them will serve long prison sentences for arson,' he replied, 'and Ernie Gill will go back to Liverpool to stand trial for murder.'

'Cyril and Arnold Burridge will be hanged,' said Marmion.

'When did you suspect *them*, Daddy?'

'There were two things, Alice. I caught Burridge looking at the burnt-out building with an air of satisfaction when he had no reason to be there. The second thing was his smugness. I met him in Green Park today and he had the complacency of a man so certain he can't be linked to the crimes that he can afford to be rude to the detective in charge of the investigation. I felt taunted,' said Marmion, 'and that confirmed my suspicions.'

'Think of the wife,' said Ellen with a rush of sympathy. 'I can't believe that Mrs Burridge was involved, yet she has to watch her husband and her son being sent to the gallows. How could any woman cope with two horrible blows like that?'

'You could do it,' teased Marmion. 'After all, it's no worse than having a daughter who joins the Women's Emergency Corps and leaves home. Those were two horrible blows for *you*.'

'Harvey!' exclaimed Ellen, slapping him playfully.

The dessert course arrived and they started to eat it. Marmion enjoyed his pudding but, after the excitement of the investigation, he felt rather flat. Keedy had shared his sense of disappointment but his spirits were soon revived when his foot accidentally nudged Alice's toe under the table. Instead of moving her foot back, she kept it where it was, nestling against his shoe. The meal was suddenly operating at two levels. Four of them were joining in a pleasant celebration and two of them had started a silent dialogue of their own below the table.

Marmion raised his glass. 'I think we should toast Alice,' he said. 'She's made two momentous decisions in the past week and we should wish her well in her new life.'

'I'll drink to that,' said Ellen, snatching up her glass and making it clear that she had no recriminations about what her daughter had decided. 'To Alice and her future!'

'To Alice and her future,' echoed the men in tandem.

'Thank you,' said Alice, laughing happily.

'We'll support you in whatever you do,' said Marmion.

'Yes,' said Ellen, warmly, 'and I'm sorry if I was too maternal. I promise that I won't try to interfere again. I've learnt my lesson, Alice. I can't live your life for you.'

Keedy wondered what Ellen would think if she could see below the table. Alice had just kicked off her shoe and was stroking his ankle with her foot. He was content. He'd not only joined in the toast to Alice's future, he was determined to be a major part of it.

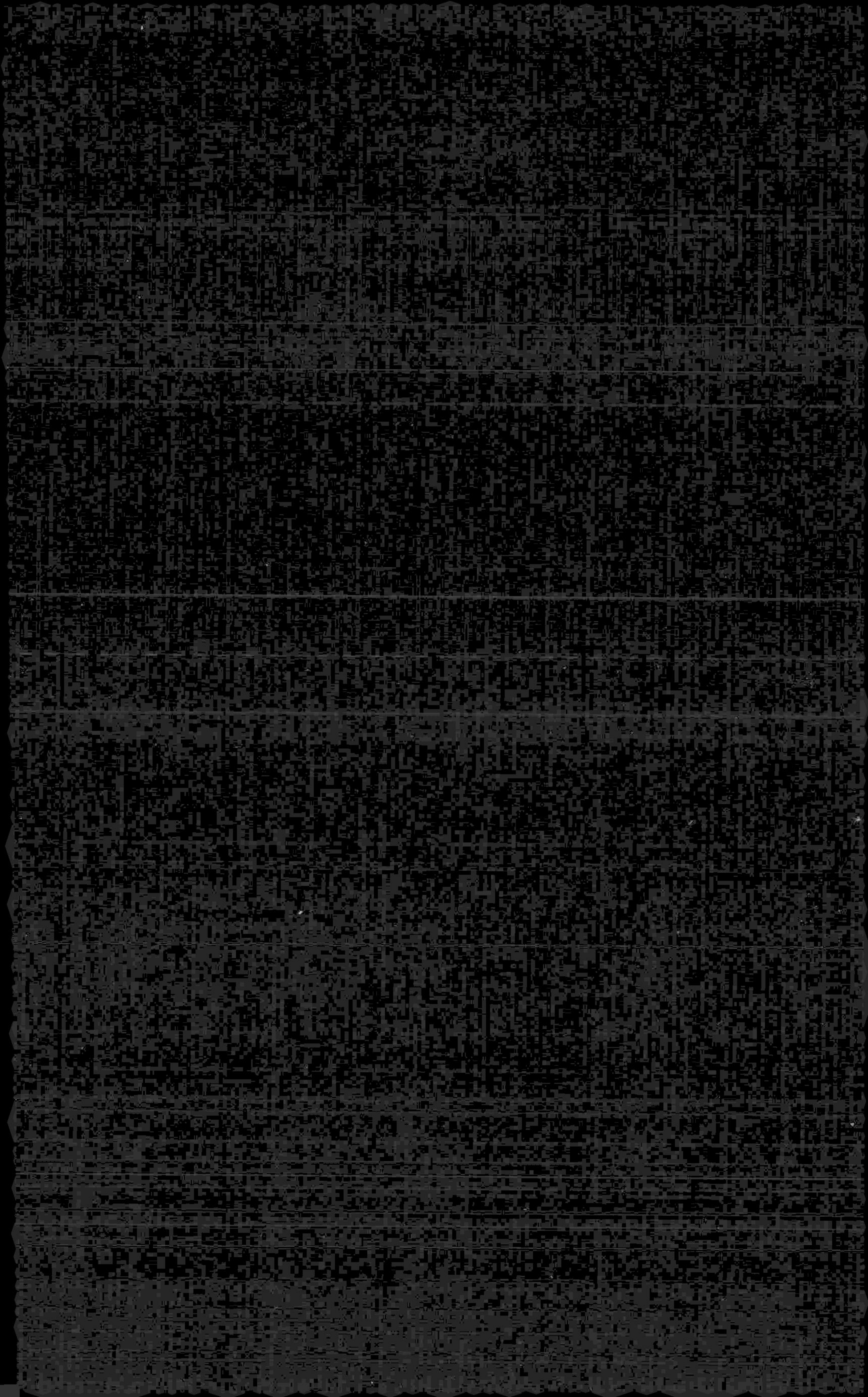